JESSICA WATKINS PRESENTS

FEARLESS 11

by AMARIE AVANT

D1407627

Want to be notified when the new, hot Urban Fiction and Interracial Romance books are released? Text the keyword "JWP" to 22828 to receive an email notifying you of new releases, giveaways, announcements, and more!

Author's Note:

Just in case you missed it from the online product description, this book is NOT a standalone novel, but a serial romantic suspense. Although, I have attempted to streamline it for ease of reading, in order to fully enjoy it, you should start with Fearless I. If you did not prefer the ending of Fearless I and were confused about what a 'cliffhanger' is, then gather your refund now. Much like the last book, this book ends with a Happily Ever After, For Now (H.E.A.F.N.) *not a cliffhanger*. This story is also full of Zariah, with her educated, but can get "ghetto" when necessary ass, and Vassili's bad mouth, full of "cunts and fucks," and of course, some good hard fucking!

Vassili Karo Resnov

Never get angry. Never get…too angry. And keep my fucking chill when outside of the octagon. That's what I agreed to do, in order to make my marriage work.

I'm seated wide-legged on a leather chair, so fucking big and plush, it was made just for me. Before me is a massive flat screen. I can be seen slaughtering my opponent with a roundhouse kick that leaves the guy knocked out in midair and falling like a rock. The KO segues into another one of my Killer Karo approved highlights. This time my tactic is a raw submission. I had Hauser in an ankle hold that broke his shit clear in half almost two years ago. I'm waiting for my call to connect, fisting my iPhone in my hand. The images keep flickering of me in beast mode, going for the kill. I'm too good at this. Too good at being bad.

She finally answers.

"Hey, baby," Zariah says, breathing a tad heavy.

Damn, I realize my lungs were overdue for oxygen during the wait for her to answer. Just last month, my wife was pressing the "away" button repeatedly and disregarding my calls. "Zariah, beautiful, you on your way?"

"I'm trying. Your child refuses to walk." Zariah's voice sounds muffled. "I opened the garage. Forgot something. Now I'm headed back to the garage with Natasha on one hip, her favorite juice spilling on me."

I tilt my head to the shiny ass chandeliers above, silently thanking God she's forgiven me for acting a fool. "That's Natasha, mayhem with apple juice."

From my peripheral, I notice my cousin, Yuri, has dropped his cane and is leaning against the doorframe. This fat, *mudak*—asshole—is eye fucking the pin-up doll for a maid, who so far has done more bending over in my face because some idiot blabbed about my impending match this weekend than readying the hotel room for my wife.

"Whatever, Vassili. I don't have time to be abused by your mini me."

"Oh, you don't?" I break into a grin. Our one-year-old is part of the reason I'm forgiven now.

Yuri turns around. "See, kazen, told you Zariah is all talk. You two are good."

My wife continues with, "I'm all sticky, and we have less than an hour to..."

My eyebrows knead.

Yuri winks. He thinks all is good. That I'm out of the dog house.

But Zariah's tone is stricken with fear, and her voice lowers, "We —we have...."

FEARLESS II
by *Amarie Avant*

My head tilts somewhat, facial expression darkening as Yuri stops leaning against the doorframe. He turns his attention from the slutty maid to me.

I ask, "Zariah, girl. What's wrong—"

"Mrs. Resnov, you've taken everything from me…" I hear a Latino male voice in the background.

Zariah scoffs, "Mr. Noriega…wh-what are you doing at my house? How do you know where I live?"

"Zariah," I shout into the phone. "Who is that!"

"Oh, is your husband on the phone?"

There are muffled noises. Yuri is silently asking me what's going on. He mouths Zariah, and I nod.

"Mikhail will be at your house in a few minutes, kazen," Yuri whispers.

I yell into the receiver, "ZARIAH, WHO IS—"

"Tell him."

She's trembling, fuck I can feel it light years away, as she speaks into the receiver. "It's Juan Noriega. I'm representing his wife in their divorce," her voice scales down. And then she's pleading to him. Begging him to allow her to put our child in the house so they can talk. And I'm... useless.

Juan motherfucking Noriega? It feels like a knife has slid into my bones. Without fail, I always force Zariah to provide me with a rundown about every case she picks up. Regardless that it's family law, I will not have my wife in a dangerous situation. There was no mention of this mudak, Noriega. I'd have refused her request to take on any case that had anything to do with the infamous Loco Dios gang member. Shit, shit, shit. Whomever she represented against Noriega was more than deserving of justice. Instincts slam into me and churn sour.

This is revenge…

"Does he have a gun?" My voice is tapered. Her fucking answer, 'yes' is enough to feel two slugs piercing into my heart. But I continue to stay calm as Yuri sends out his own message.

"Put him on the phone," I command, lips hardly moving.

"Okay," Zariah says, her voice wrapped in a fear I've never known.

"The infamous Vassili Resnov," the man's voice is callus to the core.

"Who. The. Fuck. Are. You?"

"*Ay dios mio,* you sound scary," he laughs.

I glare at the television screen. There's so much fucking blood. I'm massacring my opponent. My gaze fixates on his eyes, clouding as he taps out in my arms, so hard that the visual blurs before me.

"Sounds like I'm talking to the motherfucking Terminator. I'm Juan Noriega. I take it, you know of me. But no worries, mi amigo, I'm a nobody these days. I know all about you though," Noriega says. "Ex Welterweight UFC champ. Loved by the masses. And I also know you're a fucking Resnov. Your family isn't to be fucked with."

FEARLESS II
by *Amarie Avant*

The luxurious hotel is gone from before me. All I see myself doing is tearing this man limb from limb, killing him with my bare hands until his bones fracture, turn into powder, to dust and then become nothing. Painting my hands with his blood until my knuckles break. "Then I don't need to inform you of my capabilities. My family's capabilities?"

"No, hombre. I'm dead already. My parental rights were terminated for my ninos because of *your bitch.* My bitch up and took my house, my cars, everything I have, also because of *your* bitch. At this precise moment, I've got a nine to *your bitch's* head. But don't worry, like I just said, the bitch took my wife, and my two kids. I heard *your bitch* is pregnant. I prayed to God the two of you *were* having a boy. So, the little nina and the baby in her tummy will meet the same ending."

"Noriega." My blood slows to freezing point. I gulp down the lump in my throat. "Listen to me clearly, if you touch my wife or my daughter you will die a thousand deaths. I will beat you with my bare hands. That's already in the motherfucking cards. You've already consigned yourself to that. But do you want me to fucking murder you and revive you a thousand times, all just to have me torture and murder you again?"

"You're capable of that, Mr. Resnov. The only problem is, I no longer have a heart. Adios, mi amigo."

Click!

FEARLESS II
by *Amarie Avant*

I storm through the suite. "Where are my keys? Yuri, where the fuck are my keys?"

My cousin starts arguing with me. Finally, he halts my bulldozing through the room by grabbing my shoulders.

There's pain behind his eyes. Yuri's still favoring his one leg. But he grits through it and says, "*Nyet*—no! Vassili, *brat*. Everything will be good."

My world has tilted on a spindle. My head is chaotic, crazed. I'm seeing red. And I'm about to serve him the left hook he got when we went to jail a little while back. My bark is hard, "Yuri, move—"

He flinches, holding his palms out. "I can't. You can't. We can't fucking do anything for them no matter how much we—"

My forearm slams against his neck.

He's reddening by the second. "Va-Vassili, we are in Australia." He bites out the words.

My eyebrows crinkle. I. Am. In. Australia. My title match is tomorrow. I'm a world away from my fucking heart! I let him go, and clinch at the top of my head. There's no more Mohawk to tug. "Fuck the belt, Yuri. I don't want it."

Yuri rubs at his neck. "Okay, *kazen*, but—"

"I need to get home!" I punch the wall next to him. It's all marble. My knuckles crush against the glossed stone. The skin has pulled back and blood smears along it, leaving a trail.

FEARLESS II
by *Amarie Avant*

"That's impossible, Vassili, we are too far away. We're in fucking Australia! I have a crew on the way..." My cousin is speaking, though I can't understand the words. All I see is myself becoming a monster.

"*Kazen*! You'll have a heart attack. We will handle this. Mikhail promised to keep them safe. He is on the way to your home right now," he argues through gritted teeth. But Yuri's words hardly penetrate. I focus on God. Over the years, having faith hasn't been easy, but it will be the end of my relationship with Him if the worse occurs.

Vassili

Four Months Ago, Brazil
(After the winning Match with Tiago)

"You sure you want this chocolate?" Zariah's voice is filled with laughter. All those dark-brown curves of hers are peeking from where they're tucked into the sheets. The hotel bed is so heavily scented with our sex I almost didn't get out of it this morning.

I arch an eyebrow. Her gorgeous smile pops in and out of view as I continue with the repetition of push-ups I'm currently completing on the floor at the foot of the bed. "You'll save me a piece?"

"I guess I could." She places another chocolate truffle to her lips and then says, "How hard will you work for it?"

"*Nyet—no*, girl, I don't work hard unless I want to. I'll just eat you instead," I tell her.

"Whatever, Vassili," is her snarky reply.

I can hear her muttered chatter, damn, but that sound is good to my ears. Just recently, while preparing for our daughter, Natasha's first birthday, all I heard from my wife was arguing and snide remarks. Zariah is a lawyer, what can I expect? But I was on the opposite side of the defense team, and we were butting heads every day of the week. Yet, there's a smile in her comment about me eating her "if she lets me."

"Get the fuck outta here, baby, with that *if you let me* shit." My voice is playful. I almost crack a smile, I'm so fucking happy. The next strain to my bicep is met with a truffle she's tossed at me. It lands yards away. Instead of picking up the piece of chocolate she sucked at throwing, I continue with isolating my biceps and glance down at it. "Zariah, girl, why do I have the feeling that this is my only piece out of the entire box?"

The next view I have while mid-push-up is her lovely curves, breast bouncing as she falls back into the goose pillows in a burst of laughter. An undertone of cherry permeates her high mahogany cheekbones before I can not longer see her. She's pulled a pillow over her face to stifle her laughter. Damn, she cannot get away with anything.

I rise from the floor, sweat glistening down my skin from the repetitions I've just completed. "Zariah, get up, sweetheart. You enjoy all those chocolates." I pick up the now empty box of six. There's a single piece left, the one she threw at me. "There's only one chocolate that I crave. So, eat it all, baby. Get yourself sweet for me."

She slides the pillow away, and I'm blown away by what I see. The world's most gorgeous face, her sparkling eyes sliding up and down my muscles, and my gaze is locked onto her pouty lips. She knows just how to screw with me.

Zariah licks that pout then says, "Um hmmm, I don't need candy to get me sweet for you."

I cock an eyebrow, running my hand along the tattoos at the side of my neck. "Then you'll give your husband some love? You'll love me now…"

She sits up. The sheets tangle over her frame, covering those heavy breasts, yet with that shape, it can't hide much. "I'll always love you, Vassili, my heart isn't set up any other way. But, I will *love you* after you shower."

"That so, counselor?" I reach down, grabbing the meat of her ass and hips. The image of her on our first encounter will forever be embedded in my brain. The most beautiful sight. I never imagined she could be more beautiful. After having Natasha, Zariah had added on in the weight department. She is so damn thick, my palm squeezes on the flesh of her ass, and I swear my cock becomes titanium, hard like never before. I paw and then grab at it before quickly placing another hand under her arm and scoop her up.

"Yuck! Vassili, let me go!" Zariah argues as I bring the soft masses of her curvy naked body to my hard, sweaty chest.

"No. You once said I smelled good when I'm all sweaty."

"I plead the fifth."

"You can't. I'm your husband. You said you loved my sweat."

The mock disgust erupts into a broad smile, white teeth kissing her dark red lips. "That was after sex sweat, not dripping like a dog sweat. Besides, you loved me crazy, boy, so I was probably bragging on you and... and I'm at a loss for words, so stop badgering the witness!" Her bottom lip protrudes.

"You're my witness." I nip at her lip with my teeth. My growl causes her to shiver in delight against me, so soft and even after having my daughter, still so innocent.

We have had a hard seven months due to my torn patella. Yesterday was my first time returning to the cage, and it was met with celebration, and taking out a worthy opponent, Tiago. Slaughtering him has solidified my place back in the UFC world and placed me closer to the new title holder. My fucking belt.

I reposition Zariah. Her thick legs wrap around my waist.

"Oh, so you don't listen?" She squeezes her legs tighter around me.

"Girl, what are you talking about? My sweat smells like cologne."

"Ughhh..." she bites her lip, while eyeing my mouth.

"You want a kiss, sweetheart?"

"I guess." She squeezes again. "I'm dirty by association anyway."

FEARLESS II
by *Amarie Avant*

"Dah, well I was going to take my kiss regardless." I nibble her bottom lip. The warmth of her pussy stamps her wetness against my waist.

"Oh, you'll take it?" Her tongue slithers along mine. "How?"

My teeth sink into her lips. "Just like this," I tell her, holding onto Zariah with one arm while pushing my boxers down.

Then I grab her by the hips and position her soaking kitty at the head of my dick. The instant I slam into her, Zariah gives this haughty little chuckle, and her pussy creams onto my cock. "Oh, *yes!* Vassili tear it up," she groans.

"Oh, now you want this beating?" I position her outwards, my ten inches are glossed with her sweets, and Zariah is angled out toward me.

"Fuck me, baby!" Zariah pleads, just as I slam into her. The onslaught of my cock bruising every sweet corner of her insides has her bucking and begging. "Yes! Yes! Vassiliiiiiiiiiii!"

Zariah unwinds her legs from around me, leaving them transfixed in a V-shape. This offers me free reign as my biceps bump her up and down. My feet plant into a wide-legged stance, causing me to gather traction on the plush carpet.

Her titties, with their hard chocolate nipples, bounce up and down as I toss her in the air and slam into her over and over. My cock burrows deep inside Zariah, and I hold her there.

FEARLESS II
by *Amarie Avant*

She grabs my face, kissing me hard and rough. "Fuck me, Vassili."

In the past, she worried that I wouldn't like her pussy after she gave birth. That couldn't be further from the truth. It's fatter now, silky soft and rains like the Lena River, the longest river in Russia. Thinking about it drives me to the brink. I slow down, not wanting to nut too fast.

"Fuck you? You want me to beat the fuck out of this pussy?" I arch an eyebrow, this time my biceps push her up and down slowly. One inch at a time, my cock gets a taste, savoring the perfect mold. Damn, she's gushier inside than I imagined, as I continue to tease her insides. "Thought I was getting you all wet, and sweaty."

"Shi… shit…" she purrs. "Vassili, if you fuck me harder. I'm gonna… I'm gonna cum…"

My cock glides in and out. I lay her on the edge of the bed, position her legs over my shoulder and place the crown of my piece against those thick lips, gliding around in her sugar.

"Ohhh…" she tries to reach up. In her position, she's useless. Her eyes narrow. "Harder, Vassili … I love you…"

"Oh, you love me." My cock is swallowed by her pussy for a second and then out, heavy stiffness dragging over her clit and lips.

"Don't play!"

I slip inside again, pull out and fuck with her clit. "Don't play? You ate all the chocolate. I can play."

"I hate you, Va—" Zariah ceases her usual rant as I get to my knees and taste.

Zariah

Never thought to beg for sex until I met Vassili. Hell, I never made it enough a priority to give it up for the first time until I met Vassili. This year has been tumultuous at best. We are a stubborn pair, and my headstrong demeanor parallels with Vassili kicking ass in the octagon. Yesterday, when Vassili and Tiago were slaughtering and damn near annihilating each other, I froze. Then I ran.

Now, I realize that MMA has a special place in his heart no matter the promises he made to get the hell out of dodge when a match wasn't going too well. I had forced him into a corner when Vassili was putting a hurting on every man he stepped into the cage with. Yesterday, I learned that just like in our marriage, there will be ups and downs—on that damn canvass—and I have to ride it with him no matter what.

I cannot believe how easily Vassili has forgiven me my faults. Since he won the match last night and I apologized for running out of the convention center, we are magnetized to each other like we've always been in the past. His body, cut and ripped with muscles and dipped in gold and tattoos is the most beautiful sight. Second only to his cock. Minutes ago, as he bounced me in the air, and that thick, long, shaft smashed into my pussy, I grew hypnotized. Vassili, now is kneeled before me. I'm at the edge of the bed. My second set of lips are pulsating with the *Hulk Smash* he just performed. Now, Doctor Jekyll has become Mr. Hyde as Vassili seductively bestows butterfly kisses against the pulse at my neck.

"I hate you, Vassili," I grumble, attempting to grab at the long wavy hair of his mohawk, while he kisses a trail down my chest. His response is to nip harder at my nipple. Shit, it hurts, but the pain has nothing on the way he just screwed me. It felt good, soaring through the air, and slamming down onto his cock.

A warm, wet trail glides down to my belly button. I tug at his hair again, but he just pushes my hand away and continues toward his goal.

When his lips meet my clit, the aggression, the anger, the feign in me dies instantly. A humming sound vibrates my tonsils. That gorgeous chocolate brown wavy hair of his rises. "Fuck, that sound makes me want to slide down your throat."

I'm torn.

His cock in my mouth.

Or his lips against my clit.

I grip the sheets, unable to determine which. *"69!"* The thought pops into my head, like those old dreams I had of being a mute, naked, and about to commence my closing remarks in a courtroom. I'd finally shout something inaudible. But apparently, Vassili can read me, or I'm not so far gone that my words didn't penetrate.

Like we're on the canvass, Vassili's hard body clambers over mine. He positions his cock against my face. And before I can even begin to taste, he's devouring my pussy!

Damn, this is hilarious. I'm speaking in tongues; his crown is spearing the side of my cheek and he's eating me like an animal.

Vassili growls against my inner thigh.

Oh, yeah! He acquiesces to my begging. I grab his microphone with one hand and gobble it into my mouth. But Vassili works my goodies like an all you can eat Las Vegas buffet. Once again, I'm humming and grinning in ultimate delight.

"Zar!" His voice is testy.

I'm a little too greedy for this reciprocation stuff, and he's doing it too damn well.

I slide my tongue along the hard, smooth steel ridges of him and recall just how much I love his dick.

***

Our one week-shy of a year old, Natasha's fat little paws slap at the coffee table as she gains leverage. Her chunky legs are locked straight. She's taken a few steps before, but she's too damn eager to get around.

FEARLESS II
by *Amarie Avant*

"She's making room," my mom speaks up, right behind Natasha.

I purse my lips. "Um hmm."

"Making room?" Vassili's eyebrows come together. "Walk, sweetheart," he tells her as she shuffled to the side.

"For a new baby," mom says.

"Humph, that's a pain I still haven't forgotten yet. I don't know how anyone goes through it and..." I start laughing at Natasha's movements. She's using the table to dance now. "Okay, maybe I understand how mothers endure labor more than once."

Mom is right there as Natasha starts to fall. Usually, she cries for Vassili in frustration, but my mom refuses to let her hit the floor.

"Mom, she has all that diaper back there—"

"Girl, this is a hotel. I don't care how luxurious of a room we're in, Natasha isn't falling on the floor."

Vassili takes Natasha in his arms. He sits on the low seated chair. "Daddy was beating some ass last night."

"Daddy be... be... *ass!*"

"Vassili," I chide as my mother laughs. I swear I recall a day when she had no sense of humor. My father hardly allowed her to be comfortable in her own shoes. I can't be mad at her, so my reprimand comes with a smile. "How do you allow this baby to cuss?"

I ask her as Vassili's voice lowers. He's having a sidebar conversation with Natasha as he often does.

FEARLESS II
by *Amarie Avant*

When *they* talk matches, I know he cusses a storm. And Natasha giggles in response. The shirt he's wearing clings to his buff biceps as he does a jab into the air with her in his other arm.

Her head tosses back, she gives a wide-toothed grin, or shall I say gums. Three teeth up top and two at the bottom.

I glance at myself in the mirror, and then I look at my mom's reflection. Hell, it should be me in "mommy" sweats. My mom needs a new love. And well, last night, Vassili and I disappeared early, leaving her with Natasha. It's almost dark again.

"Mama, are you sure you don't want to have a night out? We're on vacation in a new place."

"Nope. I have Natasha. Everything I want to do is at a respectable hour." She glances back and forth from me and Vassili and adds, "Tsk, my version of respectable. Y'all two have blurred the line."

"Dang!" I sound like the teenager she used to know me as. My cheeks warm. No matter how old I get, I can't let my mother know of the freak Vassili has made me into. He winks as I pick up Natasha and burrow my face in the fat rolls of her neck.

"No! No! Nooooo!" She argues as I kiss her caramel skin. I smack kisses on her neck and start to blow, causing my baby to cackle with laughter. It's the sweetest sound, and I swear it makes this bulky husband of mine soft for a fraction of a second.

FEARLESS II
by *Amarie Avant*

"I don't mind y'all disappearing at all hours of the day and night. Long as Natasha becomes a big sister soon," Mom says, still on the topic I attempted to skirt around.

I dance around that question with, "Hmmm, we have to get you a man."

"I have one, thank you very much. Now go enjoy—"

"Who? Since when?" I ask. Natasha tugs on my shirt for attention, but I stare my mother down waiting on her answer.

"It's... new. I won't ruin it by chatting. Go out, drink, and try to have a good time. Because the two of you mix like oil and water. Have fun before being forced into returning to reality..."

"Well, damn, mama, tell me something I don't know."

She catches my gaze. "Honey, as long as you keep God first in your marriage, you two can continue clashing and loving. In fact, contrary to the example myself and your father provided, a little rebellion makes love stronger if Jesus is in the mix."

***

"This is the treatment we get when your man wins against one of the local legends," Taryn, my half Asian and black best friend, grumbles. We are virtually invisible to the bartender, who has an imaginary 'Team Tiago' stamp on his forehead. Damn, the match was outstanding. The guy put up a fight and lost, and now we lose out on good drinks.

I sigh, waving at the Brazilian. He catches my eye and continues to flirt with a young woman. "Yeah, I'm surprised the bartender doesn't add a little something extra to our drinks by way of bodily fluid, and I wouldn't have even seen the ending of the fight if you hadn't dragged me back into the stadium."

"You can pay me back in Valentino." Taryn drums her hands on the scuffed wood counter.

I scoff. "Your ass needs a job, Taryn, a j-o-b."

"Ugh!" She shakes her long hair. "Gainful employment isn't in my vocabulary."

"Is love?" I play it cool, still waving for the bartender's attention. "Hello…"

"Is what?" Taryn no longer bats her eyes and attempts to get the servers attention by leaning across the counter with her tiny tits. "Zar, what?"

We step away from the bar, and a crowd of other people engulf the spot we just had. The bartender comes over to them. I look her in the eye, and ask, "Love? You, Yuri."

She glances back at the high-stool table where our guys sit. There's no denying the sparkle in her eye. Yuri gestures for us to come back over with the cock of his beer.

Whereas Vassili is all muscle, in jeans and a shirt, Yuri is every bit as thick in the arms with a gut that slims down well beneath a custom-made suit.

FEARLESS II
by Amarie Avant

"Girls, I need some fucking water here, my tongue is hard as sandpaper." Yuri corners Taryn into his space. She's so much tinier than him. A pretty roasted almond color to his paleness, Yuri isn't a lover of working out nor is he much a fan of the sun.

"Oh, you want water, do you?" Her voice is dripping in sex. "Their vodka isn't as good as your family's. I've got something better for you…"

They proceed to caress each other's tongues in the middle of the bar.

Vassili kisses my neck and grabs his beer. Sometimes I swear, he is a super fan of public displays of affection, like the first time we screwed in a car. Though there's no way in hell I'll fuck him with an audience, those token times he devours my mouth outside of the bedroom are rare. I live for those. His dark eyes sparkle. He wants to eat me. I swear even after being married for almost three years he still treats me like a virgin in front of others at times. If you don't count the ass pawing. Every few minutes he squeezes one of my ass cheeks like his life depends on it.

Like right now, my pussy is screaming for attention when he does it. Then he leans back in his chair.

"You could kiss me like that."

"*Nyet*—no. Not here."

"Why not?" My eyebrow rises.

He grunts.

FEARLESS II
by Amarie Avant

Sometimes I want him to grab me in front of a crowd of people. Set aside my education and the entitlement my father instilled in me. Set aside his tattooed, yet, gentleman qualities. There's no denying that I belong to him. Yet, I realize that in those occasions where he is *too respectable* he is thinking of something. Perhaps how his father, Anatoly, treated his mom. Yeah, that must have something to do with his level of pause. I hope…

Vassili

How the fuck do I respond to her? Zariah turns her head away from me. She takes my lack of willingness to fuck faces as if I'm dismissing her. I went from slamming my cock into a different pussy a day, sometimes more, but my wife satisfied me in ways I cannot begin to explain. I can't just slobber her face down today. Shit, I didn't even know I was starving until Zariah became mine. But with my parents on my mind, I am in the wrong headspace for PDA. Because I'm amped up on adrenaline, and maybe because I'm paranoid like my fucking father about a few things.

Zariah starts to sway to the music. She snaps her fingers, closes her eyes. All the restraint in the world is holding me back from her right now. No need for ass shaking, my girl is too fucking beautiful just being herself. She doesn't even know that it's the little things that send my cock to a heavy rise and my heart drumming in my chest.

"Dance with me?" Zariah asks out of the blue.

Fuck, can't say I don't dance because Natasha jiggled around even as she crawled to music. I do dance, but in the few years that Zariah and I have been back together, we've only attended the VIP section in clubs. And I would bash a man's skull in for looking at her at The Red Door. There's never been a time we were dancing in the lounge when it's been open to the public.

My eyes keep zipping around. Really, have I gone paranoid, obsessively anxious like Anatoly? Someone is here…

Zariah glowers, expecting an answer. She doesn't know that I'm scanning the room with my peripheral vision because that would lead to more questions. Like the truth. So I take the dick way out…an excuse. "You don't know the words to the song. We don't know the words. Why dance?"

There. In the side, left corner, a man who resembles one of my many brothers sits, nursing a shot glass. My muscles tense.

Zariah rubs my bicep. "Vassili, baby, dance with me."

My eyes lock onto hers. "I don't fucking dance." My voice is hard as ever, iced over due to hate from a past life. And dammit, I need to see what this guy wants. "Okay, love?" My mouth tips at the edge to soften the blow.

Yet Zariah cuts her eyes, and glances away from me.

Yuri slaps a hand on the table. *"tchyo za ga`lima, kazen!"* What the fuck, he asks in Russian.

FEARLESS II
by *Amarie Avant*

"*Po'shyol 'na hu.*" My middle finger goes to the air as I toss back my beer.

As if on key, my cell phone vibrates in my jean pocket. I pull it out.

"Is that my mom?" Zariah asks. She'd left her phone with her mom and Natasha, since her mother's cell won't hold much juice.

"It's…" I glance at the screen. *Anatoly.* "Nobody."

"Nobody," she breathes the word.

"Hey, Zar," Taryn cuts in and saves the day. My wife's mouth was set for a comeback. She says, "There's a new bartender, let's see if we can get a good old' fashion Cosmo? Beer is not my fancy." Taryn lifts up her empty glass. The girls rise and head toward the bar.

"That your pop?" Yuri asks.

"*Dah*—yes!"

"So beside being a fucking '*khu i*—dick, is Zariah aware that the two of you are talking again? Because I've seen you just about pawing Zar's pus—" he stops and gulps. Changing his phrase out of respect. "I've seen you two go at it, Vassili, many times. So is that why you've hardly touched her tonight?"

I rub the scar along my jaw with my thumb thinking about how Anatoly called me seven months ago. The first thing out of his mouth was 'disrespect.' That the MMA fighter, Louie the legion Gotti, disrespected me in the cage by placing me into submission and tearing my patella. I laughed at his ass until he promised that The Gotti only had seconds to live. Meaning that one of my brothers with a particular motherfucking set of skills was probably a hundred yards away from Gotti's kitchen or living room or somewhere the fighter had to be in plain view. After calming Anatoly down and saving Gotti's life, the piz'da and I continued to talk.

"Tell her," Yuri warns.

I shake my head, and respond to my cousin, "Nah, she doesn't need to know."

"He came to you with a peace offering... you declined," Yuri says of the unnecessary ass hit on Gotti. He shrugs. "This is the longest period of time that you and Anatoly have talked to each other. He wants something."

No shit! I'm aware of exactly what that mudak wants. "Okay, *okay*? What the fuck, Yuri, am I stupid now?" I bark, still keeping an eye on the guy in the corner. There's a shadow masking much of his face, but the resemblance is all too familiar.

"First, you didn't want Zariah around me. *Me.* I'm more than blood, Vassili! I'm your brah! We are like brothers. Then my pops, Malich, and the family were off limits, okay, I saw that coming. Zariah loves Malich and the family *now*. But now Anatoly is in your ear and you're acting... Will your morals slip with him, too?"

FEARLESS II
by *Amarie Avant*

The man stands up. My hand comes up into the air, and Yuri stops talking. This idiot thinks I'll up and allow Anatoly to come around my wife and kid one bright sunny ass day! Fuck that! And he's too stupid to realize that I'm about to tear this motherfucker across the way a new one. "Do I need a lecture from you, Yuri? *Nyet*—no."

I glare through Yuri. Then I start toward the hallway that leads to the restrooms where the man in jeans and a hat just went. He has to be one of my *brats*—brothers. Anatoly keeps popping up. If this is my blood, he's getting the blood bashed out of him.

In the hallway, my pace slows down. There're two guys between me and the other Russian. There are lines leading to both the men and women's restrooms. With my hand in a fist, I bite my knuckles and glance over my shoulder. The girls are sweet talking a new bartender for some sugary ass drink. From their location, they'd be able to see me bash this mudak's head in.

There's a door reading '*Cozinha*' which means kitchen in Portuguese, with arrows that implicate it swings open, a few yards before the crowded restrooms. When the doors swing open I cock a grin. The line shuffles forward.

"You should tell her," Yuri says over my shoulder.

A deep breath funnels into my lungs. Shit, he followed me over here. "What?"

28

FEARLESS II
by *Amarie Avant*

"You and Zariah are in *good* until your dad sneaks his ass into the States. He has you worried and treating Zariah like—"

In a few quick steps, I'm around the two people between the other Russian and I. My palm stiffs the side of his shoulder and he goes stumbling into the kitchen.

My left hook goes out, targeting his nose. It's powerful enough to slide him across the room. At the last instant, I raise my elbow. My bone catches the face of the Brazilian line chef who is holding a butcher knife to the side of my face. His jaw is reset. He's out cold, hitting the ground so swiftly that his knife hardly began to clatter to the ground.

Fuck, there are seven more where he came from, all ready for war.

"What the hell?" Yuri asks behind me as he catches an angry dishwasher with a jab to his eye.

"This guy is my—" I slam my foot into my enemy's chest. The Russian's eyes widen. But his gaze isn't dark like mine—ocean blue. And come to think of it, he doesn't look shit like me. He is no family of mine. This mudak isn't even Russian!

The man is a serious golden color and his voice is off when he clutches his chest and says, "What the fuck, mate!"

He's Australian. His dialect, the confusion on his face, all of it is pure comedy.

FEARLESS II
by *Amarie Avant*

"I thought I knew you," I tell him, as I press my arms against the shoulders of another Brazilian chef and take a knee to his junk. Fuck it, they have weapons. I'm playing dirty. The knife in his hand falls.

"Oh, I thought I knew you, too," the Aussie chuckles, with effort, while regaining air into his lungs. "You're the fighter, Karo?" Now, he's gripping a frying pan in one hand. I brace my forearm, but he slams the damn thing right over my left shoulder. It sends another man clear out.

In seconds, all three of us have taken out the guys in the kitchen.

"I'm the fighter." I shrug, taking a deep breath, licking the blood from my busted lip.

"Okay, wanker, can I get your autograph, and mind telling me what had you acting like a *fuckstick?*"

His choice of words goes over my head. I was in the wrong and this is as close as we get to an apology on my part.

"Sure." I shrug, grabbing a tab and a pen from the apron of one the servers Yuri just put down.

"Dah, I'd like to know, too?" My cousin smooths the lapel of his suit.

We chat for a few minutes as the Aussie tells me his girl is in their hotel room sick, so he came down for a drink, at least I think he said that. He tosses words out like *spiffed* and *chockers* and I pat his back.

A waitress heads into the kitchen and she stops in her wake, sees all the guys on the ground, and then glances at the three of us. She grabs a plate on the counter and goes back to her business.

"We better get the fuck outta here, before they wake up," Yuri says.

"It was fun, mates," the Aussie heads for the door.

I start for it.

"*Brat*, I'm not gonna waste my fucking breath again, but tell her that Anatoly is coming around." Yuri's shoulders lift in defeat.

Without responding, I press my hands against the kitchen door, and allow it to swing open.

Nothing, aside from my marriage, is off topic. Yuri always understands where my head is at. He was a little bitch when I told him to stay away from Zariah, but in the end, he respected that. And he was right, Zariah did love the family—the half that Anatoly uses his fucking puppet master antics on from across the ocean. My uncle's side of the family is closer to me than anything. Malich has always been more like a father to me. His sons, especially Yuri, are more brothers than that of the football team of half siblings I have.

For the longest, I couldn't give a fuck about my father. Anatoly held me under the same regard. But after losing my belt to Gotti, my father wanted to intervene. And I haven't told Yuri the extent to Anatoly's interest in my life these days.

It has nothing to do with him.

And it sure as hell doesn't have anything to do with Zariah because unlike her willingness to meet and greet with Malich, Yuri and the rest of them, she will never be crossing paths with my father. I won't allow it.

I just have to get Anatoly Resnov out of my fucking face.

Zariah

A week Later…

Mom's right. We honestly don't mix at all. Like bad pancake mix that you try to make crepes with but in the end, it results in something even worse. That's the first analogy that came to mind the instant we returned to our reality. Los Angeles.

Planning Natasha's first birthday was a horror story before we left for Brazil. Heck, the seven months leading to Vassili's smackdown on the Brazilian, Tiago, trumped any season of American Horror Story, and I actually like it. Vassili hates that show. Nevertheless, every season, I lay on his chest and watch every episode, clutching him in fear or spilling popcorn on him when the gore is too good to turn away.

We simply don't mix. He likes Russian food, I have my certain favorites. However, most of it I loathe. He loves squeezing the forearm conditioner when we are arguing, and that's pretty much how we got to Brazil. His jaw tensed, mine set in a line too, sitting in silence in first class.

Now, it's the perfect first day of summer, a Saturday morning, to be more precise. And the icing on the cake? Two cakes that is. We're celebrating Natasha's first birthday. I don a colorful maxi dress and Vera Wang sandals with gemstones, while Vassili is stepping out of the shower. "Damn, girl, bring that ass over here," he tells me, as I stand in the bathroom, fixing my hair.

Dang, now there is no problem with my husband glancing me up and down while water glistens over mounds of muscles and tattoos. I woke up earlier than him, and got dressed because there are a few surprises for Natasha's birthday that in retrospect will be quite the surprise to Vassili and his pockets soon.

One, I might have blown the bank for Natasha's first birthday. Two, there's a petting zoo on the way to our home, with the clown he and I compromised and nixed, with Vassili in my face when I called to cancel. The instant he left my side, I called back and got the damn clown, including a few ice sculptures that I was told were on sale.

While brushing the waves in my long weave, I start off with a little deception, saying, "Um, I'm going to finish getting dressed."

Vassili opens the glass door and steps out of the shower. "Good, good, you can do that after I get you undressed."

I make the mistake of looking at his body. The impeccable art that was carved into his chiseled chest. The way his abs stop at a V-shape which brings my eyes lower.

Before I can make a mad dash to the exit, he wraps his arms around me, his cock hardening by the second. "Damn, Vassili, whether it's a shower or sweat, you just love to screw with me."

"I do." He nips at my earlobe. "You had my baby, Zariah. And I have to show my appreciation."

"Mmmm," I moan as he turns me around in the mirror, my ass pulled against his hard rock. His hand slithers into my low-cut dress, tugging at my nipple. "I hate you, Vassili, don't do this to me..." I groan.

"I miss your pregnant belly." He says planting my hands on the counter. "Those titties full of milk use to fucking spill out of your bra when I fucked you from the back."

The lips of my pussy are dying for him.

"And when you had my daughter, shit, Zar, no woman in the world could touch how beautiful you were that day. Not before it, not since. You are my queen."

"You are trying to play me for a piece of ass," I chortle, although he has me precisely where he wants me. All the sneak purchases for our baby girl have flown from my mind. The second he commands me to be wide open for him, that is exactly what I'll do.

He starts to descend to his knees behind me. "Girl, you and this long ass skirt, I don't like it," he says.

FEARLESS II
by *Amarie Avant*

I chuckle as he stops 'gaming me up for some ass' to argue with me. "Whatever, Vassili, I have stuff to do."

His face is against my ass, and he holds me there. Damn it if I don't want to come out of my panties and this maxi for him. I can feel the warmth of his breath through the material. My thong is drenching with each exhale. All he has to do is issue a command—

DING. DONG.

My eyes close instantly. My head falls back.

"That was nothing," he says, voice muffled as the wetness of his tongue starts to seep through the material and leaves me breathless.

"I have to go, baby," I murmur. He's wrong, it's a whole lot of something. Like I said, it might be the clown and the zoo, but it may very well be bayou princess Tiana. The Princess and the Frog themed birthday was what Vassili agreed upon. He isn't aware that I chose a celebrity chef and hand selected the food, and even though I'm in a lot of trouble once the party is over, our baby is worth it.

People say that planning weddings brings with it stressors, as much tension and irritation as tears of joy, but I swear, planning Natasha's first birthday rivaled that strain. Yet, we've managed to come home from vacation, and right now life is good.

So, I hustle away, leaving the sexiest man alive on his knees, naked in the bathroom.

***

by *Amarie Avant*

My mom has been given the task of ushering the various vendors to the different parts of our vast backyard. There's a cart, which was quaintly decorated in the appropriate Princess and The Frog theme, with a baker handing out freshly made beignets and other similar desserts. But that's not to be confused with the tier rolled fondant cake or the much tinier, princess shaped one that Natasha will get to dig in all on her own.

With the pony ride area forced to the farthest corner of the backyard, children of all ages are seated before a movie screen, almost as nostalgic as an outdoor movie theater, watching clips of Princess and the Frog.

There's a canopied section with linen tables and a DJ, and Natasha is in the photo booth with friends and cousins from my side of the family and Vassili's who all want to share the special day with her.

"So why didn't I get the memo?" I nudge my chin to my husband who is talking to his uncle while I stand next to my mentor and employer, Samuel Billingsley. They're both wearing t-shirts with Natasha's photo on them. Heck, my mom's zipping around the backyard and I could've sworn she had a shirt in her hand, the last time I saw her, too. Yuri is fixing my best friend, Taryn's, silky straight hair, as Taryn places a shirt over the tiny tee she was just wearing.

"C'mon, you're a designer girl, besides your outfit matches cutie pies," Samuel chuckles. It's on the tip of my tongue to tell him that Taryn is even more about the labels than I am, but he reads me so well, inquiring, "You still worried about your dad making it?"

Damn, my father has been in the back of my mind for a while. "You can tell?"

He nods.

I sigh. "We've been at odds for long enough. Heck, I don't care if we continue to clash, but today is about Natasha, not us or his dislike of my husband."

"Call him already," Samuel begins to back away. "And whatever his response is, breathe."

I sidestep a few happy children heading to the petting zoo, and pull out my cell phone. My father answers the call on the first ring.

"Good afternoon, princess." His voice is contrite at best.

"Dad, you RSVP'd last minute to the party, and I didn't even argue with you about bringing Berenice." I keep my eyes on Yuri and Taryn. He's like a polar bear next to her thin, model type body. They're glancing into each other's eyes as if there isn't a gang of children running around them. Be happy is what I tell myself. I cut my monologue short with, "So, are you coming before the cake is served? This is your granddaughter's first birthday." Feels like mention the obvious is required.

"Zariah, I do not need the reminder. There was a bank robbery on Century and Normandie."

FEARLESS II
by *Amarie Avant*

"So, what? You are the Chief of Police, and very capable of delegating assignments to the proper unit."

"Due to your current *employment* I am not sure if you keep up to date on *current* events." My dad never fails. When he can toss shit in your face he will. Maxwell Washington has so much to be disappointed in me for that it's a wonder we were engaged in conversation this long without him going in. Samuel Billingsley is one of his oldest friends, and ex-Chief Deputy District Attorney. My childhood mentor was the reason I chose law school, yet, let my father tell it, and I chose to become a lawyer and follow the DA route as homage to my father. It must've busted his bubble when I chose to work at Billingsley Law firm, which is a family law, after Samuel switched career routes a few years ago.

I scoff. "I work for your best friend."

He disregards that statement and says, "This robbery seems similar to the one which occurred two months ago, Zariah. And therefore, it's necessary for the department to be on one accord to determine if this is an isolated incident, or should we have the public complaining? Princess, putting work first is exactly how I raised you. Or attempted, rather."

"Oh, it's an election year isn't it. Let's not piss off your friends who want an office repeat and have helped you get to where you are. Do them a solid, since they're good as family."

I click the off button. Samuel walks over with a beignet. "We cannot allow others to ruin our mood, but we can allow food to pick it back up."

I laugh at him, and shake my head. I'm still unable to fathom how Samuel became friends with Vassili. Although he resigned from the district office, the first encounter with them together, Samuel warned me to steer clear of riffraff like Vassili. But Samuel gave Vassili a chance and learned that he's much more than the last name Resnov. A name I once feared. Samuel is the greatest father figure anyone could ever have. Sucks that I have a willing father, Maxwell Washington. He is *willing* to welcome me home with open arms, if I divorce my husband.

Vassili comes up to me, holding out my shirt.

"Oh, you are awful. Made me wait until last." I shake my head. "This shirt is awesome!"

"That pose was supposed to be mine," Samuel says. "Love that photo."

"Sam helped me choose the photos for each shirt," Vassili says.

Each of our shirts are different, but all have Natasha's gorgeous photo on them. Mine also has the writing, "The bully's mama." I recall the exact moment this photo was taken. Natasha stood for the first time, for a fraction of a second. Her hands were balled into fists. In retrospect, it looks like she was ready to go to war, cute face to boot.

FEARLESS II
by *Amarie Avant*

Just as I slip the shirt over my head, Vassili kisses me. "Now, I have something for us all. The people who design my Karo gear, and these shirts, put together a video. You promise not to cry if I show it?"

I mock pout, though my eyes are burning with happy tears. "Oh, baby."

"Nah, don't 'oh baby' me, girl. No crying. Can I use the large screen you snuck and rented?"

My face breaks into a smile. "Dang, you knew I'd go behind your back and rent it anyway!"

"I did. And instead of it just sitting there with clips of a movie we have seen a trillion times, I have something in my email that I need to pull up."

The tears of happiness continue to swell in my eyes. My husband beats strong men into submission, he is someone to be feared, but he is incredibly thoughtful, too.

Vassili pulls me to him. "Girl, you better dare not cry." He kisses me hard on the lips again, before walking away.

Vassili

I head over to the attendant manning the big screen. Children are seated before it, watching the scene were Princess Tiana turns into a frog. They have those theater bags of popcorn in their hands.

"Where's uncle?" I ask Yuri as he catches up with me. My uncle, Malich is all about family, so this will be the highlight of his day. He'd gotten his t-shirt and went to change, but I haven't seen him since.

"Igor was eating everything in sight," Yuri says of his brother. "Dad took him home. Anna is staying here with their kids."

I shake my head. Why does it take Malich to keep his grown ass son from trying to kill himself? The idiot, Igor, has diabetes. His wife, Anna, is good at keeping him on track. The different attractions around my home must have kept her entirely too busy with their children to watch her husband.

"Are you putting that video on now?" Yuri asks.

The email app on my cell phone pings with a new message. I start to click on the one titled "Baby video," when I notice a new email, the title in all capital letters.

FRANK GASPAR.

FEARLESS II
by *Amarie Avant*

I'll never forget the name.

The sea matched the pitch black of the night. My heart rate was at a resting pace as I jogged through the sand. My gaze narrowed, a dark figure was standing at the stairs that lead up to my Venice beach house. He stood in the shadows of the wooden pillars, blending well with the stair. Pretending to be oblivious, my eyes shaded somewhat, and I caught sight of a badge. It was one of those "to protect and serve" motherfuckers.

With a hard frown, I played stupid, continuing at my current pace.

The outline of a baton went to his side. In the last second, the cop lifted it, saying, "A message from—"

The baton slammed against my palms so roughly, it broke the skin on my palms as I grabbed it from my skin.

"You're gonna fucking hit me?!" I whacked him across the head with the stick determined to break the damn thing. Then I gripped him by his neck, slamming him against a pillar. His feet dangled.

"Next time you're given an assignment, back your shit up," I squeezed until he was dead weight. Fuck, what have I done?

I reached down and check his pulse.

Weak.

"What is it?" My wife's concerned voice breaks through the memory. Where did she come from? I glance around. Children are running around with cotton candy and parents are chomping on beignets. Balloons fly in the wind. I rationalize where I am.

Fuck, fuck, fuck, she can't know about him. Zariah and I have our secrets. Big ones. The first died by the name of Sergio. I murdered him slowly just to get Zariah's attention.

In a fraction of a second, I've deleted the message without opening it.

Yuri catches the slight look in my eye. "Um, the email, maybe it was sent to me instead of you?" He catches on. "Don't worry, kazen, let me check."

Zariah sighs, "Oh no, I hope you guys find it soon."

Yuri pulls out his phone, toggles the apps for a second and then says, "Nope, don't see it. Let's go make a call, Vassili. This is my god baby's birthday. The director had better come through."

Director? My cousin sounds like a liar. I shake my head, and we head to the sliding glass door.

I cock my head and he follows me to the downstairs office. Inside is memorabilia from my previous MMA fights. My first shirt with the Killer Karo symbol is framed above the back of my desk. I head to my leather chair, claiming it with a heavy heart.

"We need water?" Yuri asks, hesitantly.

I nod. From the inside of his suit jacket, he pulls out a bottle of Resnov vodka, and opens it.

FEARLESS II
by *Amarie Avant*

After he takes a swig, I grab the bottle and toss it to the head, downing much of it. Wiping my mouth, I ask, "Do you remember maybe two years ago or so, I called you over after a run near my old home in Venice?"

"No."

"Some cop came out of nowhere. It was night, and he started to tell me who he was about to beat me up for, but I got him first."

My cousin's eyes flit around with a bewildered look.

"You came over, whining about not sucking on your old lady's tits. And you capped him, and hauled him away."

"Oh, you'd dumped the cop beneath the stairs by your home. I came and finished him because you were being a pussy?" Yuri tosses back.

"No Sherlock, I just don't murder mudaks for no reason. I thought we'd figure out who he worked for."

"My dad," he says of Malich. "Your dad, or Zariah's."

"Ring-ring-ring/" I nod, sarcastically.

"So, who did the cop work for?"

My eyes bug out. "Are you serious right now, Yuri. You killed him before we could get that far."

"You were my accomplice."

"Kazen," I gesture, "I'm not wearing a fucking wire, we need to figure this out!"

"Okay!"

by *Amarie Avant*

I reach up and grab my cell phone from my back pocket, open the email account and view the "deleted" items. Then my thumb mashes onto the email entitled with the cop's name. I open it up for the first time, and just as I suspected the dead man is there. Someone excavated his body, and in the photo, the stiff is near a muddy area. A close-up photo of his Los Angeles Police Department Badge shows that he's none other than Frank Gaspar. Now I have two bodies to my name. I slide the phone over. Yuri glances at it in disinterest.

"So?"

"Some-fucking-body pulled him up from the LA River, and all you've got to say is 'so'?" I nudged my tense jaw at the phone. "Who did this?"

"Well, my pop didn't. I remember everything now, you were ready to start pointing the finger at all of us. Malich didn't do it."

"Tell me something I don't know, Yuri." I say through tensed lips. Although, I still feel bad for thinking so negatively about my uncle, he's more than a father to me.

"It leaves one of two people. Vassili, we can't take out Anatoly, but we sure as fuck can go murder Maxwell Wash—"

I reach over and slam my hand over his mouth. "Don't fucking say that, Yuri! Not in my house. My wife is that bastard's daughter!"

Yuri pushes my hand away.

FEARLESS II
by *Amarie Avant*

"And again, Vassili, I say 'so'?" He holds out his hands. "She doesn't like his ass anymore. One crooked cop off the streets is no sweat off my back."

"Maxwell Washington is the Chief of police. Bet your ass that the entire division will search for him, unlike they did for Gaspar."

"Can you stop saying his name?" Yuri inquires. "I'm not a fan of mentioning the names of people that I... you know."

"But you have no problem adding to the list?"

"Better them than me, Vassili. You have always been lukewarm in this game. You're not in the bratva, but you'll ask me to get some motherfucker in a basement just to get the attention of a piece of pussy!"

I slam my forearm along his chest. "That was my wife. I never asked you to help me torture for anybody but—"

"Dah, and you got whatever the fuck that Italian guy's name was in the basement for Zariah, as you requested. I don't have a fucking problem with helping you. But I recall a certain someone telling me to stay the hell away from his woman before you married her, in not so nice words."

I shake my head. "Really? You're bringing up old shit? I have a wife for that!"

"You have always been my brah! Fuck, a kazen, you have always been *moy brat*—my brother! So, forgive me if I recall bullshit, that still hurt. Then you call me to get rid of this cop, I do it. You call, I do it.

FEARLESS II
by *Amarie Avant*

Oh, and before this, you sent me to Atlanta to follow Zariah around like a stalker, while she attended college. I still had my assignments for Malich. And I still managed your MMA fights, Vassili. Where the fuck is my thank you for once? Calling me inside to—to argue with me about some cop on the beat, this is my god baby's birthday! Fuck him, fuck that Italian dude, fuck you! I'd say fuck your wife, but I actually like her, and she's family now. You, I don't like."

I hold my tongue. Shit, I have another assignment for him. He'll be in Atlanta for me by the end of the week. He just doesn't know it yet.

"Yuri, you are more than a fucking *brat* to me, okay?"

He almost smiles at the thought of us really being brothers. "And…"

"And." I gulp down the tension in my throat. Shit, I've only said sorry a few times in my life, in all cases it was to a female. Zariah, Sasha, and my mother. "We will figure out who dug up Gaspar's body and emailed me."

"We you say? We will work together?" His eyebrow bunches. "No, Yuri, 'manage the situation,' as you always say?"

This fool is pushing it. I rub a hand over my face. "We work together."

"And if it's Zariah's father? Do we get to kill him—shit, if you want to do the honors, I'll just dump. Igor has had it in for him for years. Back when he was a lieutenant, Washington dropped coke on Igor's wife's, brother's, best friend's cousin's, little brother's—"

"Yuri," I warn in a testy voice.

"Just want to recreate the picture. Everyone was pissed. The guy's still in jail."

"Well, fuck that. We need to get back to my baby's first birthday. When that's done, we'll figure out if it's Washington or Anatoly that is behind this email, and then we'll deal with it accordingly."

FEARLESS II
by *Amarie Avant*

Zariah

These last two weeks have been a whirlwind. Watching Natasha as she bulldozed her smash cake was the highlight of it. Second only to me promising to Vassili that I will always be there, regardless of how scary his matches can be.

We had a great time in Brazil after the fight with Tiago. His confidence brings me life. Yet, my mind continues to roam to the night after the fight. When we went to the bar with Yuri and Taryn.

Sitting at Billingsley Legal, the family law firm I work for, I click the top of my pen, listening to the rapid sound, letting it soothe my constant worry. My room isn't the biggest in the building, but it's cozy with a custom suede couch and pictures of my family all around.

I haven't been to work in over ten days, and I'm stuck on how Vassili gave me the cold shoulder at the bar, regardless of the fuck marathon we had before and the amazing sex we had after. *All I wanted was one dance!*

Usually, I can't get his hands off me, not that I'd ever want to. But every once in a while, I'm stuck with the cold shoulder. We can be out, holding hands. There are certain instances where he won't kiss me. But I swear the second we are behind closed doors, he's all over me....

Like he most often is, out in public. I guess I hadn't noticed it in the past couple of months because, hey? What can I say? We have argued about his return to the cage after the loss to Louie Gotti the damn Legion, who reminded Vassili of a man he murdered for me when I was seventeen.

We rarely talk about his parents. Damn, am I trying to make a connection here? He will become distant and need his space after mentioning something despicable his father did to his mother. But Vassili hasn't talked to his father since the night we woke up married in Vegas. He told the bastard never to call again... So that leaves me.

I glance down at myself in a designer, peach colored pantsuit. There's a little pudge to my stomach that I haven't been able to rid myself of, but I always assumed that my after-baby hips weren't too big. Heck, ass and hips are a good thing. And the thug of a man that I married never had a problem with it. *I need to work on this tummy.* With that consideration, I click faster, unable to concentrate on work. At 175 pounds, I am twenty pounds over what I was when Vassili and I met.

"I trick people well with custom suits and high heels, but damn, not in the bedroom." My thumb moves in rapid succession with the pen.

FEARLESS II
by Amarie Avant

Samuel pops his head inside the room. His thick eyebrows arch before he steps inside, a cream suit pops against his dark brown skin. The smile on his face fades. "Why so down?"

"Nothing, nothing." I place the pen on the table.

He assesses me a second longer then offers a confident smile.

"Meeting in a few. We have a new—"

"Uncle Sammy, that new guy is a dream," Connie sneaks into the office behind him. She's a redbone with a slim shape, yet lord only knows she can wear blood red and not have this sexy oomph that most women have. She's too starry eyed when it comes to love. She's the woman I never wanted to be until I met Vassili.

"Who's this new guy?" I ask, aware that whomever he is will be the topic of discussion at Pokilicious, me and Connie's favorite lunch hour restaurant, tomorrow.

Samuel regards his niece with a look. "You two can chat about Mr. Nicks after hours. I don't want him meandering down the hall, hearing anything that can cause him to file for sexual harassment. Zariah, how's Mora?" His inquiry ends the previous discussion but presents an array of questions of my very own.

"She's... good... as usual," I begin. My eyes narrow in thought. It never fails, Samuel asking about my mom. He always uses her nickname, Mora, short for Zamora. Something my dad never agreed with.

And damn it, but my mother and I can be deep in discussion or chuckling while watching our favorite show, and here she goes. Mom subtly asks about—

"Tyrese Nicks," Connie butts into my thoughts. Her light brown eyes have a faraway look.

It's on the tip of my tongue to tell Connie to stop playing 'high school' and go for the goal, but Samuel is mentioning lawsuits again on his way out.

"Counselor, you better leave him alone before you catch a *case*," I joke.

With a tiny giggle, Connie leaves me to my own devices.

* * *

An hour later, Vassili texts me, "Lunch?"

Since Samuel is squeezed in the 11am meeting, and I'm not certain how long it will take. Especially if he has to introduce "Tyrese Nicks." I bite my lip and respond.

ME: Make it late??

While stepping out of my office, there is an island of cubicles in the center of the room where the interns and secretaries sit. With Billingsley Legal, a new and upcoming law firm, there is room to grow. Larger offices surround the perimeter.

I head to the conference room, chatting with my assistant, Lanetta, about an upcoming mediation between my client and her ex-husband, when I feel someone watching me. Not with hatred or anything, but the intensity is real.

FEARLESS II
by *Amarie Avant*

Lanetta turns around as I do. "Oh, Tyrese, please let me know if you'd like any help until a new assistant can be assigned to you," Lanetta bats her fake eyelashes.

The man before us nods politely to her, although his gaze never leaves my own. Tyrese is a cool six feet, with creamy brown skin and the brother has a serious pair of dimples that place him in his late twenties at best, and also double as panty droppers. I can tell by the quality of his suit that he blazed through law school. Just like me. More power to my black brother for coming from a well to do family.

"Welcome to the team, Mr. Nicks." I extend a hand.

"Zariah Washington, you don't remember me?"

"Resnov," I correct him with my award-winning smile. "And I can't say that I recall..."

His brown orbs cloud at the sound of my last name. Shit, so now I can't place Tyrese Nicks. Nevertheless, what I do recall is the fear that slammed into my chest the instant Vassili told me he was a Resnov. Mommy didn't raise no fool. Apparently, he is aware of the name.

And he doesn't associate the name with anything good. How to continue when one minute, the man is eyeing me like chocolate pudding and the next, sneering at the surname I married into?

Lanetta heads into the conference room, as he says, "Your father and mine were partners a very long time ago. I'll never forget how… inspired you looked when sitting in on the Sullivan case. You looked at Samuel …"

The way you're eyeing me? With a hunger?

"I heard my name," Samuel cuts in.

"I was reminding Zariah about Sullivan."

Samuel offers a grunt of disgust for the highly decorated cop who murdered four women.

"I was just about to tell her that you restored my faith in the justice system during his extensive litigation process." Tyrese smiles at me, and the lingering gaze of his slowly slides away.

Samuel pats his back. "It's trials like those that made me leave the DA office. Us defense attorneys need the police to assist with evidence. Felt like I was on my own."

My mentor pats my shoulder as well. Damn, that was a dig at my father, who wasn't too keen on cuffing his own, but every word Samuel just said was fact.

My phone buzzes as Tyrese holds the door. That's a saving grace. Like hell do I want him ogling my ass as we walked in. I step a few paces away and they head inside.

VASSILI: meet at 2?

I smile and reply with a thumbs up while stuffing my cellphone into my pants pocket. Although skipping a meal will help counteract all my *extra* thickness, lunch with my husband and daughter is the cherry on top of the cupcake I shouldn't have.

Vassili

Venice Beach
An hour earlier...

The Ukrainian who I've sparred with for almost fifteen years, Nestor, taps gloves with me. We're in the cage at Vadim's Gym. This is my first practice match since leaving Brazil. Adrenaline slams through my veins, on my toes I go, keeping a tight profile.

"Tighter, tighter," Vadim, my trainer, shouts, "You ain't champ no more, keep your chin down, elbows tight!"

My eyes narrow, although I keep my eyes on Nestor. I cock my head for him to make the first move. He punches at my chin. Air zips past as I move. I jab for his nose. My thirst for blood isn't lost on him. In a split second, Nestor is saved from having to reconstruct his nose, while tucking his forearm in front of his face. I issue swift body shots to his lungs. If it weren't for the gear he's wearing, his ribs would've been slaughtered. He lurches to the left and the right, with each hit. Catching his footing, he comes back with a right hook that slides across my chin.

"Stay on him!" Vadim shouts in Russian. "Vassili, pen him."

Then I catch him with a left, right, left. Nestor's knees buckle, he grunts and slides back onto the ground.

"C'mon, brah," I wave a gloved hand. "Get the fuck up, I'll put you down again, I promise."

"Don't get cocky," again, Vadim reminds me that I'm no longer the champ.

Nestor clenches the ground. I step back to my corner, not taking my eyes off him. Like a yoyo, Nestor jumps up to his feet. He shakes out the pain and disequilibrium.

We go back to our toes, chins down, fists at the ready. I let him feel me out and imagine Alvarez, no Karsoff, that motherfucker will be my next match. Might as well have ambitions. Nestor tosses a low kick toward my shin. It's one of those filler movements to see where I'm at. Nestor thinks he's closing in on me, bringing me back to the clench. The confidence is all in his eyes. He reaches low and targets my chin, my hands press the back of his neck, bringing his chest forward, my knee slams into his gut. The padding along his abdomen saves him from the type of "knee" that realigns organs in a fighter's stomach.

"That's what the fuck I like to see!" Yuri shouts out from the seating area.

While Nestor rests, Vadim gives me the body ropes for conditioning, and I know today, he wants to break my body down until I'm resurrected. Newer. Harder.

An hour later, Vadim grips the back of my neck. "You are a beast! Your comeback is now, Vassili. Your grandfather's blood is on fire in your bones."

I dip my head to his compliment. "Who am I murdering next?" My glare roams from him to Yuri. "I need a fucking date. I'm dying here."

Yuri's fat ass is damn near swallowing the folding chair. He sits forward. "Alvarez's team hasn't responded—"

"Fuck Alvarez, I want Karsoff. Put that shit on the calendar so I can go play tea with my daughter already."

My cousin gives a huff as Vadim goes to the runner stroller were Natasha is currently sleeping. He smiles in at her. "Vassili, you got a win the weekend before last. Give people a chance to respond. And like you just said, enjoy your beautiful little girl."

I grab the hand towel from Yuri, stretch it and pop him. "You, manage the fucking situation or I score my own fights."

"Oh yeah?" Yuri's voice raises until he looks over toward the stroller in concern. Nobody wakes my daughter. She has more guts than I do. He whispers through gritted teeth. "You called Alvarez out whole hardly standing on your own two feet in Brazil. Now you wanna step over him for Karsoff? Everyone calls me stupid, though."

"Yeah, you are, mudak. Get me Karsoff or La—"

"This guy is out of his mind?" Yuri tells Vadim.

FEARLESS II
by *Amarie Avant*

My coach glares at me while addressing Yuri. "He has aspirations. All he sees is getting the belt back—"

My fist slams against my chest. "My motherfucking belt."

Vadim flicks my ear. "Close your cunt. Get the fuck outta here, Vassili. My other fighters love to talk shit when you stay a moment longer. And no matter how *milyy*—cute—Natasha is, that baby is also meaner than a—"

"*Volk*—wolf," Yuri finishes.

"You're the Godfather and you say that of my child?" My face is hard but my thick accent rings with laughter as Vadim agrees to his metaphor.

I grip the handles of the stroller and head past the workout gear.

"Yuri, anything on the email?" I ask him.

He shakes his head. Throwing a thumb over his shoulder, Yuri asks, "You want a ride? I'm parked in the alley."

"*Nyet*. I parked a few blocks away. Natasha loves to watch the singers and dancers and shit, and I'll get a little cool down."

"Fuck? Kazen, you haven't worked out enough?"

He heads toward the back of the gym, and I start for the Venice beach exit.

Outside, the sun blazes across the beach. And not one spot along the coast is left as families and couples enjoy the beautiful summer day. I start for the trail, and head off in a jog. Off in the distance, a young Michael Jackson wannabe is gathering a crowd. My baby girl will wake up soon. This is how you wake up a bully without getting into a world of trouble... music.

The boy, panhandling about twenty yards away, has the moves to boot.

The umbrella is shielding Natasha, but she kicks out her foot. Her baby shoe somersaults into the air. She's awake.

"Girl, do you know how much I spend on your shoes?" My tone is even more playful as I stop to retrieve the expensive, stylish tennis shoe that Zariah always complains about. She purchases those ugly "stride" shoes, mentioning how they assist in walking but our baby is too pretty for that.

The name brand tennis shoe is wedged into the sand. When I turn around, there's a man standing before the stroller, sliding open the partition. In a flash, I'm there.

"Who the fuck..." The threat is lodged in my throat.

A pair of eyes the same as mine smile back at me.

Grigor! One of my many little brothers is donning a power-suit. He looks ready for Wall Street, but here he is in Venice, California. I grip his lapel. "Why are you here?"

"No hug, brother?" The idiot still has the silly smile on his face.

"Daddy! Daddyyyy!" Natasha pounds a fist onto the table before her. Organic fruit puffs tremble with each hit.

"Oh, she is beautiful." Grigor reaches out, and I slap his hand. He bares his teeth, shaking out the pain in his hand. "It never fails, Vassili. You don't have to be so rude."

"Fuck You. Just because your cunt of a mother was such a simple piece of pussy doesn't mean you have to be —"

Grigor interrupts my comment with a dose of seriousness. "Vassili, dad wants to talk to you."

"Where's Semion?" I ask of my father's sister's son. Of all the damn kids Anatoly had, he only wanted me for the bratva. And he only utilizes that ugly fuck, Semion, as his lap dog. There has to be logic in that Semion is so fucking ugly, you'd have to be crazier than the devil to cross him.

"At the car." Grigor nudges his head to the side. Along the tiny street is a Maybach. My cousin, Semion's enormous square head bobs as he leans against the side of the car. Noticing the back of a head, which must belong to my father, I keep it pushing.

"You came a long way for nothing, *brat*— brother," I toss over my shoulder.

It's a quarter after twelve, and I need to shower and dress. Natasha and I have our routine, she takes her two-hour nap, during my training, including the drive to and from Vadim's gym. Usually I play hard with my child in the afternoon, because Zariah will complain if our girl refuses to fall asleep on time. We'll be pushing it as it is to pick up Zariah by 2pm.

Natasha is pointing to seagulls squawking in the water as I jog past. At least, she will get a good night's sleep, waking up early. Now, I'll have to improvise to wash off all this sweat. Grigor's impromptu arrival throws me off my game for a moment, and I almost pass the street that I parked on. In Venice, with all the million-dollar homes and tiny streets lining the ocean, one could get lost. But I owned a home in the area, prior to marrying and settling down.

At Park Street, I move the stroller off the pathway since the street I parked off, the sidewalk doesn't connect with the pathway. The wheels navigate over the sand for a moment before wedging into the ground.

"Where you wanna go for lunch, beautiful, huh?" I ask.

"Daddy, da-daddy," she slobbers.

"Oh, you're happy today, no teething?" I unlatch her from the seat, hoist her on my arm, folding up the stroller, and then heft that beneath my other arm. "Daddy stinks, sweetheart," I tell her as she begins to slobber on my shoulder.

We head through the sand, and onto the sidewalk. I lean the stroller against the front side door of my Mercedes SUV, open the backdoor, and place Natasha in her car seat. While climbing into my car, I glance

FEARLESS II
by *Amarie Avant*

back at my beautiful daughter and my mind is on the woman who made her so gorgeous. Zariah.

***

Forty-five minutes later, the sweat has salted against my muscles and my damp shirt clings to my chest. "Dad's a fuc—Dad's a mess," I tell Natasha as I place her on my hip and we enter the kitchen.

"Eat, eat," she growls.

"Yes, this is where we eat, but not yet, girl. Let me shower," I tell her, a little too excited to hold on a conversation with my child. There was a time I could go days without talking, but the baby's book Zariah read, I snuck a peek at a few pages, and learned the more I talk to Natasha the more vocalized and intelligent she will become. Of course, my daughter will become an MMA fighter like her father, but there will be times I prefer her to use her words and not her fists. "You want French fries?"

"Yeah!"

"Okay, baby girl, we will get those French fries, but don't fight me if we aren't at the restaurant soon enough."

I start down the hall to the front of the house where the double staircase is. My hand just grazes the carved wood staircase when I hear a noise. *Someone is in my house!*

Zariah

Surprisingly the meeting ends well before one pm. Connie has the task of helping Tyrese become acclimated with the office, which causes Lanetta and a few of the other female workers to sulk. Like what where these hoes intending to train him on? Filing and shit?

Damn, I'm getting a little edgy. I take this as my key to get some sustenance in my body. These extra layers of fat aren't fooling my brain. I am *hungray*!

I pull out my cell phone and text Vassili a change of plans.

ME: How about you come get me now…

I add an emoticon, and then press send.

"Zar, Zariah," Connie corrects herself, with a professional nod, "Tyrese and I are headed to lunch. You should come."

"Vassili should be here soon," I reply. And if he doesn't get the message to come early, there are a few snacks in my cabinets that have my name written all over them.

"You should really come." She lowers her voice, as we head toward our offices. "His eyes are all over your ass right now."

FEARLESS II
by *Amarie Avant*

"I'm married."

"And that wedding ring of yours compliments all the junk in your trunk. I'm sure he's aware. Flirting never hurts..."

Sometimes I just can't with Connie. She assisted me with training for the bar, having passed the October prior. Yet, her mentality can be lacking. Vassili and I are very jealous people. And I am too goal oriented to piss off my husband which means I do not have the time or the balls to cheat.

"So, are you joining us for lunch?" Tyrese catches up with us.

"Oh, where are we going?" Lanetta asks, running up after him. Damn it, I want to school her on a few things. When my father's secretary, Berenice, started to stick her claws into him, she did it subtly. Lanetta needs to learn the game.

I speak up. "Pokalicious has the best sushi, but that's our Wednesday spot. Greek Street is our favorite, for Greek," I shrug.

"Which do you prefer?" he asks.

"Depends on what you all agree upon. This is a democracy. Can't vote, I have other arrangements."

"Oh, is Vassili taking you to lunch?" Lanetta hops in.

Well, mentioning it myself seemed like bragging. I nod, and turn to strut away. And damn it, Tyrese Nick's eyes are glued to me, yet again, reminding me that the chat we need to have can't come soon enough.

FEARLESS II
by *Amarie Avant*

Vassili

My eyes close for a fraction of second as I process the past hour. Grigor and Semion had me convinced that the man in the Maybach being guarded by that dog faced fucking cousin of mine was my father. Anatoly doesn't exit from hiding without heavy security. Hence, my assumption that Anatoly was in the backseat of the car.

A familiar scent hits me. It's of lemon, fir cones, and black currant, the scent is a favorite of Putin, and my father, forcing my frown to deepen.

I kiss Natasha's soft cheek. "Don't play nice with grandpa," I tell her, recalling the first time Anatoly came to my neck of the woods. We were at a daddy-daughter day at the park near our home. She was on a swing when three SUVs pulled up.

Zariah knows nothing about that.

She never will.

We enter the dining room. There's a China cabinet to one side, in the middle is a fortress of a table. Crystal goblets, silver chargers, and other trinkets give the table a posh home magazine feel. On each side of the lengthy, custom made table, three men stand. My eyes cut to their holstered guns. Then my wrath directs to my father. At the park, he was incognito with a red wig. Yet wearing one of his usual colorful suits. Today, he swapped the bright blue suit for a canary yellow one, with an even brighter blue silk tie. Enough jeweled on his fingers to certify him as a real bitch. Fucking idiot.

"Bring her here, bring her here," Anatoly clasps his hands together. "My little Chak Chak," he says, having given Natasha the nickname of a Turkish dessert, which is deep fried and drenched in honey, and a staple with Russian tea.

"Cha... Cha!" My daughter trades teams instantly, chubby fists pumping in the air.

"*Moy syn*—my son!" Anatoly snaps at me. "Bring my granddaughter. I wasn't invited to her first birthday, have some common decency. Let's save the 'you're disappointing me' for later. Unless you're ready to agree with the only proposal on the table?"

"*Nyet.* I'm good with disappointing you, it's the norm for us," I snarl. Though I cuss in front of my child, I place my hand over her ear, the other is trapped against my sweaty ass shirt. She has this habit of picking up words that are said in emotion—or lack thereof. "Have I ever made it seem like I give a fuck about your psychotic requests?"

His hard eyes match my glare, and then they soften while he holds out his hands for Natasha. "Chak-Chak, are you walking yet?"

"A couple of steps." I turn to one of the men. "If those guns go from any of your waistbands, you're all dead."

The man's gaze falls to the floor.

"Pah!" My father scoffs. "Semion is about the only one of these fucks who doesn't care for your threats."

"Good, Good. Make him your legacy."

"My nephew?" He considers the idea with disdain, ready to argue, but I place Natasha on her own two feet, and take both of her hands. Again, I want to tell her not to play nice, but she's pressing off from her knees and attempting to hurry to the piece of a crap of a father of mine.

His praise for my daughter curdles in my ears. Though I cannot recall being so young, I remember my sister, Sasha. Out of all my father's children, Sasha and I had the same mother. Anatoly did not glance her way much of the time he came over. And no matter how hard I tried to make it up to Sasha, she chose the lifestyle my father got rich on. Drugs.

With my support, Natasha takes heavy, shaky steps down the length of the table to her grandfather.

"I like black people," Anatoly's words come out of nowhere. "Can't say this for your wife—beautiful shape— but this girl, my Chak Chak is the perfect color." He tugs out of his suit, and places his arm next to hers, they're both a golden complexion. "Fuck, I

FEARLESS II
by *Amarie Avant*

could sunbath for days and not obtain this flawless hue. Girl, you are 24 karat gold."

She laughs at his disgusting comments. My father holds out a velvet box. "Chak Chak, this is for you."

He opens it, and the diamond earrings inside are so ridiculously large that she'll tumble attempting to walk with them in her ear. The moment he leaves, those go to.

I sit on the chair next to him, and pull out my cell phone. It's almost two pm.

"Vassili," my father says my name, in a testy tone, when I assumed he always took great pleasure in saying 'my son' just to irritate me.

I toss the phone on the table. "You afraid I'll call America's Most Wanted?"

He's paranoid. Natasha stands in his lap and pulls out his handkerchief in a matter of seconds. Next, she goes for his tie. I smile as he gulps.

"Chak-Chak, too many people want to kill me. Not you, too?" He smiles at her, with a million-dollar row of veneers, while removing his tie from her tight fists.

"Cha… Cha… Daddy!" She shouts.

This mudak proceeds to gift her with all of his attention. "I have too many kids, sweetheart. Shit, you aren't even my first grand baby, but you are the most important one. You belong to *moy syn*. You are princess of the bratva, yes you are." He laughs.

FEARLESS II
by *Amarie Avant*

"She isn't princess of the fucking bratva, Anatoly." I sit back in my chair. "What do you want? I have shit to do."

With his tie removed, my father addresses me again. This time, the usual pure anger in his eyes is knocked down a few notches. "You and I have a business to run."

"Oh, you're going legit now? I may need a new manager if Yuri keeps slacking off." I am far from comedic, and my carefree stance slithers beneath his skin.

"How's The Red Door?" He mentions the lounge that I own in honor of my dearly departed sister, Sasha.

"Good."

"I see Resnov Vodka is still the prime seller."

"I have a contract." I grunt. "The family vodka is about the only legacy that I give a fuck about, Anatoly."

"Return my girls to The Red Door."

I shake my head, not even wasting my breath with a response.

"What do you want, Vassili? The last time I came to California, didn't I tell you that there'd be consequences of noncooperation."

My hand slams against the table. The sturdy wood splinters. "You do not threaten me!"

Natasha jolts, her cute little face puckers into a frown. And then she bursts into tears.

FEARLESS II
by Amarie Avant

The men become tense. Each one easing his hand along the butt of his gun.

"Pull them out, and die," I growl through tensed lips.

"Chak-Chak, your *otets*—father is a very bull-headed man. He is blood of my blood. He will get passes, trust me, beautiful, no one in this world will touch a hair of his head or your head."

"Or my wife's." I argue.

"Or your mothers of course, what sort of man would I be?"

Our eyes lock onto each other's. This motherfucker murdered my mother.

"I had nothing to do with it," Anatoly reads my mind. "I loved your mother, Vassili."

Tears burn against my eyes. My knuckles are numb. I glance down at them. Their also ashen gray due to holding them into tight fists. My breaths come short, as I think about all the crap my mother was put through by this man. He made her weak.

I hated her.

I still have him to hate for it.

"You removed all the girls from The Red Door, Vassili. Make your father happy for once and return them," his tone is callus. "You've had ample time. No, you've had more time than necessary. I was sick for a while, so you have had more time than necessary to stop being stubborn. Do it now, before *something* happens."

FEARLESS II
by *Amarie Avant*

"Dah, I'm aware of the repercussions of my actions. If we weren't family, I'd be dead. If it makes you feel any better, Malich was the one who handled anything that had a connection to you. He ensured that the cunts were safe, and the rich old fucks kept coming. All the mistrust you have for your baby *brat*—brother is bullshit. Malich plays into the rules where one must do what they're parents asks, or their older brother, in your case. But I give respect where respect is given. And I can't' recall a day in my life that I gave a fuck about you."

"Vassili," he breathes heavily, still cooing into Natasha's ear as she cries against this neck. "I tried so very hard with you. Somewhere in the back of my mind, I knew that you, and that other fucking girl were always so much like your mama. But they are both dead now." He says of Sasha and his first wife. "You are moy syn," he argues through gritted teeth. "Mine."

"Sasha. Do you even recall your own daughter's name?"

"Daughter's names? Hmmm, I don't recollect many of them by name, no."

"So, I allow you to sex traffic your high-end prostitutes at The Red Door. What's next?"

"You head it, instead of Malich. I don't need my little brother, Vassili. I sure as fuck don't need my nephew. Semion gets a snug wee bullet to the skull when you become king. Contrary to how you perceive things, everything I have ever accomplished was for the benefit of my first child." He kisses Natasha's head as she snores softly.

"I've been thinking." I stare at him for a beat. "If we took this moment in time and dissected it. Tore it away from the image of the man who had my mother tied to a street sign in our hometown and had a sign of vulgarities strung around her. If we took this precise second and forgot about the families you've had murdered, the whores you had strung out or given "the world to" in order to fuck other rich old fucks for money. What would we have? Anatoly, what kinda man are you without the power and fear?"

He rubs Natasha's back softly, and I swear the glare he gives me tells me that she is the only safe person in this house. Blood is slamming through my veins. But I won't fight him. My child is here. There was a day when I would fight my father fist for fist, only to be stopped by multiple guns to my head. In his warped mind, me being his first born is like my golden ticket to act like any other over-privileged white American boy. I can play fool. Cuss him. Fight him. Just like those Facebook home videos that some people think are funny and tear my fucking heart out because in another world you respect your elders. But not him. He'll go toe to toe with me no problem. He'll let me push the limits.

Nobody else can. Malich will suffer. Yuri and Igor will be marked. I continue with, "so what kinda motherfucker are you without the team, huh?" I glare through him, realizing he had to have sent the email. It would be too coincidental for him to come two days after. I'd ask him, but the mudak is a liar.

He bestows a loving kiss at the top of Natasha's head. "The kind who gets shit done."

"I'll think about the bitches, okay?" I lie. Because motherfuckers like him just want attention.

"Returning them to The Red Door?" His eyebrow cocks in hope. When I nod, he asks, "What's to think about? I've lost a mill a week, fucking with you for over a year, Vassili."

"Then you continue to lose a little longer." *Until I speak with Malich and we come up with a plan to get rid of you for good.*

***

"I want out," Malich's response is amplified through the speaker of my car radio. "The moment Zariah kicked my old ass out of The Red Door—"

"It wasn't like that."

"It was. She has balls. I love and respect your wife, Vassili. She's just like my..." The confidence in his voice fades for a moment. "You've got a good girl. Gets shit done. I got the boot from The Red Door. You removed all the illegal crap. Now, I want out. Should've done it years ago."

"Dyadya," I call my uncle in Russian. My hands are tightened on the wheel as I head down the street near Zariah's job. "I can't put you in this situation. I'll sell The Red Door. Besides, the second we opened for business I had nothing to do with the place. I spent millions having it designed just like Sasha dreamt." I almost laugh at the thought. "The constructor said the place would be perfect. And then I turned pussy and couldn't step into the place. Shit, you ran the day to day business and the whores until I bucked up enough to actually venture inside. Zariah just made me get rid of them, clean the place out, ya know? I still don't have much to do with it."

"You'll sell The Red door, Vassili?" He asks in the fatherly disappointment that I learned from him. "All because of Anatoly?"

I glance into the rearview mirror, Natasha is gnawing at her teething ring. "Yeah. Fuck him. I purchased that place for Sasha's memory, but my little sister will live in my heart."

"Vassili, your cousins and I will be okay. I might play the part for Anatoly, and I promise you that I have never fucked over my brother, but he has to understand that when he runs an organization, he either gains loyalty or fear."

I slap down the handle that turns the left blinker on. "Malich, I understand. You always say that there's no ruling with both."

"No, son, there is not. One day his men will turn on him. But the crew who runs his West Coast Operation won't allow him to do anything. We are Resnovs, Vassili. Boss of all bosses or not, your father won't harm any of us unless we have betrayed him.

FEARLESS II
by *Amarie Avant*

We've done nothing but retire. So what, it leaves a chair open in the big 7. Anatoly owns the big seven."

"But you have a voice."

"Did you just hear me? All the mudaks sitting at the table have no say. The seven chairs are bullshit, Anatoly rules. Do what you intended, tell the fool no for the umpteenth time, and make him understand that you will not return on your word. Keep The Red Door, one day when your glory days in the MMA cage are behind you, you may want to manage it yourself. Don't give it up."

Fuck, am I giving up? "Alright," I reply, sliding into a parking spot at Billingsley Legal.

***

Inside the building, we are made even further late due to the workers who stop to speak with Natasha. I can't take but five steps before another secretary or assistant says something.

"Oh, did you do her hair?"

"Yup." I reply.

"You are getting good at this."

"Thanks!" I respond once more.

"Natasha, you are the prettiest little girl in the world."

Another one says, "She's spoiled rotten, that's what she is. Pretty little doll."

My glare tracks just above the cubicles to the far side of the building, where a man is standing at the

76

FEARLESS II
by *Amarie Avant*

door to Zariah's office. From this angle, I can't place his face.

I'm half way there when Samuel comes from his office. "Vassili, Natasha, some of my most favorite people." I shake the man's hand and he takes Natasha. "We still on for Sunday dinner?"

"Long as my steak is ready." I nod.

"Alright, Alright. I'll bring the meats, you bake the cake?"

I chuckle. Samuel is a fan of my Russian cake. It all happened due to Malich, his love of food started a friendly competition. I made Sasha's favorite.

"Not too loud, Sam. Nobody has to know about our arrangement. But as long as you haven't forgotten about how I like my steak, I got you." I hold up lunch that I bought.

"You head on in Zariah's room. I think Natasha has a few more autographs to give out," he grins.

I turn to walk away. Damn, I can recall the day when Samuel Billingsley tried to get my cousin, Igor Resnov, to turn snitch on the rest of my family. Can't believe the same man gave me a chance, with someone so important to him. Zariah.

The doorway to Zariah's room is empty.

At the sound of her voice, my pace falters "Oh God, this is soooo good, Tyrese. Almost makes me feel bad for not recalling who you are."

"Well, we have time to catch up," comes a response that has a little too much interest in it.

"Yeah right, this place is very busy," she responds just as I step into the room.

There's a black man sitting on the chair across from hers. The mudak is entirely too comfortable in her presence.

Zariah

Where the hell did Connie go? The crew had ended up going to our Wednesday spot, since one of the secretaries hadn't tasted sushi in a while. Connie texted to let me know that we might need to search Yelp for something new the day after tomorrow, when I asked her to bring me kakinohazushi. Somewhere in the mix, Vassili texted me thirty minutes late, to tell me that Vadim had run behind schedule with his fighters. Connie came in to drop it off, but she had Tyrese with her. And that heifa knows I zone out when I'm focused on work, but she came inside and indicated that she left her purse at work.

Tyrese bought the damn kakinohazushi for me. And now he has made himself comfortable, refuses to allow me to pay him back, and is content talking about old times.

My stomach was growling so loudly a minute ago, that I set aside my typing and started to eat. I just made a joke about wishing I remembered who Tyrese was in order to give him the opportunity to cough it up already. But then, out of the corner of my eye, I see my husband. First of all, Vassili has no right to look so damn fine while jealous. Secondly, well, I should be the angry one, because I'm licking fingers and have just stuffed a gunkan maki into my mouth.

My face brightens at the sight of him. Tyrese takes that as an invitation to look at me like I've reinvented sex, so I hurry up and speak before he can come to the wrong conclusion, without even being aware that he just stepped on the hornets' nest.

"Vassili, baby," I quickly mention his arrival and place a hand over my mouth, "Oh, you brought my favorite."

I gulp the rest of the sushi down my throat as Tyrese stands abruptly. Damn, my mouth smells like uni as I rise and step around my desk to hug my husband. His tongue soars down my throat, and he kisses me in ways that make me lose my mind. Vassili's hand steers my lower back, aware my knees are weakening by the second.

As we let go, my gaze narrows at my husband, and then a fake smile plasters on my face. He couldn't fuck with my head like this when we were at the bar in Brazil? He couldn't dance with me? But now he can? Tonight, I will have words for him!

"This is my husband, Vassili Resnov." I turn to Tyrese, "Vassili, this is the newest attorney at Billingsley Legal, Tyrese Nicks."

The men shake hands and I take the glossy turquoise bag with the words Flour Bakery scrawled on the side. One of my favorite bakeries.

FEARLESS II
by *Amarie Avant*

"Nice to meet you, Mr. Resnov. I thought I'd bring your wife lunch, seems she was starving today."

Tyrese's word choice clears my mind of my anger with my husband. I know he didn't! "I actually asked Connie to—"

Vassili gestures toward the door. "Good for you. You can go now."

Tyrese looks incredulous, as my husband dismisses him. He glances toward me.

But Vassili finishes him off with, "Don't ever bring my wife anything else."

"Don't feed your wife after she's *waited* an hour for you?" Tyrese inquires.

Connie must've blabbed about him running late!

Vassili rubs a hand across the bristles at his jaw. "You know who I am? You look smart enough to know, right?"

"I know exactly who you are," Tyrese says, voice dripping in disgust.

"So now I'll ask that you don't even address my wife unless it's business related. It's a courtesy for me to ask."

"Okay."

"And you understand anything I say goes. Have a good day," Vassili turns away from him.

I offer Tyrese one of those quick grins that warns him to leave the room. He backs up toward the door as Samuel enters with our daughter. "This is her royal highness, Natasha Resnov," Samuel is well aware of the tension, but his goofy demeanor permeates the tiny area. "She's a fighter like her father. It took a while for me to gather both of their respect, Tyrese."

"Thanks, Sammy." I take my daughter from his arms. He whispers something to Tyrese that finally revs the man's engine enough to leave my office.

Vassili stands toward the window at the far side of my room, arms folded.

"What the hell was that all about?" I ask.

His pitch-black gaze glowers in my direction. "That mudak wasn't flirting with you?"

I roll my eyes at the rhetorical question. "He's new. I haven't yet had a conversation with him about…"

"No need. If he ever flirts with you—"

"What are you going to do, Vassili? Allow his opinion of you, of *our* last name, to be solidified by your choice of actions?'

"But of course, my beautiful wife. You know from past experience that I could give a fuck what most people think of me. Now eat your food." He orders, nudging his square jaw to the bag.

"So, what was with the kiss, though?"

"I'm done discussing the matter with you, Zariah." Vassili grabs the bag, and says, "Natasha, you ready for your sparkly cupcake."

"She needs to eat lunch," I tell him.

"The bakery is next door to McDonalds. We stopped for French fries, too. The little bully refused to wait." Vassili steps closer to me, lust consuming that sinfully dark gaze of his. He smiles at Natasha. "Tell mama to be nice to Daddy."

Our daughter begins to pull my hair at that. "Natasha, don't be a bully like your father."

I place her in the corner where there's ABC-123 patterned carpet along with toys for her to play with.

Vassili is right behind me when I straighten up.

"The door is open, and Natasha is…"

"Busy," his mouth finds my earlobe and sucks softly against it.

"You really were just being an asshole. And yes, for some reason that man wanted to play the fool with you. Vassili, were you stuck at Vadim's?" I stare him straight in the eye.

"Oh, your friend brings you lunch, and now you're paranoid? What kinda shit is that, Zariah?" In a snap, Vassili is helping Natasha right her balance.

"My friend?"

"Yup."

My hands go to my hips. "I don't know that man."

Vassili grunts. "Seems like he knows you and was just about to take you down a trip to memory lane had I not arrived."

"First of all, Vassili, I didn't even get a chance to correct him, you came in like a barbarian. This is my place of employment."

by Amarie Avant

He waits for a moment, and I know Vassili isn't a fan of arguing with me. Sometimes I have to force him to talk due to him not wanting to be disrespectful. I think Anatoly ruined him for how to deal with a wife. But his hard eyes flare into mine. "You are my wife. Act like it."

My lips are bunched together, they begin to twitch in annoyance. Random thoughts bounce throughout my brain. Was he at Vadim's Gym? Am I really getting too fat? Or was he with my child somewhere else? Why did the obstetrician say that I'd lose weight while breastfeeding? Hell, I just got hungrier!

And now I'm standing before this hoodlum of a husband of mine. Intuition tells me he lied. Love warns that my man would never cheat.

Vassili presses his hand against my cheeks, his palm fits along my jaw and he caresses softly. "I never mind when men look. You are so fucking beautiful it's to be expected," he says before planting a kiss on my lips. His mouth lingers on mine. "I'm a dick, okay?"

I eat every single word.

"But I don't like that guy. You can tell me later how the two of you know each other. For now, can we eat?"

"I don't really recollect where or how I know him, Vassili," I murmur. This husband of mine has me right where he wants me.

"Okay, let's eat before I get really hungry." That deep baritone of his always blows my mind.

My pussy lips jolt, crying for action. I nod and move away from Vassili. Stopped by his hand caressing mine. He pulls, and I follow, pressing my body against his rock hardness. The words are lodged in my throat to say we are still at my office, with the door open to boot, but my mouth waters for him again. This time, the kiss is succulent.

His tongue licks mine, it purely animalistic, and I can't help but imagine it's his cock as my tongue swirls around his.

"*Ya nikogda ne otpushchu tebya*—I will never let you go," he murmurs in Russian. I remember the first time he said that, although it was recently. It was after his last fight, with Tiago. I ran through the crowd with Taryn's help to catch up to him. I'd cried and made promises. And I must've made a monologue of apologies for leaving during his match.

And then, again in Russian, he'd told me this and it made my heart swell with love. Every ribbon of doubt—my weight, my concern if he has a wandering eye, it all shreds to nothing, leaving just me and him and the euphoria of the love I have for him. And the love he consumes me with.

***

Later in the afternoon I was assigned a new case and didn't have a chance to seek out Tyrese. He'd said his father and mine knew each other. I still have yet to make the connection, and during the Sullivan trial, when Samuel put away that crooked cop, nobody in the world existed. I saw myself in my mentor's custom suit as a top litigator. Justice reigned that day.

Needless to say, the conversation I need to have with Mr. Nicks will have to wait. I'm on the bicycle in our Home gym when my phone rings. It's my mom.

I place the call on speaker. "Hey, I've been waiting on you to check on me."

Her voice isn't its usual happy self. "Well, I- I had my shows to catch up on."

We've been frick and frack for the last few weeks. "Aw, you miss me already? Martin is going to kill me if I trick you into moving back to Los Angeles. Why didn't you FaceTime me, so I can make *faces* at the dysfunctional daytime soaps you love?"

"Humph," my mother replies, making me almost feel like I'm carrying the conversation until she asks, "How was your first day back?"

I groan. "I'm on my treadmill now, desperately endeavoring to undo the last two weeks."

"Who you telling? Not sure if I ate more in Brazil or during Natasha's birthday party. So how is work?"

"Good. I just have one case going to mediation and a new assignment. Nothing too bad."

"How's Sammy?"

I offer the same befuddled mask that I swear Samuel didn't notice due to Connie entering the room, gushing like a school girl, or he just chose not to bring

FEARLESS II
by *Amarie Avant*

up. At the birthday party, the two of them disappeared for a while, and now I'm truly wondering what is going on. "What's with this 'Sammy' business. Vassili's running around calling him Sam like they are from the same gang. And here you go, mom, calling *Samuel*, Sammy"

"Girl, how is *Sammy*?"

Vassili enters the gym, he nods his head to me. "Guess what, my mom is checking in on Samuel." I mouth as Vassili tells me to hustle. How fast does he want me to peddle? I pay him no attention and address the woman who raised me. "To be honest, Mom, he's good. You just saw the man 48 hours, or so, ago. But let me remind you, when you and dad divorced y'all split friends. Sammy was reverted back to previous ownership, meaning Dad has sole custody."

Now I can hear her smiling through the receiver. "Zariah, don't even. I can ask about an old friend. Sam is married every few years anyhow, so nobody is *studying* him."

"Studying him," I shake my head at her old school choice of words. "Hey, tell me about the new guy? You were gone for two weeks, Mom, which is forever for such a new love."

"Zariah, the timer just went off. I'm making a soufflé, can't let it over bake."

A familiar feeling of worry tightens my shoulders. "Mom—"

The call cuts.

FEARLESS II
by Amarie Avant

"What's wrong, Zariah?" Vassili asks.

An image of my father yanking his belt from his pants flashes my mind.

He was getting ready to beat… my mother.

"I don't know," I mumble a response to my husband, because I don't want to speak my doubts in existence. Jesus, don't let it be. "I have another mile to do."

"Don't work too hard, girl." His eyes shut in that sexy way that makes my regimen falter.

Vassili exits the room. The conversation I just finished with my mother reruns through my cognition again. Her tone was a bit lackluster. But what person is happy after returning from vacation?

As a child, I had my job cut out for me in getting her to laugh. When I jokingly mentioned that she and Samuel cannot be friends, she seemed to laugh about it.

She got off the phone with me way too quickly.

I started to dial my older brother, Martin, but quickly think better of it. Because, dang, it's past ten pm there, and unlike my mother who has her TV shows and some mysterious boyfriend to keep her company, Martin and his wife are on a regimen with their children. Their sleep schedule is set for nightfall.

I head out of the gym, in search of my husband, to talk over this uneasy feeling. I need Vassili to tell me I'm imagining things or worrying too much. Our bedroom is empty so I call out for him.

"In the kitchen," he replies.

Vassili

The conversation between Zariah and her mother is still on my mind. There's too much for me to do besides spying, but when I walked past the gym, my wife had just placed Ms. Haskins on speakerphone. The list of crap I need to review with Yuri faded from my mind. Her mother's tone was missing something.

That reminds me, when is the last time I checked on her? Though Zamora Haskins was in our presence for two weeks, I have learned to make it a habit to ensure that everyone my wife loves is safe. The girls have such a good relationship with each other that she's flying to California every other month or so. Her brother, Martin, is a family man, and with a nine-to-five, and a wife and three kids to take care of, I suspect he isn't available all the time for Mrs. Haskins.

While warming my borscht soup on the stove, I pull out my cell phone and dial Yuri.

"I'm still looking into the email, Vassili. Alvarez has sent the contract, what do you want to negotiate, we can't have everything?" he says instead of hello.

"Fuck you to, Yuri. You act like you're being run like a lap dog." I argue, although I am about to add more to his plate.

FEARLESS II
by *Amarie Avant*

"Did you review the contract? The fight's in Atlanta, mid-July."

"Nah, I didn't look over that shit, Alvarez can suck these hairy balls for all I'm concerned. He's nobody." I stir the copper pot as the soup begins to simmer.

Yuri sighs. "You say you want to fight. Then you hound me about when, where, how. Shit, Vassili, the venue is enough to offset the bone he's willing to throw you."

"Look, I want you to go to Atlanta."

"We can fax back the contract."

"Net! Yuri, listen, this is about Zariah's mom." I grab the remote, and turn on the television which is near the sliding glass door. The low drum of a sitcom sets my nerves at ease. Can't have Zariah hearing what I'm about to say, no need for her to be worrying. "I think she might be getting punched around—"

"Ms. Haskins?"

"Yes, idiot, Zariah only has one mother."

"By who? When?"

I pull the phone away from my ears. I'm getting fucking investigated through a loudspeaker, here. "Zamora has a boyfriend, I don't know his name yet. But she and Zariah Facetime during every single call except tonight. When we were on vacation, she didn't mention much about the bastard. Just now, they were talking, and Zamora blew her off. They're too close for that shit. Something isn't right."

FEARLESS II
by Amarie Avant

There's silence at the end of the receiver for a moment. "Alvarez's camp is gunning for the Center Stage Theater—"

"Why you bring him up now, huh? Yuri, we're talking about Zariah's mother and you bring up that disrespectful *mudak*."

"Vassili, breathe," he cuts in. "We'll go check out the venue and see about Ms. Haskins. Best case scenario, she makes my cookies, we come home. Worst case scenario, you handle the fuck who's crossing the line with her, and I toss out the trash."

My eyebrows crinkle. "What the fuck? I just gave you an assignment."

"Remember your daughter's first birthday two days ago. You said we were a team, so teammate, should I get the tickets so that *we* can go check on her, or will *you?*"

I sigh heavily, recalling the whining Yuri did in my office that day. He's right, I need to handle this myself. "Fine. You get the tickets, though."

"Should I bump him? You dump him?"

"*Nyet!* I'll handle the shit myself. Nobody touches a hair on my loved ones, Yuri."

"That's what I wanna hear, *kazen*."

"Baby, what's wrong?" Zariah murmurs from the entrance to the kitchen.

Fuck, what do I tell Zariah? I hate it when she worries.

Zariah

Vassili looks up at me, almost as if he didn't hear me enter. From my view of the kitchen, while walking down the hall, he'd been discussing something serious. His brow is furrowed, his sexy lips set into a frown.

"Yuri," he says, tossing his cellphone onto the marble countertop. "He sent me a bullshit contract from Alvarez, says we can fight at this convention center. I've never had a match there. But he believes I can make more than enough money selling my shit there."

It's a new day for my husband if he agrees to the proposal. Vassili talks way too much shit, so I ask, "So, you're gonna agree with the contract?"

"I'll go to Atlanta, check out the scene. See if it's worth signing the papers."

My heart sinks. We just got to a good place, how will we stay there if he leaves so soon? "Aw, can't you virtual tour the center online? I hate when you go away. We just got back from vacation but you're already on the run."

"C'mere," he orders. The sexy thickness of his Russian voice seems to wrap around me from yards away as he says, "I'll just have to fuck you so hard you can't think until I return."

"Oh, that defeats the purpose of me staying home and going to work," I grin at him, while heading over. "One day I won't allow you to fuck me into submission. Sex doesn't make everything better."

"Pft! It's either I fuck you brainless or feed you borscht?" he jokes.

"My palate isn't fit for that soup, and you know it." I tease.

He grunts. "I know exactly what your mouth is fit for."

My tongue dips out and plays across my bottom lip as I stop before Vassili. I inhale the scent of him. It's perfect, the epitome of masculinity. Fresh woods and patchouli scented. My eyes close as I breathe in more of his strength.

"To your knees, Zariah," he commands, right here in the middle of the kitchen.

I'm obedient of his request, and kneel in front of him before his long, venous cock flops out. Looking like it weighs a ton.

"No hands, girl." His hard voice plays somewhere between sinful and sultry. "I bet that mouth of yours is so fucking wet, just as wet as between those thighs."

My body melts. My pink tongue darts out to lick the lengthy curve of him, riding along the wide planes of his dick. When my mouth sucks him down my throat, Vassili's groan is likened to the sound of a tiger's deep, low, powerful, rumble.

My mouth holds him in a snug fit, slides up and down the entire length of his cock, wetting him even more.

"You wanna use your hands, don't you?"

I sigh as response.

"*Nyet,* beautiful, not on me. You can fuck yourself if you'd like."

A trickle of honey flows from my pussy. I bang his cock against my tonsils, in a repetitive motion, needing his seed to fill my mouth, to slide down my throat. Needing him to satiate me.

"Zariah, fuck yourself." His command slams through me.

My hand slips into my runner shorts, past the soft hairs of my pussy and right to my swollen lips. When my palm caresses along my clit, my throat moans against the head of his cock. I start to gather a rhythm, my fingers pressing deep inside my ocean, my mouth a second ocean for his dick.

"Stop, Zariah."

My brown eyes rise, glancing past ridges of tattoos on his six pack, up to his chiseled jaw.

"No," I murmur, taking him further, while taking myself further.

"Stop, beautiful. This is about me blowing your mind, Zar." He takes my hand and I arise. "You're sweet, right?"

FEARLESS II
by *Amarie Avant*

"I'm so wet…"

"Let me see how sweet you are." Vassili grips my wrist and brings my hands to my mouth. His tongue flicks out, mine does too. I taste the juices that I've made for us, he tastes them as well. Then his mouth meets mine in a kiss.

"Fuck," he says, "You ready to go crazy?"

I've hardly bobbed my head once, and Vassili has me over his shoulder. He carries me into the den, where a bear fur rug is on the center of the floor. Vassili lays me down and has me out of the sports bra and shorts in a second.

"Wai… wait…" I try to grab at his mohawk, but his head is dodging for the sweetness between my thick thighs before I can remind him that I just did four miles on the bike upstairs. My left leg gets to jerking as his tongue spears inside of my pussy, thick enough to get the job done and zeroing in on my g-spot. My first orgasm slams through my body, leaving my eyes shut tightly, and a falsetto piercing from my lungs.

"Vassili…" I scream.

He doesn't offer me a moment's reprieve as he licks away at the cum squirting out of me. My skin goosebumps and burns as Vassili rubs a hand up along my waist and to my breast. He's furious in his eating, and my hips have risen off the floor to match the vigor of his tongue. While he snacks greedily on my pussy, he tweaks my nipple, and I swear that my pussy must taste like the world's best pie, because he's working another orgasm to the surface. I can feel it rising from my toes, my leg tenses again. I grab at the fur beneath me, and scream aloud.

"Shit, damn—shit, damn, motherfucker," I can feel my body begin to cave into the floor, but Vassili lifts my ass up, and continues to dig in. "Shit, da-damn, motherfucker," I shout again. *Wait a minute, that's a D'Angelo song.* The crooner was losing his mind with rage in that song, and I'm losing my mind with desire all the same. My fist clamps onto Vassili's wavy brown hair as I slide my hips around. It feels like his chin is pressing against my asshole as he keeps it lifted up.

He mustn't need air?

Why exactly did I just think of that?

My lungs are burning. I realize that, hell, I need air.

Vassili eats my pussy until I'm weak. Tears stream down my face, and I have clawed at the bear fur until it's probably missing patches. "Vassili," I cry, whimpering, sniveling, the works.

"*Da krasivaya,*" he responds in Russian. I'm beginning to learn. That means "Yes, beautiful."

Vassili climbs up my body and I plant my face along his neck. "Baby, that was so good, I'm gonna cry now. I'm sorry, but I have to cry." I break out into a sob. My husband hates it when I'm drawn to waterworks, and I rarely am. But the dam bursts and tears fall as the glistening, wet lips of my pussy whimper with proof of my desire.

He just screwed me seven ways to heaven, and it's over. I sob. This husband of mine. He's murdered for me. He tears men limb from limb. And he loves my body. He cherishes me. How did I deserve this? The tears of joy rattle through me.

"Don't cry," he catches a tear with his mouth, kisses and licks it away. Vassili places himself between my legs, pressing my ankles over his shoulders. I shiver in anticipation as Vassili lines his cock with my pulsating entrance. He leans down, his face burrowing between my breasts. He blows hard while letting his head wriggle around.

I laugh through the tears. "Fuck me, Vassili," I beg. The wait will be the death of me.

"God, your pussy is soaking wet," Vassili growls, while allowing his rock-hard cock to glide along my wetness. I arch my hips, ready to aim for my own target, but he just gives this boisterous laugh that reminds me who the hell is boss.

"I hate you, Vassili," I reply. I might not be in my right mind, but I'm begging like a 90s R&B singer, he should screw me crazy…. Crazier than I am now.

"You hate me, eh?" the head of his cock thumps my clit.

I hiss, shit that feels good. My hands fist the bear rug, and I know without a shadow of a doubt, the damn thing now probably looks like it could use a couple bottles of Rogaine.

His cock slams into me, the muscle stretches my insides, and as he works his hips back and forth, each drive goes deeper. Tilting my hips as much as I can, I channel my inner yoga, well whatever the damn position I'm in is called, as I welcome the depth of his cock. Sweat slicks across his muscles as he goes out and back in. My tits shake up and down, and I snatch more fists full of fur, while screaming. My throat is becoming raw, and I like the sound of my sultry Beyoncé voice—maybe I'm delusional enough to think so, but hell, I like the sound of my voice. I may or may not sound like a scalding cat instead, as Vassili's cock pummels my g-spot.

And… then… Vassili… sits there. His cock living within my wet walls, loving the mold he's made. My breaths are ragged, my throat is dead. He starts to rock into me slowly.

The tears have returned. He kisses those away, while his cock glides inches in and inches out. Ten inches in, and ten inches out. My lashes flutter, kissing my cheeks. I'm aware of every minute second of it. And I die within his arms as he screws me slowly.

When we come together I'm delirious enough to say, "Baby, get me pregnant…"

He kisses me hard on the lips. "That's what I'm saying, girl. Let's get you pregnant again."

FEARLESS II
by *Amarie Avant*

We chuckle together as his hard muscles sag into my body.

***

It's almost midnight, way past my bedtime on a weekday. My body is glued to Vassili's as we lay in our sex. Somehow, he ended up on his back, my breasts are against his muscular chest. The Kremlin from Moscow is shaped in a crown along his hard muscles, and my index finger follows the trail of it. The artistry still knocks me out, although the menacing wolf head atop it still scares me. The lifelike design seems to leap from his skin.

I mumble the Latin words, "*oderint dum metuant* below."

Then my finger trails down to those X-rated matryoshka dolls, which the cross of Jesus, conveniently cuts through.

"You know what," I murmur, half asleep.

"What?"

"I want all these titties off your back?"

"What titties?" he responds, thick Russian voice sounding too sexy. The bastard knows what I'm talking about.

I roll off of him. "Um-hmm, you can cover that shit up with my face."

"All you have to do is ask."

I lay on my side. Vassili turns to spoon me now. Once more my eyes close slowly, but I jerk my head awake. When I do, my sight adjusts more. I glance around me at the chocolate brown fur patches on the ground. "Damn," I pause. What the hell was that? Okay, so maybe I really didn't sound like Beyoncé meets Billie Holiday, but instead like Rupaul.

"What is it?" Vassili's cock begins to stiffen against my ass cheek.

I wiggle my buttocks, and then say, "Besides me sounding like I have balls between my legs, look at the floor."

"Girl, if you had balls between your legs, you'd be dead." Vassili leans his head up, and glances around. "Fuck, between you and Natasha, I can't have shit."

He settles down and I punch him softly, although his joke wasn't too far from the truth. "You ready to go to sleep, Zar?"

"Nope, Yuri just texted that you guys leave tomorrow. I hate missing you like crazy, so I'll stay awake."

He kisses my forehead. "But you're falling asleep."

"I'm not."

The arched eyebrow looks he gives is enough to rest his case. I sigh heavily. "Remember when I was eighteen?"

"Shit, I fucking thanked God you weren't jailbait. You were the hottest piece of ass I'd ever laid eyes on."

Fearless II
by Amarie Avant

I pout. He kisses the corners of my lips until they curve into a smile. "Talk to me, Zariah. You never stop thinking."

"I was just thinking about all those years I spent giving you a hard time."

"Seven."

"Thanks for the reminder." I offer something of a smirk, but my eyes are getting heavier. "Let's look at those old videos."

"Again?"

I grin. They say the way to a man's heart is food, but Vassili and I are still cultures apart in that regard. So, I know how to motivate, uplift and love my husband I reply, "Yes, again. The ones from matches when you were still a cocky asshole, before you had the title that you'll be snatching again soon enough."

He grabs my face and bruises my mouth with a kiss. "This is why you are my wife."

Vassili

Atlanta, Georgia

Zariah and I stayed up until the sun peeked over the Hollywood Hills. Natasha and I sent her to work with her favorite Dior sunglasses and most beloved canister of coffee. After picking up Yuri, who has no reservations with wearing a suit in the summer heat, I dropped off Natasha with Taryn, and we head to LAX.

Now, it's late afternoon, when the guy at the car dealership escorts us to a supercar. My knucklehead of a cousin squared away everything. I take the keys, and we get into the shiny red Acura NSX.

I ask the idiot, "Shit, kazen, God forbid Zamora is being smacked around. How will we look knocking him around and driving away in a $150 thousand-dollar car?"

"First of all, if Zariah's mom is being treated any other way than right, we're gonna kill the fucker and drop 'em in a ditch with his own car. And yeah, $150 'kay.' Should we have upgraded?" Yuri asks. His ugly mug is set in a smirk.

"*Nyet.* This is good. I need speed." I rev the engine. The rental car representative gives a fist pump. Fucking idiot. I can't open this bitch up, not in this area, and I sure as fuck don't need a cheerleader to get 'er wet. The purr is perfect. I head to the exit, saying, "When I need to think I'm on my Ducati. Seeing that there's no way in hell that your fat, ugly ass is fitting on the back of one, this is how we roll."

"Speaking of ugly motherfuckers. Did you narrow the list down?" he asks.

I stop at the final checkpoint, and hand over the rental car agreement for it to be stamped. "Narrow what, Yuri? There's only Anatoly or Maxwell who'd send that email. Why?"

"Dah, why?" he parrots. This is exactly the reason that I don't work with people. I delegate shit, but let my cousin tell it, he's been butt hurt and we have to be a 'team.'

I grab the stamped paperwork, hand it to Yuri, and make a smooth getaway. "My dad wants The Red Door. And that mudak will do anything to get it. Maxwell, man, I don't know. She tried to invite him to Natasha's birthday. The bitch didn't even come see his first grandchild by his only daughter. Of course, that mudak would gain satisfaction from locking me in jail, but why now?"

"Why now? Yeah, that doesn't make sense, Vassili. Zariah's father waiting this long? Brings new meaning to trying to catch you off guard. The timing is right for your father. I can see Anatoly pushing you into a corner for defying him, but he'd make a request."

FEARLESS II
by Amarie Avant

A sea of yellow cabs mixes and mingle with various Lyft and Uber drivers, while we all navigate toward the airport exit. I breathe heavily. Is this idiot listening to anything I've said? "Anatoly made a request."

Yuri eyes me in curiosity.

"The Red Door, fuck, keep up."

At the stoplight, I GPS the location to FTNT (Fight Nite) Radio Station, a local subsidiary of the Ultimate Fighting Championship (UFC). With talk of an impending match between myself and Alvarez, although I'll make the mudak sweat before I sign that contract, FTNT has invited me for the afternoon.

"Maybe we should eat something before we—"

"*Nyet,* we're late enough as it is. Tell me something."

"Something," Yuri barks back, annoyed over lack of getting food.

"How do you manage me, yet are unaware of various timeframes of the shit that you've scheduled?"

"I can't think when hungry," is his snappy reply.

***

An hour later, we're in the break room of FTNT. Long tables are stationed throughout, with more food than even my cousin can consume. With fingers shining with chicken grease, Yuri pats my back. "You are my favorite."

I shake my head.

"Eat," he says in Russian.

"I'm going on in a few minutes, and I had a shake for breakfast. Gotta have my mind clear. You know these piz'das love asking about old shit."

"Do them like you did Alex Brown." He mentions one of the most famous television sports commentators. It never fails that motherfucker comes at me with something that Yuri or I previously told the producer was not to be discussed.

They all do it.

I'll be asked about Gotti, if there's enough time. *How do you feel about having your belt snatched away by Gotti? Why the fuck didn't you tap out?* Yeah, something dumb like that. *I can do this.*

A young Japanese woman with a microphone in her ear and a clipboard in hand pops her head in. "How're the sliders?" she asks Yuri with a wink.

The mention of the tiny cheeseburgers got us in here. Not sure how I'm gonna get Yuri out, unless he eats it all while I'm on the radio. He traded in and up for barbecue wings and tacos.

"Good. Good," I tell her since Yuri is polishing off more food and unable to speak.

"We're ready for you, Karo." She grins at me.

I head to the door. Yuri washes the food down with a coke. "I'm getting nervous," he says.

I flip him the bird and head out. The reverse psychology he just attempted crashes and burns. But I take a deep breath and head into the studio.

FEARLESS II
by Amarie Avant

Inside, there's enough gadgets and contraptions to overwhelm and keep Natasha busy for days. I'm introduced to the radio personality, Lizelle "Black Zombie" Jackson. He's Atlanta born and breed, and at age 40, this is his new normal, cauliflower ears and all.

"Killer Karo, I've waited too long to have you in the building. I've been a fan of every match, every match."

I nod my head. "Last time I saw you, you were taking down the War Machine."

"You saw that?" His voice is heavy with surprise.

"Live." I nod.

"Bruh, it was him or me."

"Close match." Shit, I'm warming up. They like when you say more. I'm not there yet.

"Yes, sir, close match. It takes guts not to tap out to any old submission hold. Most of these young bloods will…" he taps the table, "soon as you touch them."

I chuckle at that.

"Look, I'm not one of those motherfuckers that just spring shit up, but can I ask about Gotti? You've probably explained it a thousand times before, but my fans want to hear it from your mouth. Will you give me that?"

"No problem." I respect his gumption. Lay it on the table from the start. I prefer that to a weasel popping it in without asking.

He explains how long the show will go and that it's satellite radio, no censorship. It seems like only a few minutes have passed, but the Black Zombie alternates from presenting a commercial, to introducing my arrival.

"What up ATL, it seems every time we talk I'm introducing someone great. But truly, truly, I tell you we have greatness in the building. None other than Vassili Killer Karo Resnov. So, hit those chat buttons. Call in. Leave us a question. I promise to give you all the *deets* on Karo, past, present, and future."

We chat for a while about my younger years. Surprisingly, Black Zombie has my stats down.

"Karo looking at me like I'm a creeper or something, he didn't know. I'm a true fan. I've been representing way before Juggernaut was put to sleep. That ankle lock submissive on The Hauser—still the talk of the town. He had a big mouth, you shut that shit down, and tore into that leg!"

"I remember that." Still not many words, but fuck it, I actually like this guy.

"The beef you two had during promotions, I swear it was priceless. You're one of the few young bloods who doesn't talk shit without backing it up."

"I had my days."

"Shit, you have 25 TKOs, 10 subs and 2 losses. I only have one problem with that, Karo." He pauses for effect. "What took you so long to get with the submissions? Those TKOs under your belt had folks shitting bricks, but the subs! Man, the submissions! Oh, look here, Arnold from Decatur, he's agreeing with me. When you started really getting into submissions, the world…it was a more beautiful place."

I laugh with him. "I was a hot head back in the day. I always thought power was in here." I punch my fist into my left palm.

"Karo, buddy, they can't see you. But I'm telling y'all, there's some serious bromancing going on here. The question screen is lighting up like no other time before. There's no way in hell we can take them all." He pauses to read one and I take the lead.

"So, anybody want to know where I'll be fighting soon?"

"Shit, yeah. Half these calls are about you taking down Alvarez, and this is his hometown. I'll have him on the show in a week, hope he isn't listening now." The Black Zombie chuckles again.

"I might be fighting him," I say, not all that interested. "I'm ready for Karsoff."

"Yesss, I see where your head is at. Karsoff is a few steps away. We need you to get that belt back. Karsoff, if you're listening, I bet Karo can have you to bed by—"

"Damn, have him to bed? That's a little bit much."

"Then lay it all out, Karo. How will you take down Karsoff?"

"He has a big mouth, but I shouldn't. Should I…"
I joke.

"TKO? Come on, Karo, you're better than this."

We laugh like two drunk motherfuckers drinking Resnov Water.

"Then I'll hit him with a triangle choke."

"Old school?" he says, processing it slowly. "Simple. Classic. You might want to bash his head in, KO 'em as your old MO. He'll be studying all the ways to get out of the triangle choke. Although, it will shut his mouth real good…"

***

After the show, The Black Zombie and I chat for a while longer. I get his address in order to send him some of my beloved vodka, and Yuri takes the keys so we can head to Ms. Haskins home. I glance through my phone. Zariah has texted me nonstop throughout the broadcasting.

ZARIAH: Aw my baby is playing nice for the first time ever!

ZARIAH: He's right, that ankle lock was gangster.

ZARIAH: He should be your hype man, I swear he was auditioning to be one of your hype men.

ZARIAH: I miss you already…

I chuckle at her messages, and call her up.

"Beautiful, I'll be home late tonight. You still sleepy?"

FEARLESS II
by *Amarie Avant*

She yawns on key. "Yes, all day. But that won't stop me from waiting up for you."

"Don't wait up, girl. I'll wake you."

"I bet you will. Get to the airport with plenty of time, Vassili."

"I love you, Zariah." I turn away from my childish ass cousin, and my voice lowers as I reply, "*Nyet.* I love you more, *krasivaya.*"

I hang up. Yuri makes kissy faces and I wave him off. "That's how you are with Taryn…" *and in your case, you shouldn't be…*

***

The housing track that Zamora Haskins lives on is full of summertime action. Kids roam big front yards, and get into some gold old-fashioned summer trouble.

There's a mixed-race boy, wide shoulders, running a scrimmage. He stiff arms everyone on the opposite team, and makes a touchdown.

"Yuri, I've gotta fucking have myself a son, soon." I grumble, considering Zariah's recent agreement to get pregnant for me again.

"Maybe you only have girl?" He reaches over to flick my ear, but I catch his hand, twisting it swiftly. "I'm driving, piz'da!"

"Who's the cunt now?" I let his hand go in enough time for him to switch gears and turn the corner.

He parks in front of a tan home with slate stone. Having only visited on a few occasions, I'm sure

Zamora's cooking kept him from his usual forgetfulness.

Ms. Haskins opens the door with sunglasses on. Who wears sunglasses in the house? Yeah, it's hotter than back home, in St. Petersburg, will ever be. But she could've slipped the shades on while stepping out.

Instantly, I'm floored at the idea that a man placed his hands on my wife's mother. I place my hand on the roof of the door, and get out of the car.

"Hi boys, I didn't think you'd make it by." She hugs us and invites us in. "Yuri, your cookies—"

"Oh, Ms. Haskins. You didn't!" He's somewhere between 350lbs and six-foot-three, yet sounds like a kid in a candy store as we all head to the kitchen.

She moves faster than a rookie's knees lock up after a busted nose. Zamora removes mittens from the drawer and opens the wall oven. "Isn't your flight home soon?"

"A little later," Yuri offers. "Allow me," he adds, taking the mittens from her. Shit, we Russians can be nice when we want, and we sure as fuck are gonna figure out why Zariah's mother is flighty and shrugging off people. She's one of the most genuine people I know—and I can only count the rest on one hand.

At a loss of what to do, Zamora Haskins still hasn't removed the sunglasses from her eyes, yet continues to chatter. "I wish Zariah had come with you all. I know we just came back from vacation, but I have missed time with my baby girl."

"Can you do me a favor?" I finally speak.

"What is it, Vassili? Why aren't you guys eating these cookies? Sheesh, you aren't even mentioning healthy eating when I make the peanut butter cookies." She's her usual chatty self but something's off.

"Please." I gesture to the shades. "Remove those."

Her head tilts somewhat. Zamora touches the shades, as if she forgot they were on.

"Please, I'm worried about you," I tell her, wishing to God I could look her in the eye, so she understands I'm real.

"Worried?" Zamora waves a hand. "You are a good man, Vassili. That's all that I ask."

"And I will continue to be a good man."

Yuri places the cookies on a marble block on the counter. Her gaze slides back from me to Yuri.

"What's the name of the guy?" he asks.

"He didn't mean anything by it." Her tone is hardly audible. She turns away from us, passing the time by removing a spatula.

"Ms. Haskins," I speak up.

"You've started calling me Zamora, Vassili." She purses her lips. Embarrassment creeps up her throat as she leans back against the counter. "Will you tell Zariah?"

"If it happens again. But we need his name. And I would like to see your face if you don't mind."

FEARLESS II
by Amarie Avant

"She'll be disappointed in me." Ms. Haskins' lips bunch together as she gingerly removes the shades.

Fuck, she isn't sporting a typical shiner. Her eye is swollen completely shut.

Yuri's face is to the ceiling. He strides away for a moment, huffs and then comes back. I'm shocked still. Though I've witnessed my father and his goons beating on my mother and sister a thousand times, this shit kills me every time. This world is fucked.

"He was angry at me for Brazil, and then I forgot to tell him I'd be in California the weekend after for cutie pie. He thought we weren't serious—*I* wasn't serious enough about us. Like I had been traveling with someone— another man." She speaks to the ground. And God, if there isn't something in me that wants to hug this woman and tell her thank you for striving as long as she did.

I blink and realize that Zamora Haskins-Washington is not my mother.

But fuck it, she birthed the love of my life and I have too much respect and too much to thank her for anyway.

"We won't tell Zariah. What is the man's name, please?" I speak through tensed lips.

"Matthew Overstreet."

***

Mr. Overstreet works at the Commerce Trade Center. The woman in the lobby said he always leaves his office around 6pm. A quick check of his Facebook account indicates that he hits Crunch Time Gym at 6:45 promptly, only to leave an hour and a half later. He's a man of routine and he loves to catch the female trainers in his selfies, though he doesn't get too many likes from his friends because he doesn't have many of those. A regular old douche bag is what he is.

It's a quarter past eight pm, and I have to hand it to my cousin. I underestimated his capabilities because with his assistance, I'm seated in the back of Matthew's car, hands clenched tight. Yuri is in our rental, parked a few rows away. I contemplate on my mother. She gave up on Sasha and me, leaving us with one of Anatoly's bitches, but earlier today, I recalled the time she had more than herself to care for. She'd taken up sanctuary, when I was a tot. Most of the time, I keep the woman who birthed me from my mind. Why not? She gave up. But I begin to fixate on the past. Darkness surrounds me and life in Russia pulls me under…

The lights flash as Matthew hits the alarm button. My stone sculpted outline is lit up and instantly drowned back in darkness. He slides into the front seat, without realizing that when Yuri got into his car earlier, the music was playing. It's not now.

He shuts the door, and his finger is poised for the 'push to start' when I speak. "Don't."

Matthew's shaky hand yanks away from the button. He grabs for his keys to hit the alarm. I snatch them first. Stiff as a board, he leans back against the driver's seat, eyes closed. I settle into the middle seat in the back again.

"Go ahead, Mr. Overstreet. Turn around. You're thinking I will rob and not kill you if you don't see me."

He lifts up somewhat and tugs out his wallet, tossing it over his shoulder in my general direction. Without so much as moving a muscle, I listen as he stutters, "There's at least four-four hun-hun... hundred. I... I can take you to the bank."

"Money is the least of my concerns."

"Oh-kay." His shaky response is hardly audible.

"Turn around, Mr. Overstreet. I'm here because you touched the hair on the head of someone I love. Have a good look into my eyes. Know my motherfucking face, because if you ever see me again—" I cut myself off. I'm not Yuri, shooting them, bagging them, and tossing them ain't my thing. "Turn around!" I bark.

"Okay, Okay!" His stiff neck cranes awkwardly, and moments pass by as he believes that the lapse in time will result in me having a change of heart. When he makes eye contact, my glower pierces through his, where he can't seem to choose an eye to connect with.

"You like to hit women, Mr. Overstreet?"

"No!" The word expels from his mouth without so much as a stutter. "I love Zamora, I'd never hit—"

FEARLESS II
by *Amarie Avant*

"You're lying to me. Isn't it a universal norm that people hate liars?" Damn, I sound like my wife, "universal norm." "Have you seen me before?"

His eyes close then he nods. "Yes, sir. You're a fighter."

"You piss yourself?" I ask. "C'mon, I smell fear off my opponents in the cage. I can smell piss, too."

"I'm sorry."

"You are sorry."

My fist slams into his face. The crush of my knuckles against bone tells me that his forehead will always and forever be indented in that precise spot.

I get out of the car, and zig zag around the cars to the lane Yuri's parked in. The driver side window zips down.

"What the fuck you doing, kazen? We can't just leave the body," his voice lowers.

"He's alive."

"Should I?" He starts to open the door.

"No," I shake my head. "He won't hurt a fly in the future. I'm sure of it."

"But that mudak touched your mother in law, Vassili," Yuri replies through gritted teeth. "Put him down!"

"And now they have matching eyes. Or in his case, his face is—"

BEEP. BEEEP. BEEP!

My narrowed eyes turn toward the Chrysler. That fool is slamming a hand down on the steering wheel.

FEARLESS II
by *Amarie Avant*

"Oh, should I manage the situation?" Yuri snarls the sarcastic line that I'm usually telling him. Then he goes off in Russian about "getting it over with."

"I'll handle it!" I cross back to where Matthew is parked.

Through the rolled-up window, his eye that isn't swelling widens. He slams his hand down onto the steering wheel again. I try the door. It's locked.

"Open up," I tell him.

He sounds less like a pussy when shouting, "Fuck you!"

Seriously, does he believe a door will double as his savior?

My fist slams through the window, glass shatters down around my feet, and Matthew ducks as even more shards spray toward his face.

A woman who so happens to be walking by with earphones, jumps. Must've noticed me from her peripheral.

"Don't mind us. He beats women," I tell her.

She jogs off to her car.

Matthew dives for the passenger seat when I reach through, grip his muscle shirt and yank him through the window.

"You wanna act like a bitch, huh?" With my left hand snatching the collar of his ultra-tight shirt, I yank him toward me.

There's no fucking way Matthew's gonna run from this ass beating. My right fist sprays like bullets

FEARLESS II
by *Amarie Avant*

against his face. My target is crushing his skull in where I had just smashed his forehead before. Then I jab at his neck and ribs. Matthew slams against the trunk of his car. He's not as heavy as before. I realize I'd been holding his entire weight.

"What happened to all those personal training sessions?" I pause, my left fist clenching his shirt, and now his legs are doing a two-step before me. "You not gonna save yourself? Fight me, dude. I'm just a few inches taller than you. Fight me!"

He tries to speak, blood splashes from his mouth. "I'm sorry…."

"Fuck you and your apologies." I let Matthew go. His feet clop like a horse, noodle legs hardly able to sustain him. I hit him with a right, then a left elbow that sends him back in the other direction, and finish him off with another right.

"Ne smotret'! Ne Smotret, moy rebenok—Don't look, my child," My mother shouted. Men walked past, they spat at her, and called her the names that were strapped around her neck.

"Shluyukha—Whore!"

"Piz'da—Cunt!"

My eyes were glued to her pale white face. I hadn't seen her since she ran off on Sasha and me. And so I stared at her, my face dead from any sort of emotion. My father stood next to me, a freshly rolled cigarette in his hand.

"She left you, Vassili."

FEARLESS II
by *Amarie Avant*

"And you beat her, and look at these people. They laugh at a Resnov! Who laughs at a Resnov, huh?" I argued with him, not a single hair on my chin, and I shouted at my father.

"I didn't beat that bitch," he puffed air in my face. "She's no Resnov. Just the first woman to have a child for me."

"Let her down, now!" I shouted. The people along the street laughed, his men cackled as I pushed at my father. I was a skinny motherfucker, and yet my mind didn't make the connection that I couldn't put him down. That I couldn't kill my father.

I started toward her, and before I could place a hand on the straps binding her to the street light, Anatoly grabbed my shoulder and pushed me to the ground.

"I said, she's no fucking Resnov."

"But she's my mother."

"Vassili, what happened to 'fuck her?' She left you, didn't she?"

My ears burned in shame. Yeah, I said it. A bruised ego rots the mind, makes you forget. "Prosto idi— just go," My mother said, her face was too carved and disfigured to smile, but I felt it. She wasn't mad at me. I'd forgotten about her first attempt to get away with Sasha and I, a few years back.

I reach out to hit Anatoly. He clasps my hand, then tossed me to the ground. Pain slams through me

FEARLESS II
by Amarie Avant

as he kicks my ribs. Then his team jumps in, kicking me in the back.

"You hit your father over this cunt?" Anatoly finishes his statement with another kick. I roll into a tiny ball, with the sound of my mother screaming for them to stop.

A siren is screaming. Had to have been for a while, because my eardrums ring as the top of my head is being pushed down, like protocol requires when being tossed in the back of a squad car.

"What the fuck are you doing to my kazen!" I can hear Yuri shout from behind me.

With the handcuffs behind my back, I'm cranking my neck much like Matthew did a few minutes ago. Through the rearview mirror, Yuri can be seen resisting arrest. It takes four cops to get him down to the ground as he argues that Mr. Overstreet, who's on the asphalt nearby, and isn't even attempting to get up, is the person at fault.

Zariah

Earlier in the evening…

After work, I fight traffic to Taryn's house, since she offered to watch Natasha today while Vassili is in Atlanta. We do not believe in childcare while our daughter is unable to fully articulate her feelings and opinions about the person in the position to care for her. Taryn's father is in government and with an African model for a mother, she has it made. Natasha's godmother spends her days shopping, and is a godsend in times like these.

I stop at the gates where a hut houses a security detail for the governor, her father, who my friend still technically lives with. Aware of my car, the guard opens the gates while waving me through.

I consider stopping at the mansion of a home Taryn's father lives in before heading to the pool house that she moved into years ago. Well, hopefully, she and Yuri marry one day, so after years of hoeing, he can make an honest woman out of her.

The front doors of the mansion open, and I veer to the left in order to get around a humongous cement fountain. It's Taryn's mother, who rarely is ever home. The model is at least half a foot taller than her husband. They make an odd pair. His tiny eyes peer straight through you. She's ultra slim like Taryn, and her looks blow her husband away.

"Hi, Mrs. Takahashi." I start to get out of the car.

"Hello, Zariah." She grins. "Taryn is in the house with Natasha. Come on in."

Ms. Takahashi offers one of those 'loose' hugs where it seems she doesn't want to ruin her Italian silk dress or smudge her perfectly set makeup, that makes a person seem to shrink within themselves. No matter how much I think I slay when waking up and spending extensive amounts of time dressing in the morning, looking at Ms. Takahashi reminds me to hold my head much higher, and to work these stilettos.

"How is your mother? Your father?"

How is my father? Hell, somebody tell me. Damn, Mrs. Takahashi and I haven't crossed paths in years. When I was younger, realizing that my father had a crush on her was a shock to me. I mean, dad and I share the same rich dark skin. I love the skin I live in. But my mother is as light as they come, and the women who came after! You can toss cooking grease on them and kick them out of a safari in Africa; there'll be no frying. I didn't think Maxwell could look at someone of our color, and Ms. Takahashi has us beat with beautiful jet-black skin. But there was this one time where Ms. Takahashi wore a silk dress, much like she is wearing now, and her tits played a game every time she strutted from hip to hip. It made me see fire when my mother didn't backhand his ass across the room like he use to do with her—for some trivial reason.

"My mom is well, happy," I smile.

"And your dad? I'm never on the same continent for more than a week or two. I miss those barbecues."

"Tsk, my father is operating an entire police station while I do me." I place my hand on my hip as Ms. Takahashi stops.

"Hmmm, Maxwell ran the police station on Grand Avenue before becoming Chief. So, does what you're saying have something to do with that delectable man you married? I owe you a gift."

I wave a hand. She owes Taryn a sweet sixteen gift and more. But damn it, Mrs. Takahashi is like one of those good friends where no matter how much time passes, when you come together, she can read you like 'Baby's first A-B-C Book.' "Yup, my father believes that I settled..." *Fell and am slumming it, rock bottom.*

Her lips set into a line for a moment. "Fathers want the best for their daughters. I defied mine and married a Jap—shhh, can't say that too loudly, but those were the words my father said, when I did not return home to marry the man of his choosing. There's nothing like a father's love. At times, it's overwhelming."

My eyebrows rise. That's the understatement of the century.

FEARLESS II
by *Amarie Avant*

Mrs. Takahashi waves her slender manicured fingers. "Maxwell will get over himself. Now, come in. We have had so much fun with Natasha."

We pass a foyer. The black-and-white checkered tile is dotted with just as many vibrant pink designer bags with highlighter yellow tissue sticking out of them. "Goodness," I reply as she tells me to watch my step.

I can hear my daughter's happy banter. "Daddddaaaa, Daddaaa, mommmma, Fry!"

"She can eat," Mrs. Takahashi says as we enter their grand kitchen.

Taryn is zapping a frozen corn dog in the microwave, while Natasha sits on a highchair. "Girl, this baby wants French fries. I ate the first corn dog because she kept turning those fat cheeks to me."

"That's how she rolls. Can I trouble you for a few Cheetos or cheerios?" I grin. "Vassili did his best to get Natasha interested in his raw fruit smoothies, but she acted a plum fool one day because someone I know bought her McDonald's. Now, she's a junk food eating monster."

"Look at me like that, if you want, Zar." Taryn bites her lip. "I'll continue to blame McDonald's on my cuddles."

"Your cuddles?" Mrs. Takahashi asks, while heading toward the door to the wine cellar.

"His name is Yuri Resnov." I squeeze in. "And I think your daughter is in love." At least, I hoped.

There were too many occasions when Taryn and I were in high school where I had to remember more than one boyfriend name from one date night to the next.

"Oh, another Resnov. Hold that thought." Mrs. Takahashi opens the door and disappears down the stairs.

"So, are you in love?" I corner Taryn as she grabs another tiny, plastic plate for Natasha. My hand on my hip doesn't intimidate her one second as she skirts past me, opens the door to the refrigerator, which looks like the rest of the walnut wood shelves. Taryn grabs condiments out before pulling the hotdog from the microwave.

"How many times will you ask me that?" she finally inquires.

"Until you tell the truth."

"Yuri isn't the type of man to fall in love with, Zariah," she murmurs while placing her index finger over the breading of the hotdog to make sure it isn't too hot.

"How can you say that? You see what Vassili and I have, and you encouraged me to run after my man two weeks ago, in Brazil! Taryn, you and Yuri are magnetic."

Mrs. Takahashi comes from the cellar with a bottle. "Pinot Noir. And I've seen what Zariah has with her husband. It's is pure hotness, needs to be on the cover of a magazine. Can that be said about my daughter and 'Mr. Cuddles?'"

"Mom," Taryn huffs while placing the plate in front of Natasha, who promptly pushes it away. "Please, sweetie pie, eat it," she coaxes, holding up the corndog. My child playfully paws it away. Had it been me, Natasha would have slapped the damn thing across the room.

Taryn's mother and I wait for her response. She's always been overly confident when finagling a few men at a time. Bragging about who is wrapped around her finger and just how captivating men comes naturally to her, yet she opens the refrigerator, retrieves a string cheese for Natasha, and then makes a beeline to another cabinet to get three wine glasses out.

"What's wrong, Taryn?" I ask.

"Yes, if you care enough to give the man a nickname, Cuddles, then you must like him. Although, I can't say that I'll ever be attracted to someone who's..." her mother pauses. "Cuddly as in a lot of muscle?"

My head tilts somewhat. The governor is pleasantly plump. She has to be attracted to her husband.

"Mom, you don't understand. Heck, when this heifa says Resnov, that doesn't even ring a bell, does it?" She offers a pathetic laugh, while heading to a table, with plush, studded chairs.

"No, can't say that it does." Ms. Takahashi uncorks the bottle as I sit down.

"Their family has been known to dabble in … mafia stuff," I speak up, taking my drink and downing a good, long sip.

"Zariah, they *are* the Russian mafia. They are the fucking bratva!" Taryn takes her drink and sips.

Mrs. Takahashi shrugs. "When I was younger, I fooled around with a Kenyan drug lord. Might not have been a good thing to do in retrospect, but dangerous sex is…daring, passionate."

"Vassili isn't with that." I stumble into the conversation. Why did I speak up? Her mother is glamorizing a lifestyle that I don't condone. So, I sit confidently in my beliefs.

Taryn glances at me.

"Well," I start, "is there something I should know?"

"No, Zar. Yuri says that his father has slowly cut down on assignments. Malich no longer controls the San Pedro port. But your husband is the son of," she makes an elaborate gesture. "Girl, your husband is in it for life, no matter how much he busies himself with MMA."

I huff. "You really believe that?"

"I do."

"So then why do you continue to fuck with Yuri?" Oops, I forgot that her mother was sitting here.

Fearless II
by Amarie Avant

She doesn't say a word, just waits for a response as well.

We receive a lethargic shrug. Taryn downs the rest of her wine. "I can't stop. Yuri treats me like a queen. His cock is monstrous." She holds up her hands.

"Ohhhh," Mrs. Takahashi claps her hands.

"And when you feel—cock aside—that the life is too much what will you do? How could you string him along?" I inquire, almost in lawyer mode. Removing my feelings from the equation, I glance her directly in the eye.

"Yuri would never hurt me. When we connect, the world stops, and he isn't participating in any illegal activities. Shit, I got that from you, Zariah. It's a job and a half for him to assist Vassili in securing matches, Karo merchandise, and everything that goes along with the MMA world. But there will come a day when Yuri and I can't be together. And you ask if I love him. Nope, I can't do that to myself."

I finish off my drink, the smooth taste supports my desire not to make a comparison. Damn, Vassili tells me that I overthink things. And the dynamics of my relationship with him are the same for Yuri and Taryn. Heck, she just implicated that I'm in a worse predicament. I watch the dark crimson liquid fill up into my glass again, while ruminating over the time I assumed Vassili was Malich's son. I wished to God he wasn't. The joke was on me. I fell in love with danger.

FEARLESS II
by *Amarie Avant*

"Okay, Taryn, I can't fathom how easy it is for you to play with your own heart in that manner, but if you don't love him, then you don't love him."

"Stop being so closed minded, damn," Taryn says. "My parents are in an open relationship, and they dole out their time to whomever they please. We're good at not allowing our heart to become involved. Don't judge me, Zar."

"Humph, my only endeavor is keeping you from breaking your own damn heart, Taryn, no Honorable Judge Resnov here. You're right about one thing, though, Vassili would kill me if I considered adding another man to the equation, and I would only be obliged to do the same if the tables were turned. We are jealous people."

"You're like your father," Mrs. Takahashi says. "There's nothing wrong with that."

I all but scoff. Like hell can I be compared to my father. Instead of acknowledging and redirecting Taryn or her mother, I tell them something I am certain of. "My heart isn't set up to be played, so I married Vassili through good times and bad times."

"The two of you are too young and in love to know a thing about bad times, not yet." The model shakes her head.

I beg to differ. This past year has been hell. "Well, I may not have the ability to predict the future. Regardless of the cards stacked against us, I'll be damned if I spoke vows into the universe about my love for Vassili in vain. Shotgun Vegas-style wedding or not, I'll snatch him up myself if need be."

Taryn starts to chuckle. "Heifa, you need to be in somebody's *gotdamn* courtroom, with all of that arguing. Are you pregnant?"

My glass perches along my lip. Am I? "No, I can't be pregnant."

"You two aren't screwing?" Mrs. Takahashi asks, and damn it if I don't sputter on my wine. My mother and I have always had a good relationship. What made having a father in the police force such a good thing is that when he didn't want to be bothered, mom and I hit the road on the weekends. And my older brother, Martin, inundated himself in high school, so he was only there when we needed. But it was nothing like this level of openness. They wait on bated breath.

"We are definitely screwing," I respond giving a giddy little chuckle myself. I should've declined the second glass of Pinot Noir, since I can hardly drink my husband's family's liquor. Thinking about him, I calculate that it's going on 8PM in Atlanta right now. So, I text him a quick reminder about his late flight tonight…

Vassili

"Can I have my phone call, *now*?" I ask the guard as he places me into the community cell. The place is crowded, but the closest people standing near me are a young man with too much eyeshadow, another dude who smells like he bathed in rum, and my cousin. The processing took a few hours, and each time I asked, those mudaks acted like I spoke the words in a foreign language.

The guard locks the gate without so much as offering me a glance and heads toward the security door.

"Who? Vassili, who the fuck will you call?" Yuri asks from behind me.

I let go of the bars and turn around with a snarl. For a man who has known the backseat of many police cruisers, the cops had to force him into one of the many cruisers surrounding the local gym. Shit, this motherfucker is the reason the cops treated us with extra force.

Either the death glare in my eye doesn't penetrate or Yuri goes postal when cooped up in small places, because he doesn't shut the fuck up. He continues to taunt. "Who, Vassili, huh? Who the fuck are we gonna call? My dad wants to be out of the game. He can't make demands without collateral. Igor is sick as usual. This mission isn't for you know who." He mutters my father's name beneath his breath, as if I ever been in a predicament that Anatoly fixed. There'll never come a day. He finishes with, "You gonna call Zariah, so she can chew you a new one? Ha! And we sure as hell aren't in our area to make demands."

I rub the back of my neck and take a seat on the cement slab. "We'll be out soon."

He stands in front of me, still flapping his jaws with, "Our return flight leaves at 11PM, Vassili."

"You, get the fuck outta here with all that arguing," I roar. "If I say we're leaving soon, we are. I just need to make a call."

Air swooshes past my nose as Yuri slaps a hand toward my face. Although deadly with a gun, my cousin is no fighter. It's funny how, despite being older than me, Yuri can turn into the pesky little brother I never knew I wanted until hanging out—and bumping heads—with him. I toss a stiff finger at him. "Do it again, you'll be on a gurney just like that motherfucker we just left."

"Oh yeah?" He glares down at me.

I stand to my full height, chest puffed out, lips sneered. Yuri is just as menacing, in his coal gray suit and shiny shoes. The crowded cell is divided in half as the guys smell a fight coming on. We toe around each other, sizing each other up, as if this is our first fight.

FEARLESS II
by Amarie Avant

"I'm fucking tired of you calling the shots, Vassili," he says.

"Shut your cunt, do something, then!" I'll allow him to toss the first punch. Then I'm gonna punch his face in!

My cousin goes for a cross hook. Too bad there's a faint glint in his eye which reads exactly what he's intending to do before he strikes. My hand catches his fist, and then I smack it down.

His stance is all wrong as he issues a sloppy uppercut. The hit is thwarted by my forearm. I laugh just as my cousin slides his shoe between my Nike's, tripping me up.

The readymade crowd cheers as Yuri's heavy body lunges toward mine. I counter the takedown with a knee to his jewels. The cheers are followed by heckling. Fuck them, I wanted him to stop with the pussy monologue.

"Fu—" Yuri stops breathing, grabbing at his balls.

"See, I was just waiting for you to shut up, kazen."

He lowers himself, bullrushes me with his head spearing toward my abdomen. Like a wave, the tight-knit group of guys move to the opposite side of the cell. My hands gather into a tight fist above my head, and I pound against his spine as my own slams against the cement wall.

FEARLESS II
by *Amarie Avant*

"Fuck," I gasp, hardly able to get the word out myself.

Yuri starts pounding against my lungs. Shit, I've taught this fucker too much while he watches my practices and my matches. I reach beneath and grab his neck, spinning him around. When Yuri's ass hits the ground, his eyes are wide with shock. I have him in a triangle choke hold, the one I promised to Karsoff for his mouth. Well, my cousin's mouth is even more annoying. So, I continue to choke, and watch his face shake, his lips gloss with spittle and him gasping for air.

CLANK. CLANK. CLANK.

A baton grates along the bars. The noise aggravates my ears, so I let go of my cousin. He falls face first on the ground.

"Hey, you boneheads, break it up or no calls," the guard says.

I hold my palms out, as innocent as they come.

"Resnov," he shouts, "Which one of you fucks is Resnov?"

"Right here," I nod, holding my side, as my cousin croaks.

"Well, who wants to make their call first?" He glances between us, the pathetic pair that we are.

"By all means," Yuri wheezes out at me.

The electronic bars slide open, and I determine who's more than capable hands will get us out of the mess that I've made...

Zariah

Fog surrounds my brain, yet I feel like I'm clinging to something entirely too soft to be my husband's frame. The scent fusing into my nostrils is faint although it sends another moan roaming along my throat. Vassili's musk surrounds me. The thought hits me that the scent of him is a day old, and I rouse myself awake.

"Vassili," I grumble, pushing away his pillow. My eyes begin to adjust to early morning as I mope. "Why didn't you wake me up when you got home last—"

I sit up. His side of the bed is empty. The digital clock reads 4:10AM. Where the hell is my husband? I reach for my cell phone and the charger that I could've sworn was connected to it, but the cord slips between the bed and the nightstand. Damn, I didn't plug my phone in all the way last night.

I press the home button of the iPhone. It has no juice. My attempt is in vain. While sticking my hand between our custom-made bed post, I bump my temple on the edge of the nightstand.

FEARLESS II
by *Amarie Avant*

"Zar, wake up girl." I can hear my husband's usual response within my psyche. It's too early for a macchiato, and he should be here.

Leaning down, my fingertips feel for the charger, and I finally clasp it. Sitting back up, I connect it to my cell phone.

The brightness of the white screen burns my retinas, and for a fraction of a second, the burgeoning bump on my temple no longer exists. I start listening to a stream of voicemails. There's one from 9pm from an Atlanta area code. Since the number isn't familiar, I skip it, and click on my mother's message. What was she calling me for after 2am?

"The boys missed their flight, honey, don't worry." Her indication not to 'worry' unsettles me.

There's a voicemail promptly after hers from Vassili's phone number. I listen as he confirms the *alibi* my mom previously offered. "Uh, beautiful, we will just stay the night at your ma's. We... couldn't get back in enough time."

Hmmm, his thick Russian accent mixed with the 'got my hand caught in the cookie jar' tone further sets my intuition at work. I click on the oldest message from 10PM.

"Sweetheart, I need you to call me at this number." Vassili seems to be treading water. "Soon as you can, girl, call me."

Due to him not utilizing his cell phone to "call me," I dial the strange number. When I hear a greeting about the 'county jail' my heart flops in my chest. What the hell is going on?

I dial Vassili.

The call transfers straight to voicemail. "Boy, call me when you get this," I say through gritted teeth. "Are you in jail?" Damn it, I'm so rattled that I'm acting like my mother from circa 2010, when I was a senior in high school. She'd leave elaborate voicemails with questions and seemed hell bent on an answer. "Call me." I get the words out again and mash the END call button.

Next, I dial my mother's number. It's a little after 7am and I swear if she doesn't answer, my fury will be unleashed.

"Good morning, honey. What are you doing up so early?"

The usual background soundtrack of pots and pans clanking around settles me for a moment. My mom is safe and at home. But what more can I expect, she's a creature of habit. "Mom, where is Vassili? Is he there or is he in jail?'

"He and Yuri spent the night. They missed their flight. I have more than enough room. You received my message, right?"

My spidey senses are blazing. She disregarded my statement about jail. Nobody just lets something like 'so how are you doing, did you just get out of jail?' slip from the conversation. It's something that you correct to clear your name. At least, I believe so.

FEARLESS II
by *Amarie Avant*

Instead of demanding answers, I inquire, "How did they miss their flight?"

"Okay, Maxwell Tavion Washington *Junior*, what's with the questions? You should be sound asleep. They're still asleep. I'm making breakfast. If you've completed your interrogation and would like to talk to me or provide a message for him, I don't mind..."

"Mommy, I am going to ask you one more time," I assert myself, in a respectable tone. "Did Vassili take a trip to the jailhouse, lose his phone there, get rob..." Wait, I can't see my husband as a victim of a crime, let alone imagine a viable robbery scenario. "Was he in jail anytime last night?"

The sounds of banging pots and pans continues. "Hmmm, let me think back."

"*Momma!*"

"I bailed them out. It's not like my alimony checks couldn't cushion the blow, but Yuri transferred the money back into my account. It was nothing, honey, nothing at all."

I grumble and gripe for a moment. Damn it, my mother is covering for my husband's antics. She bailed them out.

Is Taryn right about Vassili's undeniable connection to his family business?

Did he and Yuri …

What the heck have they been up to?

FEARLESS II
by Amarie Avant

"Oh god, did they…" My throat is constricted, which is a saving grace because *Nancy Grace* has nothing on me when it comes to taking names and asking questions. And damn it, I cannot have this conversation over the phone. I begin to hyperventilate. Can I have this conversation over the phone? It implies that my husband is part of a criminal organization. I press my head back against the bedframe, and sigh heavily.

"Zariah, stop over thinking everything. Girl, I can hear your mind churning a thousand miles away. All is well."

I scoff. "My mother bailed my husband out of jail. This is some bullshit. Mom, forgive me for cussing with you." I shake my head, considering the conversation that I had with Taryn and her mother yesterday evening. There was no such thing as censorship with regard to their mother-daughter relationship. "I just can't believe this, dang."

"Honey, breathe."

"Oh, trust me, if I'm capable of communicating, then I'm more than proficient at breathing, no matter how much of a feat it is at the moment." I grip the phone in my hand and grumble more. "You tell that man to call me when he wakes up. I have a bone to pick with him."

"Zariah—"

"No, there's a couch with his name on it if he wants to go gallivanting around ATL! Shit, he's in the dog house. Love you, Mama." I hurry to end the call as my own imagination begins to take me under.

Through thick and thin… good or bad… I have to lead with my heart, and Vassili owns it. My breaths seize up at that thought. He's my eternity, no matter what…

***

Natasha is grumpy all day. I consult with Samuel after telling him that I need the day off. Damn it, but I just came back from vacation. There's a man whose perception of my last name 'Resnov' needs correcting and here I am, calling off work.

Samuel said he had friends in the department and would look into why Vassili and Yuri went to jail. Yes, I'm aware that the public database will allow me access to whatever shenanigans they've been up to. But hearing the story from the horse's mouth is my aim. And then, with the assistance of Sammy, we will fix whatever foolishness those two have caused.

When I arrive at LAX, I don't resemble the respectable black girl my parents raised me for. I'm in yoga pants and a camisole, holding Natasha. She's dressed to the nines—come to find out, all those pink designer bags in the foyer of the Takahashi mansion belonged to her. Taryn's mother said she 'just couldn't help herself' and I'd be damned if Natasha didn't have more clothing to wear than possible before she grows out of them. So, we are a pair. She's positioned on my hip, and I'm at the bottom of the escalator, frown set,

FEARLESS II

by Amarie Avant

waiting for Vassili to come down so I can smack him a good one.

He always trends on Twitter and Facebook during a match, but today, he's being slammed for fighting an unarmed man. That much I gathered from the Facebook newsfeeds on my cell phone. I told Samuel that his hands are registered, and he broke the bad news earlier. Vassili will have to return to Atlanta to speak with a judge next Tuesday. For fighting.

I am livid. I am going to listen to his story, and then I am going to rip him apart for being so stupid. There is no amount of foolishness in the world that can cause a man to need to use his hands on another. Unless someone disrespects my mama, I handle my shit in a civilized manner.

"Natasha, I'm going to talk to Daddy until he is sick and tired of my voice, yes, I am, cutie pie," I tell her. She smiles at me, all because I mentioned her father's name. Little traitor. "Daddy's in trouble."

"Daddy," she giggles.

"Trouble." I accentuate the word, through tensed lips, though it doesn't resonate properly with our daughter. With the imaginary 'angry black woman' stamp on my forehead, people have steered clear of me. Yet in this crowded place, the anger resonating from my body pales as I feel *him*. Vassili is here. My gaze ascends the escalator, and there he is.

The chocolatey waves of his mohawk caress ever so softly against his brutal dark eyes. He looks like the badass he was painted as. And he's wearing the same jeans and shirt he wore when leaving yesterday morning. Our eyes connect as the escalator brings him closer to me. My lips twitch with how harshly they are set. He looks happy to see me. *Keep your anger. He's in trouble. Don't give in, Zar, don't do it!*

"Daddy!" Arms open wide, Natasha tries to lunge from my arms. In her glee of seeing her father, the danger goes over her head. I grip at Natasha's knees in an attempt to save her. Vassili is at our side in seconds, scooping her up before she can fall.

"Girl, you are not ready to jump yet." His ropey, strong arms grip her tightly. She kisses his cheek as he tells her how much he missed her in Russian.

Yuri is behind this beautiful pair that melts my heart. When I see him, my eyes narrow again. "Hello." I eye the two cousins.

Aware of the storm that's brewing inside of me, Yuri nods subtly.

"Zariah, girl, don't look like that." Vassili's sexy voice tempts me to forgive him as he kisses Natasha's cheek, and she settles her arms around his neck. He reaches out to kiss me as well—

On the heels of my tennis shoes, I go, turning around without offering him a word.

Fifteen minutes later, we have walked through the car garage, with Vassili attempting every other minute to rouse a 'friendly' conversation out of me.

"You want me to drive?" he asks, once we're a few yards away from my car.

"Do you want to explain why you beat up Matthew Overstreet? I don't know of him. Explain that to me—"

"She doesn't know?" Yuri grunts.

Vassili gives him a look.

"Oh, so you two are trading signals now." It was a stiff finger into his face. "Yuri, talk to me, buddy. What kinda fun where the two of you having last night, that lead you to—"

"Zariah," Vassili's voice booms against my chest cavity. His tone startles Natasha into a frown which brings an onset of tears. He kisses her cheek, mumbles something about 'chalk chalk' that makes her smile. "It was not like that. I will talk to you about it later. That's a promise."

Yuri gives him a look.

"You want to tell me, Yuri, go ahead." I fold my arms.

My husband passes our child like a bag of potatoes to his cousin. He gets in my face, "I'm not fucking talking to you right now. You gave me the cold shoulder, Zariah. Allow me to mention, there'd be hell to pay if the situation were reversed. You'd have a problem with me ignoring you, but I won't dish the same shit you just served. We will have this chat later." He grabs my arm firmly and escorts me to the passenger seat, while Yuri straps Natasha into her car seat before sitting on the opposite side of her.

"What possessed you to fight the man, Vassili?" I ask once Vassili navigates the freeway for a time.

"Girl, I just tried to have a conversation with you, you refused. Now, you will wait."

"*Boy*, you might have jeopardized your career. How am I the only one making logical sense? So, what the hell's next, Vassili, since you just might have sent your ass to jail for fighting a civilian. You can't fight a common citizen off the streets!"

He gives me a stiff shoulder.

"Will you follow in your father's footsteps?" I argue. It was a low, way below the belt comment, but Vassili understands the type of woman I am. At least, I assumed he knew that I want better for him. When you love someone, disappointment is a hard pill to swallow.

And I know he isn't like his father, but Vassili has jeopardized his career and love... the MMA world... for fighting so I must be a bitch.

Vassili

"My father?" I spit the question while rubbing at the stubble along my jaw. I had less than three hours of sleep last night. When Zamora bailed us out, I once again reiterated my promise that I wouldn't tell Zariah about her relationship with Overstreet. Now, I'm in a fucking predicament.

And now, my wife just compared me to that piz'da? "You believe so little of me?"

"I apologize." Her shoulders rise and fall slowly. "Toss me a few facts, Vassili. Make me believe otherwise. So, we can get you out of this mess you've made."

"Uh, Zariah," Yuri speaks up from the backseat. "We didn't do shit. That douchebag provoked us."

"Did he now?" She scooches around in her seat, voice dangerously content. I almost tell my cousin not to speak. Anything he says is incriminating. My wife has this built-in lie detector test, and I'm still stuck on her fucking statement about my father.

Instead of letting Yuri taste his own foot, I throw the ball in her court. "You'd compare me to that motherfucker? You think I'm like my father?"

FEARLESS II
by *Amarie Avant*

"Don't yell at me." Her chin juts. "I'm trying to help you."

"Tell me, Zariah," my hands tighten around the steering wheel in disgust, "How the fuck am I like my dad?"

She's silent for a moment.

"Huh!" My bark sends her shoulders jolting. "First of all, you're good at keeping secrets."

I grunt and turn toward the road. Fuck, she has me there. "What else?"

"You're acting like a heathen, fighting people. Can we just go back to an hour ago, chat this out, Vassili, please?"

I shake my head. My father has people to kill people. And my wife is throwing elbows at me for a measly fight? "Girl, I'm a professional fighter, so come with it. Come harder. How the fuck am I like Anatoly?"

She snaps, "You—"

"You guys," Yuri says. "The daughter that the two of you had *together* looks like she's about to cry now. Can you knock it off for a while?"

We're back to silence.

***

Later on, I spent hours getting Natasha to fall asleep. Every time I sang the Russian ABCs, which is usually her favorite, she'd fall into a fitful sleep, only to awaken.

FEARLESS II
by *Amarie Avant*

"You worried Daddy's gonna leave?" I ask, rubbing her back. My daughter smiles up at me with her few teeth. Only one of her eyes closes, just a further reminder that getting out of the nursery, without her being in a deep slumber, might be the hardest thing I've ever had to do.

"Should we start on our story? The one about the princess and her ogre of a father?" I ask. She gives a sleepy little coo. Since Natasha was eight months old, and fighting swollen, teething gums, I started on a super exaggerated story I made up just to hear her laughter. While I'm adding dragons to the story, I hear a doorbell ring. My stomach rumbles. Good. I heard Zariah making a call to Taiwan Chang's, one of our favorite takeout spots, when I'd given Natasha a bath.

Thirty minutes later, I tiptoe to the door of the nursery. I consider washing the day off, but head downstairs instead. Zariah is in the den, seated in my leather chair. She's got her legs folded under her, and those freshly showered dark brown thighs look creamy in just a pajama shirt. There's a carton of chow mein in her hand. She's eating it with chopsticks and offering me an angry stare. I head to the kitchen, pick up the brown paper bag from the island. It's empty.

Really?

From the open kitchen/den floor plan, Zariah grumbles. "Don't be so dramatic, Vassili. Yours is sitting in the oven. Although, I considered getting your least favorite."

FEARLESS II
by *Amarie Avant*

I grab my food, and instead of going near my wife, I sit at the table. We eat in an ocean of silence.

I'm finishing up when Zariah heads into the kitchen with her empty container. Though I made a promise to Zamora, I'll try to explain my rationale for bashing Matthew's face in to her daughter. He's an asshole should suffice...

"You ready to chat, Zar?"

"Are you and Yuri done with the deception?"

I scoff. "Are you fucking kidding me? Deception? Okay counselor, that's left field."

"Then you'll tell me everything? Vassili, you have my heart. I'm scared, okay? I can't be without you."

"You're mine, Zariah. I love you." My tone is hard, raw, confident.

"What possessed you to beat some man, on the street, within an inch of his life?"

There's longing in her eyes as her hands plant on her wide hips. She must notice the slight hesitation on my face because Zariah returns to her spot. She clicks on the DVR list, choosing a Lifetime Movie.

I can't fucking tell her that the mudak whose skull I bashed in was beating on her mother, so I head upstairs to take a shower.

A few minutes have passed, moisture plumes around me as hot water slams down from the rain spout.

"Will you turn down the heat?" Zariah asks, standing wide legged, arms folded.

She's watching the water glide over my chest. My cock rises at just the sight of her in that long t-shirt that swallows her curves. I fist my cock in my hand.

She licks her lips. "I'm still angry with you."

"Okay." My wrist glides slowly. I imagine her lips sliding over my shaft. No, her pussy or that virgin ass, skimming up and down my cock.

She gulps. I turn down the water temperature, and the shirt goes over Zariah's head. She starts for her short-panties, the ones that cling to her ass, and leaves the bottom of those thick cheeks out. I love those fucking undies more than when she wears a thong. I grasp her hand and pull her inside before she can remove those.

"Vassili," she scoffs.

"Don't act like you weren't already wet," I shoot back in my thick accent.

Water waves up her thick weave. She caresses my cheek, and I glance down at her.

"Vassili, should I be mad, truly angry with you? I'm sorry for earlier, but should I be angry?"

I kneel, planting a trail of love against her gratifying lips, down her flat stomach, and to the top of her panties. The panties are soaking wet. I bet it has nothing on her soaking pussy though. I bite the back of her ass where it falls out of the bottom of her panty shorts.

The rain shower masks much of her moan. Zariah places her hands against the glass wall for support.

With effort, I peel the material off one hip at a time. With a shaded, lustful gaze, I admire all that ass in my face. I slap one cheek and then palm the dark meat in my tan hand.

"Fuck, you are thick in all the right places."

Then I rise. I can feel her heart slam into her throat. I turn Zariah around. "You still mad, girl?" My hand smacks and cups her pulsating lips. My fingers delve into silk curls, seeking out her clit. Her pussy lips tighten and contract.

I press fully against her, dominating her soft body. Her nipples are hard against my chest. "You wet or are you mad, girl?"

"Both."

I nip and then murmur in her ear, "I like that."

Once again, I press her up against the wall. My chest now to her back. Her hips rise, her ass thrusts back, spearing my cock against her left ass cheek. The attitude she has causes me to chuckle. I clamp a hand along her neck, and command, "Tilt that ass more, Zar."

Her hips curve, her ass rises. I bend down again, getting a good look at the angle of her butt.

"Tilt more or I'm gonna have to fuck that ass, sweetheart. Angry as you are, you're still scared of it." I grunt in laughter.

Her eyes flash at me. I cock a grin up at her. From the side profile, I run my hand over her buttocks and then my thumb stretches out in search of her pussy.

FEARLESS II
by Amarie Avant

Yeah, she's afraid of me screwing that tiny little hole. My thumb finds her wet, sopping pussy with ease. I stand back up. My hand once again claims the back of her neck.

The side of her face is pressed to the glass. I kiss her lips and ask, "You ready for me to fuck you?"

"Fuck me, baby!"

My cock is harder than titanium as my legs take on a wide stance. I clutch the back of her neck, and glide in.

She's angry. I can feel that shit way down in my bones. I grip her neck and drive my cock into her pussy, letting her ass cheeks slam against my dick.

My other hand swats against her ass so hard that Zariah almost straightens. "Keep the motherfucking position," I growl. She has a bone to pick with me. Fuck that, me too. She compared me to my father. My dick slams into her, balls deep.

Zariah

The water pours down on us in torrents. My nipples slap against the cool glass wall with each thrust. I'm on my tippy toes, as Vassili hits it from the back. The angle of his cock slaughters my walls, making my pussy release mini orgasms with each driving force. I can't even count how many times he's taken me to heaven while bettering me with his dick.

Mmmm, I love that pain.

"I'm beating the fuck out my pussy, Zar."

"This pussy is yours, Daddy." I gasp, my lips against the glass. It's pure greed, that has me leveraging myself to slam back against him. "Fuck me."

"Shit," he grunts. "I'm gonna break this pussy."

I scamper to clasp the walls, wanting to pull my hair out. He's screwing so deep in my tummy, that my future walk will forever be changed. "Harder," I beg. Each thrust clears my mind of all the red flags. He's dangerous. Everything about him is dangerous except his promises.

His swat along my hip brings stars to my eyes, and death to any thoughts of him being like his father. A sharp breath escapes my mouth as he flogs the same spot. The hurt catches fire from the center point of my pussy and expands it outward. The instant it reaches my hair follicles and toes, my mind goes dumb. And I beg for more hurt.

"Shit, Vassili, fuck." I once again feel like a drunken woman, steadying herself on weak legs and tiptoes.

The way he screws me insides sends me to another galaxy. It's enough to clear him of a thousand misgivings. I reach between my body and the glass wall to fuck with my clit. My fingers work the shit out of it. I'm still angry. The pain becomes my haven.

With strong arms that have beaten many of his opponents, Vassili turns me around. He's screwed the tension right out of me. My legs go around his hips, as he buries his dick deep inside me. Our hearts implode against each other's chests, creating their own drumming symphony.

"I don't give a fuck how angry you are, Zariah," he whispers in my ear, cock sitting deep in my juices. "You belong to me."

I reach my arms around him, pulling the Russian stone God to me, and kiss him hard. "I belong to you," I solidify his claim while our tongues dart together.

He drives cock inside of me one last time. His warm seed is so strong that it erupts deep inside my pussy. I cling to him, neither one of us is ready to let go.

***

by Amarie Avant

My cell phone alarm awakens me. The clock we use is on Vassili's side of the bed because he's always up at the crack of dawn for a run, and I feel like I've exerted too much energy rolling over and turning it off when he's gone.

"Zariah, baby, turn it off," Vassili kisses my lips.

I'm still submerged in a contented shade of black. My eyes are closed. They're not ready to open yet.

"Hmmm," I grin, blindly, feeling my husband looking at me.

"It's Saturday, sweetheart. What's with the reminder?"

The reminder? Oh, yeah, dread seeps into my heart. I open my eyes, reach over and turn off my cell phone. "We have to meet with Sammy before he leaves for a seminar this afternoon."

"We? I thought he was cooking us dinner tomorrow evening? Sunday dinners are his thing."

"He is, but I can't wait until then, Vassili. We need to go over your case."

There's a hint of hesitation in Vassili's demeanor. Then he scoops me up, and plants me on his waist. "Didn't I tell you not to worry?"

While straddling him, I offer a faint smile. "You did. But I can't stop, Vassili. I love you."

***

There's a vein pulsating in the side of Vassili's neck. Doesn't he know that this is the wrong time to bump heads?

FEARLESS II
by *Amarie Avant*

We're at Samuel's Venice Beach home. The beach surrounds us in a 90-degree angle. The furniture is perfect for a man who doesn't have tiny terrors running around, ready to stamp a train of dirty fingerprints everywhere.

I can't believe, almost two years ago my mentor was eyeing Vassili during his jog, and telling me to keep away from the riff raff. Now, he sits on the low-seated chair between the two love seats that Vassili and I have claimed.

My leg is crossed, my foot rattling with irritation. Samuel attempts to rationalize with him. "The more you tell us now, the more we're able to defend you."

Duh! Sammy's voice is too friendly. He's offering my husband a choice, one that he doesn't have. I will help regardless of what nonsense is going through Vassili's mind.

"Vassili, you have two lawyers here ready to build a titanium case for you." I sit forward in my seat. "I love you, let me help you."

"Girl, I won't have you as my attorney." His chuckle is contrite. "I've already said it. End of discussion."

"Why? Because I'm not seasoned? Sammy is, talk to him." I gesture.

"No. Zariah, I believe in you," he sighs. Rubbing the chain link tattoo on his forearm, he turns to my mentor. "Sam, this meeting ... I don't need it. I'm going to handle the situation myself. Come Tuesday morning, I'll be dressed in a suit, and will speak to the judge myself. Zariah and I'll see you for dinner tomorrow. She's wasting your time."

"Are you sure?" Samuel asks.

"He's not," I butt in.

"Judge McKinley is a hard ass," Samuel tries. "My connections will not be of any use without your side of the story—"

Again, I speak up. "Yes, his side of the story. I'm sure you told my mom why she had to bail you out of jail, Vassili."

His lips bunch into a frown.

"Well, if he won't give it, then my mom will." I snatch up my leather purse.

My husband is cussing in Russian underneath his breath. Then he addresses me, palms out in a truce. "Zariah, c'mon, beautiful, stop the madness. Do you want to get your mother into this mess?"

"Zamora?" Samuel arches an eyebrow. "What does Mora have to do with it?"

"Hello, Mom," I place her on speaker. "I need you to tell me what happened the night Vassili and Yuri were arrested."

Her voice rings loud and clear and hesitant. "Tsk, honey, they didn't do anything wrong."

"Mom, please explain it to me." I can feel the tears slithering down my cheeks. Vassili's eyes warm with concern before he leans his head back and takes a breath. His dark as sin eyes glower, causing me to feel hot coils against my skin. What the hell did I do? I'm trying to save him!

"Ms. Haskins," he cuts in. "You don't know anything."

Samuel glances around in consideration. My husband's comment was leading! Totally leading. Heck, he really sounds like a Russian mobster, prepared to cap a potential witness.

"Honey, are you crying?" My mom asks.

"Yes, mom. My husband is in more trouble than he realizes. Vassili, you aren't as invincible as you think. Think about Natasha. This is a crucial time in her life to be gone." An image of him behind bars pops up on an imaginary projector before me, whisking away the deep blue sea. His love has me drowning. "Someone tell me something!"

"Okay," My mom speaks up.

"It's nothing," Vassili says just as she admits to knowing Matthew Overstreet.

The muscles in my abdomen knead, twisting rapidly, and a sinking feeling overwhelms me.

"Is he the man you've been dating?"

"Yes, honey. We were dating for a year."

"That's a rather long time without introductions, Mom. You know how I am, queen of interrogations. 21 questions an all." I scoff, more anxious than I let on.

My husband shakes his head at me.

FEARLESS II
by *Amarie Avant*

But I still ask the question I'm highly suspicious I already know the answer to. "Does he... does he hurt you, mom?"

There's a heavy silence. Samuel breaks it, his distraught matching my own. "Mora, love, does he—"

"Sammy? What are you doing there?" The embarrassment in my mother's voice rings into my ears....

***

The community park near our home is an upgrade from when I grew up, and I'm not just mentioning the switch from seesaws to a sandbox, which teaches outdoor science. I also grew up in a well-to-do area of Los Angeles. But our park is child developmentally friendly. The sections are for early development, middle grade, and even the skateboard sections a few blocks down are fit for that crazy sports channel Vassili watches sometimes.

I'm halfheartedly pushing Natasha in a swing, with an extensive seatbelt contraption. These rich mothers can never be too safe. Who am I kidding, I've seen more au pairs than bio moms at the park. My mind is inundated with other things.

"I'm awful, aren't I?" I ask Vassili as my mother's story twines in my ear. She told the story about her relationship with Matthew Overstreet to save Vassili, and I know it broke her heart that Sammy listened to every word. If she could only see his face. "Vassili, answer me. Am I awful?"

FEARLESS II
by *Amarie Avant*

"You are," Vassili says, grabbing Natasha's feet. She's angled with her frizzy hair blowing in the wind. "Now, move. Our baby is a stunt double."

"Dang, tell me how you really feel," I grumble taking a few paces back.

"You're in trouble, no discussion needed. You'll pay later," his voice is ominously sexy. And I'd like to see myself pay later, if I didn't feel like a jackass. In the next instant, the frown is expunged from his face, a smile in its stead. As Vassili lifts Natasha's feet higher, she's damn near upside down. Then he says, "Swoosh."

"Daddy!" she giggles before being flipped back. I have to move further as Natasha soars higher than I've ever attempted.

"Boy!" I shout a warning which lands on deaf ears. Natasha vaults back toward him, fat fists waving around like she's preparing to go to war. She loves it. Natasha swings back and forth a few times before Vassili catches her legs and repeats, sending her higher into the universe.

"She needs a helmet," I grumble.

"*Nyet,* our daughter loves it."

***

Vassili plants me on the kitchen counter after we've double teamed—fed, bathed, and put Natasha to sleep. "I need a shot of Hennessey," I tell him.

The sexy laugh that comes from deep in my husband's abdominals makes my body wet. He places his thick waist between my thighs, and pulls off his shirt.

"*Got damn,* Vassil, I'm asking for a petty party. Which means you have the tools at your disposal to get me drunk. This is a once in a lifetime opportunity."

"Okay," he moves away. My hands barely have a chance to caress the eight pack of his. He pauses, then in a sarcastic voice inquires, "Oh, can I get your drink, your highness?"

"Humph, you're still being an asshole, aren't you? Earlier, my only thought was saving you from joining the Aryan nation in jail—"

"What the fuck?" His thick eyebrow rises.

"Hello, you're white. There's only one place for you in the pen. So that's my excuse for setting up my mom. I feel like middle school, there was this one time when Ronisha, you remember her?"

"Of course, Zar."

"Tsk, my mind is frazzled. There was this one time when Ronisha got me on the party line—a phone call with random kids. Needless to say, I was too 'white girl' for most of the people on the call. I blindsided my mom with Samuel's presence. Now, I need copious amounts of liquor to help me forget. Which, might I add, can be how I repay you." I bite my lip as my hand slides over the smooth ridges and then let my index finger glide over the KILLER KARO tattoo which is spread across his chest.

"Oh, you think you are allowed to state how your punishment will play out?"

"I'm offering you the grand opportunity to get me drunk as fuck, Vassili, be calculating and ambitious."

He moves back into my area, brushes a kiss along my neck. "When I give you an order, you have to start listening."

"Yeah, you told me not to have the meeting with Samuel. I'm wrong, can't admitting my faults be punishment enough." I feel myself tearing up. The hurt in my mother's voice while explaining how Matthew Overstreet treated her, didn't exceed the pain of knowing Samuel was aware that she was in *another* abusive relationship.

He kisses my lips. "I'm your husband, Zariah. You must trust that whatever action I chose to take is for the best interest for our family."

"Wait," I grab out for him as he pulls away again.

"No using me like a piece of ass." He goes to the refrigerator and pulls out the vodka.

"Oh no, I want some brown, brown persuasion. That stuff will have me acting a fool."

"Maybe I want you ready to be committed, Zariah. The crazier you are the easier it is for me to get to certain parts of your body, i.e. your true punishment." He opens up the Resnov Water and gestures for me to tip my chin. Vassili pours some into my mouth, a small bit trickles down my chin and neck. He licks that up. My pussy starts to rain down in my pants just like the vodka that was just dripping down my neck.

"What sort..." I shake my head to help ease the burn. "Shit, no more. Now, what crazy stuff are you considering?"

"The kinda shit that requires me to get you good and drunk." We chuckle as he pours more in my mouth, this time, I don't swallow. He places his mouth over mines and drinks.

"So, where you headed?" I inquire, feeling my reaction time fade by the second. Damn, I only had about a shot and a half.

He grunts. "You want me in that tight, wet pussy, don't you?"

My head bobs up and down slowly. "Yessss..."

"I wanna," he begins, voice slow, deliberate, and powerful, "get in that ass." Vassili takes the bottle to the head, and then he hands it over. "You ready for me to get in that ass, girl?"

"Nope." I sip at the bottle. This shit feels like liquid fire, slamming all the way down, inside my chest. Vassili tips the bottom of it, and I end up guzzling down more than I anticipated.

"Take off your clothes."

I press on my palms, intending to jump down, but the ground sways slowly. I chuckle.

"*Nyet,* don't get down, Zar," he tells me, while brushing my lips with a kiss. Vassili places my hands over my blouse. I slowly start undoing the buttons.

FEARLESS II
by *Amarie Avant*

"Damn, girl, you'll be forever." He grips the silk material and pulls, buttons go popping everywhere.

Did he just? Cognition slowly trickles in as I glance around at the buttons scattered across the marble flooring. "So it's like that? This is my favorite shirt!"

Vassili unbuckles my pants, and gathers my panties with it, sliding them together down my hips. My ass is now on the cold marble slab. He's still in his army fatigues.

"Take yours off, too," I pout.

"In due time." He grabs the bottle, offering me more. I turn my head and he asks, "What happened to you getting drunk?"

"Boy, I am good and drunk!" I slur.

He pours the vodka along my chest. "One day I'm going to cum all over your tits and make you lick them off."

"You can now."

"Nah, I've got other things up my sleeve."

I chuckle, and then realize the extent to his response. "You want me to be a bad girl…" I grip the chocolate waves of his mohawk as Vassili licks the vodka from one of my tits. It takes ages for me to realize that my fingers won't be gripping the marble countertop. As he applies pressure to one of my nipples, I moan. My hands press backward, as I lean back for him. I pour more vodka onto my body, the cool liquid rushes over my breast, into my belly button, drenches down to my pussy, mingling with my own wetness.

As I groan with delight, Vassili licks up every trail the vodka makes.

"Can you stand?" he asks.

Dang it, but I giggle, again. Vassili holds out a hand, I take it, and move at a snail's pace until my left foot touches the ground and then my right.

"Turn around," he orders. "Hands against the counter."

Feeling my body mellow even more, I am quick to do his bidding. My hands go to the marble ledge. Before I can lean back, wet liquid shoots down my lower back and between my ass cheeks.

"Mmmm," I purr. Vassili bends over and licks me down below. His tongue prods against my asshole. "Shit, that feels good," I murmur. I rock my hips back as he eats my ass out. Then he slaps the inside of my thigh, making my stance wider. His tongue nudges my pussy as his fingers work their way into my ass. Again, my ass is begging for his penetration. I work my hips until more of his fingers slip into my hole.

"Oh, so you want me in this ass?" The drum of his voice is delectable.

"Yeah, Vassili," I cry out. "Keep fucking my ass."

"I'm not fucking you yet." He removes his finger, and then his tongue slides up my pussy to my asshole before he gets up. Vassili stands right behind me. The sound of him taking his belt off is titillating to my ears.

"Fuck me, baby," I tell him.

He pushes his pants off with the heel of his barefoot, kicks them away. His belt is still in his hand. Vassili swats my ass with it. Pain shoots through me, and I'm so ready for him to replace it with a pain that I have never felt before. His cock.

Vassili enters my pussy from behind. My mind starts to catch up, it's on the tip of my tongue to tell him to fuck my ass. Screw me with his big, white cock. "Girl, you are fucking wet for me," He marvels. "You should see my cock."

"Can I taste it?"

"Nah, I have other things for you to do."

I whimper at his refusal. Vassili continues to screw me, my back arching perfectly as he grips my ponytail. "Keep wetting my cock with that thick, sweet pussy, girl. You got that pussy wetter than the ocean for me."

I force my hips back, meeting him thrust for thrust. Until he pulls out. His cock slides up my labia and to my ass. I gyrate, gliding his hardness across my tiny hole. "Vassili...don't stop."

His cock nestles against my butt.

"Girl, you should see how beautiful your ass is," he tells me, smacking a cheek, before he rubs the pain away. "Now, drink that vodka."

I reach over, grab it, and guzzle it down. Then my hands grip the ledge as he slowly works that glorious cockhead into my ass. "Shhhhhit, Vassili," I growl. It hurts so good, I love it.

Vassili

Her asshole is puckered and tight. I've fit four of my fingers into that tiny little hole before, and loved how her pussy came on my cock. That's what I'll do now. My cock moves back down from her ass. I bang inside of her wetness again and again. Zariah works her ass back against me, slamming my cock till it sinks deeper and deeper into her pussy. My balls clap against her sweetness. Jaw ridged, I fight not to explode inside of her miracle pussy.

I lean back on my calves. Cock at attention. Zariah turns her head just as I slam the belt down on her hip.

"Fuck, Vassili!" She glares.

Again, the belt swats along the same spot. Her eyes spark with fire, this is a pain she just has to take. Once more, the pinnacle of my manhood brushes against the tight entrance of her ass. It's so fucking beautiful, my cream-colored cock, nestled between her dark chocolate globes. I can see cum squirting from her pussy and down her legs. Damn, I want to lap it up like a dog. But, now is not the time. I lean against my calves once more. Causing the head of my dick to slither across her swollen clit.

FEARLESS II
by *Amarie Avant*

"Shit!" Zariah screams. "Fuck me, baby. You can screw me. You can fuck my ass," she growls. "Just fuck me."

My lips spread into a smile. Her excitement is contagious. Zariah wriggles her ass back against me.

"Hold still." I grab a bottle of lubrication from the table that she hadn't noticed me pull from my pocket, earlier, while sucking on the vodka bottle. Like hell am I going in my wife's ass without any extra protection. She isn't one of the bitches that I used to fuck with, and despite her eagerness, there's an art to stretching her tight hole.

"Vassili," she whimpers.

While opening the bottle, I give her pussy another jolt. My thumb's loving the tightness of her asshole now. I work against the firmness of the inside ring of her ass, my cock is a piston in her ultra-wet valley. She bucks like the most gorgeous Arabian horse and rides out another orgasm. An ocean of her sweetness rushes along my cock as Zariah comes harder. My toes tuck underneath and clench, the tension abets me in my desire not to explode inside of her because tonight I'm headed into her ass.

She moans and groans and sags something fierce against the marble counter.

Damn, my dick is sloshing inside of her cunt now, and my fingers continue to widen her out while she recovers from that hard orgasm.

FEARLESS II
by Amarie Avant

"Baby, I want it…" she feigns as my thumb and index finger tweak and stretch her hole.

My cock slides in and out of her channel as I entice her with this response, "Yeah, I know you want this cock in your ass, beautiful. I'll give you that now." I slip my cock from her pussy, picking up the lube again. I coat my already soaking piece.

My slick cum-coated cock lodges at the puckering of her butt.

Hands skimming over the side of her hip and up her tiny waist. Now she's silent, no more begging, but this gorgeous body of hers speaks volumes. She's ready. She trusts that I'll fuck her good in the ass and that I'll do my best to love her without hurting her. The crude mushroom shaped head of my cock kisses ever so softly against her asshole. I slowly push my way in.

"Mmmm, Vassili."

"Don't tense up, Zariah. I promise you'll love this. Just breathe, my beautiful wife."

The whimpering transforms into a heavy sigh as my cock inches inside and past her tight entrance, for a heavenly fit. I make leeway and then give her time to breath.

"Mmmm, Vassili, I love you…" she breathes the words.

"I love you, more."

For every inch I take inside of her ass, I caress ever so softly at her lower back. I listen to her body.

FEARLESS II
by *Amarie Avant*

About three inches of my cock is in her now. She's too beautiful to force it. I reach beneath her hip to rub softly against that tiny, little bulb if hers. The action of me working her clit, sends her pussy lips to shiver.

I pull out of her ass, this was enough for now, and slide into her pussy. This time, I fuck Zariah until she bucks back, and I cum deep inside her…

***

Monday morning, I stand in the bathroom, after a fresh shower, and grab the waves of my hair. "Time to get rid of you my old friend," I give a cocky grin, determining to be the image of a pristine 'white' boy.

Fuck, this is for Zariah. Nobody in this world can force me to change my image. But for her, I'll play the part tomorrow. She was worried about me being locked up. I grab the clippers and plug it in, ready to look like a brand-new man… Well new enough.

Come tomorrow, I'll have a freshly shaven face and a suit covering my tats.

On the 30-inch flat screen TV across from the sink, MMA Sportscaster Alex Brown mentions my name. "The Anaconda Alvarez has decided to pull out of the contract binding himself and Vassili Killer Karo Resnov."

What the fuck? How did Alvarez pull out of a contract that I had yet to sign? We never did take a trip to the convention center in Atlanta, like I told Zariah we would in order to consider the retail value of fighting him for pennies. I grab the remote and turn up the television.

"This news has come in the midst of Karo's recent assault of an unarmed man," Alex says, his face sneered into a judgmental frown. "Karo, if you're watching, call in. I'm confident your fans are interested as to why you'd beat up an innocent man."

He begins to bash my name. "Yeah, well fuck you." I flip the bird to the TV screen, grab the hair at the front of my head and buzz it off. I recall the last time I was interviewed by Alex, that bitch was riding my cock, raving about my latest fight. And I promised him that Juggernaut would fall in less than—what, 8 seconds? I think it was eight seconds. The crowd used to be my bitch. Now to hear from him that neither Alvarez nor Karsoff want to fight me due to my current legal matters? He can suck a diseased cunt!

"Boy are you in there grumbling and griping?" Zariah calls out from bed.

Fuck, I realize I am mumbling.

"Go back to bed, Zar."

"Humph, I'm glad you are aware that I still have an hour before I need to dress to go into the office. Thanks for turning up the television as well."

"Then go back to bed." I buzz off another piece, my brown waves fall into the sink. With a frown, I nod at myself. Wait, need to get rid of the frown as well. Samuel, Zariah and I finished the discussion about how to get myself and Yuri out of the heat. He came through saying he'd have both of our cases seen by a judge who sympathized with domestic violence. The clean look will just solidify that. Yuri isn't much for tattoos, so basically, it's just me needing to cover up and fly straight.

"Baby," Zariah calls out once again, this time her voice seems preoccupied.

"*Dah?*" I take a warm towel and rub it over my buzzed head.

"C'mere, now," she orders.

When I enter the bedroom, Zariah is laying there with her cellphone in a horizontal position, listening to some dude whose cussing likens me to a saint instead of a sinner.

"Girl, what are you listening to?" I ask just as I hear my name.

"There's this short clip of you from the other day..." She smiles as her eyes land on me. "Oh, lawd, what is going on? What happened to my thug?"

I rub a hand over my head, again. "I knew you secretly wanted a square."

"You aren't even capable of sounding like one." Her eyes are full of life as she gestures for me to come closer. I climb into bed on top of her, and Zariah speaks in a tone filled with mock fear. "Can I-can I touch it?"

"You sound scared," I say just as she laughs, again.

FEARLESS II
by *Amarie Avant*

Her lips softly plant onto mine. Her tongue comes out, and she licks before nibbling on my lip. At the sound of more cussing and joking, my eyebrow rises.

"Oops, I had it on repeat. Rodney is funny as hell. When I'm at work and need to de-stress, I'll click on his Facebook page." Zariah digs around for the discarded cell phone and I cuddle next to her. "He has this habit of assessing the craziness going on in his world. You made the cut."

She clicks onto a YouTube video. A black man comes onto a split screen. On the right side of the screen, Rodney is sitting in a chair, and must be streaming from a laptop camera. On the opposite side of the screen is a fuzzy video from the night I beat down Matthew. Whoever took the footage didn't catch me in the backseat, but the camera starts rolling with Matthew honking his horn.

The honking slams and fades from the screen with extra sound effects. Rodney speaks up, "Man, I mean, really? Does this dude think that some buff personal trainer is going to come out of the gym to save him? I mean, look at his face." There's a still-frame close up on Matthew. Rodney can hardly speak for laughing. "His forehead is lodged wayyyy into the back his throat. I don't know if he was able to drive away, but I'd be damned if I'm going to create a scene after somebody punches the motherfucking breaks off me! Just wait a minute though!"

FEARLESS II
by *Amarie Avant*

Rodney laughs so hard that all is visible on his side of the screen is teeth for a second. "Look, really close, somebody tell me if this dude was born with a brick to his face. Man, he's so ugly I would say my face hurts, but it can't hurt anywhere near as much as his does. He's gonna need a lifetime supply of Tylenol for that bullshit."

The comedian glances at the right side of the screen and says, "Just wait. Y'all, just wait."

On the opposite side of the screen the freeze frame has ended, and I'm returning to the car. "Karo, seriously? You beat the man into next week. Why come back and serve him with another beat down? And I mean, some-motherfucking-body call Triple A, he beat the breaks of this man. The guy's name is Overstreet, but I swear he needs to change his name to *just Street!* Had him blending in with the pavement. Wait, wait, look—"

Rodney pauses as I pick up Matthew from the ground. Somehow the comedian has added sound effects to the fight. Every hit seems to SPLAT, POP or CRUNCH.

I squeeze my arms around Zariah's midriff. "You listen to this bullshit?"

She stifles another bout of laughter. "It's funny. Matthew Overstreet deserved it. Wish I was there."

"Like you'd have been good with me trying to knock his head off?"

FEARLESS II
by *Amarie Avant*

"Humph, you *did* knock his head off! Under the circumstances, I might have run up, kicked him, and ducked out of the way."

"No need to run, I got you anytime you need to let off steam."

"Oh, so we should just hit the streets, knocking people's block off whenever we're stressed?" She can hardly kiss me for grinning now.

***

Judge Styles is supposed to be a softy, at least Sam told me she would be when he received favor by switching her out with Judge McKinley.

But when I take my seat next to him and Zariah, looking fit for a fucking J. Crew suit listing, she starts harping about how I have a higher level of accountability as a fighter.

My voice is tapered, "In my defense—"

"Don't' speak," Samuel says under his breath.

Imaginary horns pop out from her blond hair. Ironically, she's sitting in front of the great seal of Georgia. Wisdom. Justice. Moderation. My ass.

Styles jumps on me with, "This is *my* courtroom, Mr. Resnov. It's my time to shine not yours. I saw the video of you wiping the *streets* with Mr. Overstreet, and the DA is ready to lock you under the cell for using such tactical strategies on him."

Fuck, this could be pure comedy. She has that mudak, Rodney, beat with her reference to *street*. But she continued to carve me a new one. "Mr. Resnov, you are a weapon. Your hands, your feet, your body! Now, Mr. Resnov, what do you have to say for yourself?"

Shit, I would say that I didn't kick the motherfucker, but do I get to speak. Zariah nudges me in the side.

"Oh," I begin, fixated on my thick Russian accent. "I would like to say that Mr. Overstreet deserved every single hit—there was no kicking involved, your honor. I didn't use a takedown, none of that, I just used my hands." Fuck, this isn't helping.

"Your Honor," Zariah speaks up, "may I be allowed to approach the bench?"

"Humph, would that be a waste of my time?" Styles inquires, ice blue gaze still glaring through me. Then she turns her attention to my lawyers. "Billingsley, Washington, I respect you, but I'm baffled at how can you convince me that Mr. Resnov is not a threat to society?"

I try not to grit my teeth as the judge just called Zariah the wrong last name, and if it were my turn to speak, I'd let her ass know that, too!

"Yes, your honor," Zariah holds up photos. "I believe these photos are relevant to the case."

Judge Styles gestures toward her bailiff, the beefy fucker eyes me, my 'good' boy persona slips for a second as I frown at him. He takes the photos from Zariah and heads to the judge, who gasps at the sight of what she sees. "Ms. Washington, these are some very despicable photos? Please state the name of the person in these photos for the record."

"They're photos of Zamora Haskins Washington, my mother." Zariah's voice breaks. "My mother is—was dating Mr. Overstreet, Your Honor. As you can see, there are many bruises inflicted on her person, which were all at the hands of Mr. Overstreet. Each photo is time stamped below."

A moment passes before the judge's pursed lips loosen, she glances at me, and then at Zariah. "And where is your mother, Ms. Washington?"

Zariah turns. "She is here, your honor."

"This court will take a temporary recess." The judge slams her gavel down, the sound rings out throughout the cherry wood walls of the courtroom. Styles gestures toward the District Attorney and then to us. Samuel and Zariah start to rise when I do, but they tell me to sit down. Now, I'm twiddling my thumbs like a useless idiot for half an hour. When court is resumed, Samuel beckons for Yuri, whose case was being called separately from mine, due to his resisting arrest.

Zariah sits next to me. I reach over, caress a few strands of hair behind her ear. "Girl," I whisper to her. "Tell me something."

"Shhh," is all she will say, while squeezing my hand beneath the table.

I sit back, bite my tongue and twiddle my fucking fingers like a lapdog, with no orders as the Judge drones on and on about how I must be held to a higher standard.

It's either I tap it out or go off. Not that I expected special treatment, but Zamora Haskins didn't have to add herself into the equation. I fucking did this, poured out her life of abuse for Zariah to see, Sammy to see, the whole damn courtroom to see. Regardless, any person, man or woman, should want to retaliate. You don't go around smacking people—unless you're me, of course, and in a cage. If I tune into Judge Styles, I'm liable to tell her something she doesn't want to hear.

"Vassili, baby, respond," Zariah murmurs.

My eyebrows knead together as Yuri nods, "Yes, ma'am—uh your honor, of course."

"This is the good old state of Georgia, Mr. Resnov, and Mr. Resnov. We don't have vigilantes around here, so I suggest the two of you return to California post haste."

What? So, I am free? I nod my thanks, standing up as Zariah, Sam, and Yuri do. I whisper to my wife, "What the fuck just happened here? She's been riding me hard."

"You are too easy to ready, Vassili. All that 'I'll handle it myself.' Boy, bye! You really pissed of Styles, but we fixed it." Zariah hugs me tightly. "We are a team, Vassili. Next, time keep me in the loop, so we don't have to wait until the last possible second to *team* up."

FEARLESS II
by Amarie Avant

Damn, so Zariah held off before garnering sympathy from the judge. Her look tells me, it served me right.

I growl in her ear, "You're in trouble when we get home."

"Better be the kinda trouble I like."

***

We all head out of the courtroom and down the corridor to the exit. I hold Zariah's hand and fall back a few paces to align myself with her mother, who hasn't said a word this entire time.

"Thank you," I tell Ms. Haskins, placing my arm around her shoulder and giving her a hug. She's just as humble as my own mother had been in the past, offering a soft smile before waving off my show of gratitude.

"You're my son now, Vassili, and I love you."

"Aw mom," Zariah is teary eyed.

Yuri is opening the door, and I hardly get a chance to tell the woman who birthed the love of my life, that I love her as well, before a microphone is shoved into my face. Yuri is at my left, and Zariah is to my right.

There's a mass of reporters, some are held at bay by a few police officers in an attempt to keep the peace. And even more have caught up with me, asking their own questions all at the same time. I tune into the closest one.

The reporter says, "…. Alvarez, Karsoff, The Jedi…they're all ready to give you a shot in the ring, Karo. Your fans around the nation are elated that you've sought after justice for your mother-in-law."

That's right, mudak! I want to call out sports commentator, Alex Brown. That bitch tried to drag me through the ringer, but none of my fans had anything negative to say. A few of them tweeted that Overstreet had to deserve it.

Jaw held high, I respond, "I'm thankful for the fans who stuck with me even though they saw me placed into a negative light. I want everyone to know I don't condone bullying. Never have, never will, so yeah, like you just said, maybe I'll handle it another way in the future, but this situation hit closer to home than I anticipated."

"Who will you fight next?"

"Killer Karo is going after the best," Yuri says.

"Karsoff." I respond, my face doesn't even spread into a smile. But inside, I'm elated like a kid at New Years, the most popular holiday in my homeland. Alvarez is beneath him, Jedi is a bottom feeder, and neither one of those mudaks would win in the cage with me, but as Yuri bitched, I have to work my way up. I'll start from the middle because my belt will be within my grasps sooner rather than later.

"Mrs. Resnov," the reporter, "we're also told you were of assistance during the court proceedings, acting as both Mr. Resnov's attorneys. Is that true?"

"Yes, I and attorney Samuel Billingsley were available, although due to the special circumstances of the case, the guys pretty much pulled through without us."

"Will Matthew Overstreet be charged, and what will those charges be?"

"Sorry, I cannot communicate about an open investigation." Zariah grinned, providing the reporter enough ammunition to know that Overstreet isn't getting off scot-free.

"Thank you, the two of you are a winning team." He nods.

Zariah squeezes my hand again. "See, baby, keep me in the loop and you'll never go wrong…"

Zariah

Despite my elation that I won't be living the single-mama life, due to the judge dropping all charges, the feeling of shame surrounds me. I unknowingly added Sammy into this mess. My mentor and my mother don't fool me, they have feelings for each other. Deep ones. And Samuel's awareness of how she's been treated probably hurts her more than anything that asshole, Overstreet, dished out.

Sunglasses masks much of my mother's humiliation, yet her glance is to the ground, and her lips are in a hard line. Mom broke out of that bout of melancholy when Vassili thanked her. One would swear she's never received much acknowledgement from the male species. And now she's as quiet as ever as Samuel drives us in a rented Escalade.

"Can we at least have lunch before the Judge wants us out of Georgia?" Yuri asks, having commandeered the front passenger seat.

"Mora, what do you suggest?" Samuel asks, glancing through the rearview mirror.

She shrugs. "Anywhere is fine."

FEARLESS II
by *Amarie Avant*

Damn, I thought I'd never see the day again when her tone of voice hardly reaches above a whisper. Her eyes are on Martin Luther.

"This is your hometown, Mora. You know where all the good eats are." His eyes are the perfect mixture of playful and hopeful.

Since I have the middle seat in the back, I offer my mom a tiny elbow nudge.

She speaks up. "What are you in the mood for?"

"Anything." Yuri sounds like a kid. "I'll die if I don't eat soon."

"Fat fuck." Vassili shakes his head, and then apologizes for cussing in front of my mother.

"Humph," she says. "We know good and well, Vassili, that you cuss like a sailor. Now, I can recommend barbecue chicken, upscale Italian, French, and—"

"Ribs." Yuri makes the call for everyone.
***

We end up in this hole in the wall joint where a canned soda pop is served with your meal or you can pay a quarter for a Styrofoam cup and tap water. But with an "A" grade, and a to die for homemade barbecue sauce, I cannot complain.

When I come out of the bathroom, Vassili and Yuri are pushing two tables together. Samuel is at the station where my mother is grabbing napkins and forks. He appears to be talking to her, but her level of interaction is uninspiring. In the past, I've had to narrow my eye and watch them interface for a while, before determining that they may or may not have a thing for each other. Today, I'd require more evidence of any chemistry the two shares.

I stop myself from heading over to them. First, I have no idea what to say. Second, my mom is a pro with the cold shoulder. So, I'm about as helpful as a public defender on the first day of the job.

My brother, Martin, shows up. His eyes target my mother, and I corner him toward the exit before he can confront my mother about her lack of judgment. We're half masked by a life-sized pink piggy, standing on its hind legs in an apron, with the restaurant name along its hefty chest.

"Hey, Zariah, we need to talk to Mom, now." He pulls off his prescription glasses, rubs them on his polo shirt, and is just about to walk off when I plant myself in front of him again.

"I understand where you're coming from, big brother, but now is not the time. Sammy's here, we're all just hanging out for lunch—"

He cuts in, "I just heard that our mother was being..."

"I know." I try to calm him from crying. There were so many times where my father and brother went pound for pound after Martin grew up and got tired of Maxwell going upside her head. "Listen, I invited you to lunch so we can all get together while I'm in town. The conversation you're mentioning is inevitable.

FEARLESS II
by *Amarie Avant*

Nevertheless, now is not the time. Not in front of friends."

"What should I do, Zariah?" He turns his wrath on me. "Pretend to be oblivious! I'm sure in the eyes of most people watching the news, a professional fighter going off halfcocked was the reason this made national coverage. The domestic violence is not that important to them, but that asshole hurt our mom. We can't allow her to keep screwing with—"

"Martin, I'm not saying pretend to be oblivious. And look," I nudge my chin to our mother and Samuel. She's slowly beginning to blossom. "Sammy's a good guy. Would be nice to have someone like that for mom."

"Samuel is married to a different woman, every five years or so."

But it would be nice if they gave it a shot. I huff. "You know what, last week when mom asked me about him, I made the same statement. Maybe he hasn't found the right woman."

Martin scoffs. "And the right woman is his ex-best friend's *ex-wife*? Zar, you stayed with dad when they divorced. You don't know what mom needs, I do."

Mom begged me to stay with dad. I've never mentioned her reasoning, so I clamp my mouth shut.

"Zariah, baby." Vassili heads over to us. "You are hogging your brother all to yourself." He wraps an arm around me, instantly pacifying the tension in my shoulders. "How you doing, *brat*?"

They shake hands. Maxwell replies, "Not too well, man. I owe you for what you did to that asshole. Zariah and I need some sort of intervention with our mother. She's too old to be a punching bag."

"I see." Vassili nods. "Your mother is such a beautiful woman. How about you have that chat with her at another time, though. She's sitting with an old friend, and this is sort of a celebration. But, I promise you, the day won't end before you two have that talk with your mother."

I breathe easy as Martin nods. The three of us head to the tables. It isn't until we all have a basket of ribs set before each of us...well Yuri has two...that my mom eases back into her fun-loving self. She sets aside a rib that has been utterly demolished, not a trace of meat is left, and asks, "Who's this Karsoff that my son is going to put a can of whoop ass on?"

"Mom, 'can of whoop ass?' What do you know about Stone Cold Steve Austin?" I chuckle.

"What do *you* know?" Vassili feigns jealousy, kissing and nibbling my jaw.

"No, Stone Cold didn't coin that term. It was Chuck Norris," Yuri says. "Had to be him. I watched his movies and shows. When Malich would be angry that I wasn't studying, I'd tell my pop, that Chuck taught me enough English."

Our entire table is rowdy and laughing now. All except for Martin, I have the feeling he is becoming empathetic to the notion of waiting to discuss our mother's domestic violence situation, away from friends. My brother can be so uptight, sometimes his reactions are long overdue, too! I had called him with a hunch, after I returned to California. He just said mom was alright. Now, he's ready to start an intervention as he chews his food in silence.

"Wait, wait." Samuel speaks up. "I think it was Popeye, had to be Popeye. That's from back in my day."

My mother is teary eyed with laughter, and I hold my sides. Martin almost chokes on a glass of sweet tea before he caves and lets a good chuckle take over. Damn it, but I wish I was capable of refuting Sammy. I can't stop laughing to debate with him, and tell him that Popeye was a television cartoon, and couldn't have possibly said those words.

***

Life's good. I've taken the rest of the week off work, and have not been assigned any new cases, in order to attend Vassili's training practice where media is available for him to officially announce his fight with Karsoff. My man is going to break the German fighter's head off, and I'm ready for it.

We're in the middle of Vadim's gym. Some of the other fighters are crowding around the cage. I have to hold Natasha on my hip or she will literally attempt to run to the fence. Though she can't, our one-year-old is stubborn enough to forget to learn to walk before trying to run.

"What song are you coming out to?" One of the fighters shouts.

Vassili stands on the canvass dripping wet with sweat, and damn it if I wasn't holding our child, I'd be just as hot and bothered. "Where's the DJ?"

My husband gestures to me. I come closer to the cage, and look up at him. He takes Natasha from me.

"Yuck, you're so sweaty," I tell him.

"Tell the DJ to play Trace Adkins, *Whoop a Man's Ass*."

"Huh?" I bite my lip. The singer doesn't sound familiar. Lord knows I've had it up to my eyebrows with underground rap music, foreign and domestic.

"Trace Adkins," Vassili tells me.

I head over to the DJ who is stationed where the free-standing weights usually are. She has purple hair, that's shaved off on the left side, displaying a skull tattoo. She offers a bewildered look when I mention the singer.

"Is it country? I don't have any country, give me a sec." She pulls out her iPhone and starts searching for it. "Got it."

"Thanks." I head back toward the cage area, and my pace stops. I turn back to the DJ, and she shrugs her shoulders at the sound of a guitar. And the man belting out country lyrics, who I assume is Trace

Adkins, crones about having to a whoop a man's ass sometimes.

"Oh no." I shake my head, and shout over the music, "Hell, no Vassili, you are better than this!"

"Kazen, I like this song, that mudak is gonna underestimate you, with this bullshit. You really got to…" Yuri sequences his wording perfectly to shout the chores with Trace Adkins, "whoop a man's ass sometimes."

The DJ shouts through the speakers. "I'm gonna remix this, Vassili. Still can't have you going out like that."

When Vassili steps down from the stage with Natasha, she has her hands over her ears.

"Oh, I thought she was a ruffian like you," I tell my husband, kissing his lips. "I might not like country music, but I can see you whooping some ass to this song. Boy, you love making a statement, don't you?"

He lifts an eyebrow as his only response. Cocky bastard.

Vassili

On Monday morning, Natasha and I take a trip to my uncle Malich's home. She's in the playroom with his son, Igor's younger children, while I sit with my two cousins in the kitchen. Every time Yuri passes the bottle, I smack the back of Igor's head.

"Kazen, you cannot have any," I warn him through gritted teeth. "Let your pops go a day without taking care of your grown ass!"

"Just a little taste," Igor says. He's a diabetic, and with Malich as a father, who loves to cook and was once a doctor in our hometown, Igor has this warped, untrained mindset. Malich enables him, and then saves his fat ass.

"Ask again, and I'm going to punch you into that wall," I grit out.

"*Nyet, brat,* you don't need any of this," Yuri says, pouring himself another shot.

My wrath lands on him, dark gaze, and lit with anger. "This is your big brother, Yuri. Don't wait until I correct his ass to step the fuck up. Okay?"

"Man, he'll do what he wants in spite of what we say, Vassili. You can beat him to a bloody pulp—"

"Hey," Igor cuts in. "I don't need any of you piz'das speaking for me."

"Who you calling a cunt!" I bark.

With a softer voice, Igor asks, "Are we playing cards or what?"

"Nobody said we were playing cards, man." Yuri huffs. "Isn't it your time to head down to the pier? It's Monday, Igor. How am I more aware of your schedule than you are?"

Malich sets plates in front of us. "He's not going to San Pedro. No one is."

"Dad, what do you mean..." Yuri unclasps the top button of his suit. "Every third Monday, Igor goes, if he's sick then I go."

Malich slams a hand onto the table. "We're out, Yuri. You haven't had to assist with a shipment in months, and guess what, Igor still makes himself sick. Shit, son, you were out a long time ago. Managing our champ here," Malich says, patting my shoulder, "is job enough."

"Did you tell Anatoly?" Yuri asks.

"We stopped receiving his shipments last month. Albeit, there's no telling him. My big *brat*—brother— thinks that he can bully us into it. Anatoly is wrong. Our lack of response should've gotten through that thick skull of his by now."

"Nobody told me shit." Yuri pushes his food away. "I have things to do. I could use the extra funds. What about the art dealings? I've handled those requests every quarter?"

by *Amarie Avant*

Our family has an artist. One of my half-sister's can freehand the Mona Lisa with her eyes closed. It seems my father is capable of investing time in his children when they have a select skill that benefit him. We have a connection at Smithsonian, and receive an inventory of new shipments to the West Coast Museum. With Yuri's assistance, my sister replaces the originals with her own knockoffs, and he places them on the black market.

Yuri huffs again. "I need money."

Malich puts his fork down. "What's wrong, son? I cannot see the two of you going broke anytime soon. The matches. The Killer Karo clothing and memorabilia. The sports water. Your commercials still play, Vassili?"

"*Da!*" I nod.

"What's with you, Yuri? Have I raised you to be greedy?"

"*Nyet, otets*—no, father." He rubs a hand over his face.

"What the fuck is wrong with you then?" I ask, feeling my cousin's anxiousness.

"I'm proposing to Taryn, shit, is that okay with you?" he argues.

"Fuck, yeah. That doesn't have anything to do with me. You sure, though?" I glare him straight in the eye. They're inseparable when we double date, however, he's even more of an idiot than I thought for even considering actually settling down with someone like Taryn.

"What do you mean, *am I sure?*"

I place up a hand, not one for arguing. *Make your own mistakes with that bitch,* my face says it all.

"I'm proud of you, my son," Malich tells him. "Ready to make an honest woman out of your girl. When I made the decision to remove myself from my brother's grasps, it wasn't with the heavy heart I had expected. Your mother pleaded with me a thousand times before she died, to cut ties with Anatoly. He had just taken over, after your grandfather died, and I just couldn't see myself leaving such a hot head to rule the bratva."

"It's all about respect not force," I mumble in agreement.

Malich nods. "*Da!* It is. That numbskull is unpredictable. Anatoly would've been dead a month as the boss, without someone to smooth the waters for him. Too slimy," his eyes apologize to me for talking about my father. I shrug. "I've always told my sons, you too, Vassili, to never have regrets. I didn't pull out soon enough. Regrets like that stick to your heart, never go away."

"You were trying to save Sasha." I wolf down my food, feeling uncomfortable for having such strong emotions around my cousin and uncle. But with Malich's face getting all long while contemplating the past, I had to speak up.

by Amarie Avant

"Yes, myself and your aunt continued to support Anatoly after Sasha was born because we saw the way he treated your mother. He was rapidly changing. He needed us in America. We saw that as a prime opportunity to take Sasha. If only he'd let us raise the girl. But…"

"My piz'da of a father wouldn't allow it." I frown.

"So yes, we will always have a few regrets, trying for a better future isn't one of them. But, not removing myself from the fold soon thereafter will always be on my mind. Now, Yuri, you are a millionaire. I am, of course, wealthy enough with the money I have made helping Anatoly build his empire over the years. But with that being said, what type of ring do you want to purchase this girl?" Although Malich is cushioning the truth with a joke, I feel that he isn't too keen on Yuri settling down with Taryn. The bitch is a gold digger, plain and simple. Telling Yuri the truth won't help at all. Some people cannot be told. They have to see it for themselves. So, if he wants to drop money hand over fist, like I did with Zariah, I hope he simmers the fuck down until he realizes how unworthy she is.

"I want a ring made, like Vassili."

I bite my fist. *This isn't gonna work well for you, brah.*

"And you love this girl?" Malich inquires. Something in his voice is desperate for his idiot son to see the light. Every once in a while, Yuri gets pussy whipped. Tore the fuck down over some sour cunt.

"Is the bitch worth it?" Igor asks, plain and simple.

Yuri growls, is already on the defense, and so I keep my jaw compressed. Really there is no help for him.

"We love each other," he says.

Yeah, whatever you say, kazen, is written all over my face. "Uncle," I change the subject to something more important than Yuri dishing out money he won't be able to have returned for a custom-made ring. "I need your help with something. Yuri and I have been trying to handle it for about a week, but shit got in the way, and we're no closer to finding out who sent this email."

I slide my cell phone from my pocket, and Malich appears relieved. There'll be more fatherly pep talks before Yuri attempts to go for broke. My uncle places on his prescription glasses as I tell him to open the email regarding Frank Gaspar.

"Who is this little shit?" he asks, glancing through the photos of the decomposing body.

"A rookie cop," Yuri says. "I don't recall Anatoly ever wanting us to put anybody on the beat on payroll. Only Detectives and higher ups. Have you heard of him?"

FEARLESS II
by *Amarie Avant*

"Frank Gaspar? *Nyet.* Never." He places down the phone. "But we will know everything there is to know about him by the end of the day. You killed him?"

"Vassili punched him around a little, I did the deed." Yuri shrugs.

"Well, he looks like a nobody, but I'm assuming this email implies that somebody wants to make something out of nothing?"

We both nod.

Malich sighs heavily. "You think your father did this to rattle you? We aren't picking up his shipment. And he went ahead and sent it anyway. Hmmm, he'd be mad at me, not you, though, Vassili."

"Then it's Zariah's father!" Yuri slaps a hand onto the table.

"You're still having trouble with Zar's pops?" Malich's eyes widen in surprise. "We're all family now. What's going on there?"

My shoulders lift a little. "Zariah and Maxwell aren't on speaking terms. He hates me just as much as I hate him. Zariah sent him a birthday party invite but the mudak didn't come."

"Jesus," Malich says. "That beautiful baby and her gorgeous mother don't deserve the silent treatment. He'd miss a grandbaby's first birthday because he hates you? That's bullshit. Shit like this makes my blood pressure increase. I'll make the call, figure out who this Gaspar is. See if he works for Anatoly or Washington. We'll go from there."

FEARLESS II
by *Amarie Avant*

***

Later in the day, Malich is in the state-of-the-art kitchen again. The aroma of his famous meatball mozzarella soup wafts through out the room. It's the same soup that set Zariah's nerves at ease the first time she met with the majority of my family, months after we were married. He picks up a plate of Russian bread and comes to sit down next to me.

"Uncle, you cook like we're celebrating a holiday," I tell him.

Zariah, who arrived after work, sits next to Igor's wife, Anna. The women hold their own loud ass conversation. Anna smacks Igor's hand as he reaches for a pelmeni—a Russian dumpling.

"You've had enough," she reprimands him, and then she's instantly back to laughing and chatting with Zariah. One of Igor's oldest daughter's is sneaking a third pelmeni to Natasha, and the rest of the family is crowded around.

"So, uncle, any update?" I ask. He offered to cook dinner this evening so that it wouldn't be suspicious for him and Yuri to come over after I'd been in their company all day. The subject of Frank Gaspar isn't something to be discussed over the phone.

He nods. "I just got a response while grabbing that last plate. You want to finish eating or talk?"

"Talk," I respond. I have a month to make weight for my match with Karsoff. Camp week is hell with a

French fry loving daughter, and a wife who had no problems cheating on me with Fatburger in the past.

Yuri rises when we do. My wife hardly pays me any attention as she and Anna have switched subjects to some sort of new facial wash.

We head away from the loud house and out onto the patio. Yuri leans against a column, and I pace the area while glaring at the turquoise lap pool.

"Okay, so for starters, Frank Gaspar isn't named Frank Gaspar. And he's not a cop," Malich says, sitting at the patio table.

I stop pacing. "Who is he?"

"An actor, a nobody. That automatically clears Washington." Malich drums his fingers on the table. "Knowing that crooked mudak, he'd just have his own come after you, not hire an actor to pretend to be a cop, and put him in a uniform. The real Frank Gaspar is on the force, just not in Los Angeles where it would be easy for Washington to send someone after you. The real Gaspar is alive and breathing and working at a precinct in Fontana."

Yuri and I exchange glances. He rubs the back of his neck, and determines, "We had a few matches in Fontana, back in the day. Vassili is too big these days for that area. But who the fuck would still be angry with you, brah? What have you been up to?"

I shake my head. "I haven't been to Fontana, since firing that slimy ass promoter. Shit, the last time I was there, you were, too."

"Oh! The promoter who skimmed off the top, the bottom and the middle?" Yuri chuckles.

"You two done chatting it out?" Malich asks.

"*Dah*," I grunt as Yuri sits across from his dad.

"Good, because I'm aware of who did it. Danushka. So, either your father was desperate to scare you, or she's parted paths with him."

I sink down into the chair to my cousin's left. Can't have a daughter without a son was always my father's motto. There was a time where the mudak forgot about me, because he had babies popping up all over Russia. But Danushka is his second born. Just a few days younger than me. Shit, my father always jokingly said, if he had a girl first, he'd break her neck and start over. No matter how badly my father treated Danushka as a child, her tenacity was astounding. She worked her way up in the bratva, snatched assignments from others, in order to be recognized in our father's eyes besides being viewed as just a bitch. Shit, she thought me, and my sister, would disappear after my mother finally got the guts to run off with us.

"You aren't sure if she's working for Anatoly?" I finally ask.

"Nobody knows. But that's just how she rolls, Vassili. Take a breath." My uncle encourages. He adds, "We've seen her in action. In the past, I'd heard about your father asking for a political figure in Italy dealt with, for example. Prior to a member being appointed to the task, the guy or girl is dead. Danushka signs her name."

"Dah, that cunt loves to catch my father's eye when he least expects it," I scoff. "What the fuck does that bitch want with me?"

"There isn't a shadow of a doubt in anyone's mind, Vassili, your father still wants you to be his successor. That's why Danushka is fucking with you."

My hands slam against the patio table with so much force that Yuri has to push back in his chair to get out of the way. The legs of his chair snap as he falls back, in order to remove himself from the path of the table as it flings across the grass. It leaves tracks of mud and grass in its wake, and slams into the pool. I catch my breath as the table sinks to the bottom. "I am not fucking with the bratva! Anatoly needs to get it through his head, Malich. I refuse."

"Nephew, take it easy," Malich's voice is tempered. "Blowing a gasket will not stop your father or change his beliefs. You are his first born. Good as royalty in his mind."

"Where the fuck is this cunt? Where is my half-sister?" My wild eyes rove back and forth from the two of them.

"Nobody knows," Yuri says with a grunt, getting up. "I'd call Anatoly and ask him what the hell is going on, but that motherfucker is incapable of a straight response." I stand up, and start pacing over the cement slab. My fists swoosh out before me as I punch, cross, jab into the air. "You think he sent her?"

"Would be better that he had," Malich says. "She's a wild card. So if he sent her to screw with your mind—like she's clearly doing—then he would have her on a leash. If she's acting on her own accord…"

My voice booms, "I don't want her around my wife and children."

"Have you told Zariah about her?" Yuri asks.

"Fuck yeah, I showed Zariah a photo, everything. She knows to stay away from Danushka…"

Zariah

Only a few months have passed since I met Danushka Molotov and we've connected in such a short time. We crossed paths on one of the lowest days in our lives. We were two melancholic wives in the alcohol section of Whole Foods, in Beverly Hills. My husband was pissing me off, because at the time, I just couldn't fathom how he'd want to return to the cage after a torn patella. I'd tortured myself with YouTube videos of the worst MMA fights to ever occur, where the men were breaking their legs and having their skulls cracked. That was the worse time in my marriage with Vassili. I was so very afraid of him returning to the cage. And Danny, although Russian, was dealing with her own demons about marrying a fellow Russian. We talked for a few moments. It was a start of a relationship that I needed. I have Taryn who isn't married, and I suspect may never settle down as long as she still has her looks. Where I'm from, too many friends are a bad thing, and so I didn't have any married friends until I met Danny.

I know, I know. She has the same first name as Danushka Resnov. And my husband's forehead vein pops out each time he reminds me to steer clear of his sister. I've done my due diligence. Background checks and everything. And his sister looks like the Terminator. Pale. Brown hair. Big nose and muscular. Danushka Molotov looks exactly like Kate Moss.

I'm shuffling along with the hubbub of Los Angelinos to work when Tye Tribbett's latest CD is interrupted by an incoming call. Starting off my day without praise and worship is something I wouldn't wish upon my worst enemy. I'm a mess and three quarters without a sane mind! But I stop singing along and press the touchscreen to accept her call.

"Danny? I received your text last night, are you really back in town?" I gush into the phone.

"Yes. And I'm hijacking you at noon today for lunch."

"Ha, that's fine. So, did you get the house?"

"We did. As you know, my husband and I traded in Bel Air for Italy for a few months. Our new home is in escrow now. We're vetting potential caretakers for our home here."

"Humph, look no further, I don't mind moving into your home while you're away." I joke. The home I share with Vassili is large in its own right, but Danny's husband has a hand in the steel industry and international banking. Aside from how busy he is, their home in Bel Air could entertain a person for a year from grand courtyards, to a theater and bowling alley. They have a baseball field, there's no reason to leave their home.

"I'll pencil you in for an interview," Danny joshes back. "Horace is conducting background checks and all. But I want to invite you to Italy."

"Girl, I told Vassili that we have to take a trip to Apulia one day soon. I'm so happy that you guys are working out, and we will come to your housewarming if you have one," I say, traveling down the street, Billingsley Legal is a few blocks ahead.

"Oooooh, we bought the house with furniture in it, but I wouldn't mind having friends over for a week or so. Horace could spare at least a week to entertain. I have you to thank for that, Zariah, I wasn't much of a talker before."

"That's what marriage is about. To compromise, you have to talk it out."

"My family is different. We are old school Russians, and I've had such a negative mentality. I knew that if I married one of my own, it wouldn't work out. *Russian men*," she says in her thick accent, and I can just imagine her dash crunching. "But I fell in love with one. And, here we are, Horace and I are working out."

I pull around the cars, which are headed into the Hot Chilly's drive-thru line, across from the law firm. These idiots sure know how to *act* when it comes to good food.

"Alright, Danny, I'm heading into work. What time and where should we meet for lunch?" I ask while maneuvering around the tail end of an illegally positioned car.

"I have actually learned to cook. At least I attempted to. Horace and I took a class. If you are feeling courageous enough to try one of my new recipes, meet me at my place at noon? We can always go out instead, my treat."

"I'll meet you at your place." I swoop into a spot.

***

At Billingsley Legal, I seek out Tyrese Nicks. He exuded the wrong kinda vibes when we crossed paths last week. From his eating me with his eyes, to the distaste he has in my last name. And what's up with the history we have and the assumptions he's made?

It's been over a week since Vassili cornered him in my office, and due to my husband's recent acts of aggression which sent us to Atlanta, I had no time to correct Mr. Nicks. Until he has chosen to promote or move on to other endeavors, we have to work together in a common accord. With the legal firm's main goal to edify families, all of the attorneys and members of Billingsley Legal get along together, well, we try our best too, anyway.

I find him in his office, typing away.

"Good morning," I assert myself at the door.

The typing stops. His gaze drags over me from head to toe and back again. I'm wearing a dress that accentuates my curves, and stops mid-calf, yet is appropriately fashioned with a thin cardigan. High heel peep toe booties and bangles finish off my ensemble. Those dimples of his are resurrected as he grins and says, "Come in."

Eh... that's not entirely necessary for what I need to get across, but I oblige and take a seat across from him. "So how are you liking the new job?"

"Pays the bills." Flippant fucker as if I can't tell his navy-blue suit doesn't hug his muscles in a way that screams it was made specifically for him. He comes from a good black family, and I am not aware of that due to any sort of knowledge of him, but his diplomas behind him. He offers a half smile. I don't match that. "I'm learning how to sympathize with people, Zariah. My previous professor suggested that I give a damn about people before I become..."

"This big bad wolf?" I cock a brow.

He nods. "This place serves two purposes. I learn to communicate with quote-unquote victims, before I move along to DA."

I can appreciate a man with confidence, but he just made our clients seem like *nobody's.* "What better way to do it than with the ex-Chef Deputy District Attorney and working with a demographic that actually needs people to give a damn."

"Precisely. Is that still your plan as well?" he inquires.

This is the perfect opportunity to insert myself. "No, my original plan would've caused me to burn out before I made enough money to give a damn. So my father once worked with yours? And apparently I know you?" I cross my legs, lean forward, and await his response. Usually it makes a man choke when I'm too forward.

"Damn, woman, you truly are an attorney. We either lie or bite. That hurt." He offers a killer smile. "You don't remember me, whatsoever?"

He asks questions for my questions. My lips set into a line. This is a man's world, but baby, I play well. "Do you have a problem with my husband? Or just my last name in general?"

Tyrese rubs his clean-shaven face. I can't stand a man whose face looks like a babies' ass. "This conversation is headed exactly where I anticipated. Zariah, I'm just astounded by your choice in a husband."

"Elaborate," I grit out, unable to fathom why I'm having this idiotic conversation with a man who has no relevance in my marriage. But I'll let him build his case? And then I'll be the lawyer, hell, I'll play judge, jury and executioner on his ass. I see my father through his gaze. So judgmental.

"You always wanted to get the bad guy when you were a kid, then you married him."

Who the hell is this man and why does he believe he knows me?

Tyrese's desk phone rings on key. The motherfucker has the last word as picks up the headset he offers a greeting into the receiver.

FEARLESS II
by *Amarie Avant*

"Put whomever you're speaking to on hold," I order.

"Excuse me for a second." Tyrese places a hand over the receiver. "We can finish this conversation later. How about lunch—"

"Now!" My index finger slams onto the mute button. "Let's start with an apology because apparently, you're learning to become apologetic while working with victims of spousal abuse and whatnot." I huff. "Oh, and while we're on the record, damn it, I apologize that you were *forgettable* when we were teens. I'm actually making that assessment based on how old you look, mid-twenties like myself. So, with that said, I'm going to be apologetic enough to forget you're a misjudge of character. My marriage has nothing to do with you. If I were to become a defense attorney, believe that whomever I'm set to prosecute will receive the same service as the next man or woman and so on and so forth! While you came to the conclusion that I lost my fucking mind and married a hoodlum, I'll go ahead and grant you that assessment. Cause Vassili will knock you down to size for continuing to flirt with me."

"Zariah, I'm not trying to be a dick—"

"That concludes this conversation. Have a blessed day." See, Tye Tribbett and the gospel choir have assisted me with starting off the day.

***

FEARLESS II
by Amarie Avant

Danny has a humongous knife in her hand, and she slices and dices like she's worked at a butcher shop. She's a pale blonde, with a thin yoga body and I assumed that our lunch would consist of all veggies, as evidenced by her cutting more cucumbers and zucchini for the salad on the counter. But it's almost 1pm, and I'm nursing an expensive glass of wine, with a name that I cannot pronounce, while sitting in a kitchen so large its comparable to my master suite becoming a walk-in closet. And the aroma in the oven is to die for.

"Almost ready?" I ask. "Girl, that lasagna has my stomach rumbling.

"Let's see…" Danny peeks inside of the oven, mumbles in Russian and tosses her mittens onto the Italian marble countertop.

"Maybe I should've taken you to lunch instead?" She gives a wry smile while heading back to the chair across from me.

"No worries, here. I could lose a few pounds," I say, comfortably seated in the plush chair. Ironically, I'm constructing the perfect tiny sausage and aged-cheese slices on a square cracker. These damn things are good.

"I really did learn to cook. Horace, too. Albeit, we always had the chef there to instruct us." She chuckles. "Because of you I'm not frowning, and life is good, you know?"

I nod. "I really am happy for you."

"My favorite line use to be *Russian Men, pah!*"
She makes a face at that. "I can't believe Horace swept
me off my feet. I can't believe we are a year into our
marriage. It's crazy."

"It is crazy, in retrospect. How we were raised." I
shake my head in thought.

"Yes! You should be with some anal-retentive
businessman. I should be with … someone not
Russian."

"Humph, I met the perfect guy as far as past
expectations go."

"Like your father?" she asks. I nod. When I nod,
Danny scoffs. "Rigid beliefs. High expectations? Say
it isn't so!"

"Yes, we have a new attorney at Billingsley
Legal. He knows me from back when I was a rigid
teenager—well, that's how I suspect he knows me
based on his *disappointment* in my choice of
husband."

"What?" Danushka offers one of her signature
frowns.

"Well, this asshole comes to me with this notion
that I've lost touch with reality due to the man I
married."

"Oh goodness. I dated a football player once. My
family expected him to be uneducated and…" she
leans back in her chair. "And I didn't care how the guy
treated me as long as he…"

"Wasn't Russian?" I finish her sentence, tasting the crisp smooth wine.

"Yup. This is why I love you, Zar. Not only do you finish my sentences. But we both married men we couldn't fathom spending the rest of our lives with."

"We stepped out on faith and it paid off." I agree with her wholeheartedly. My soul is settled having a friend like Danushka who, unlike Taryn, fights for something good. In my past, I never saw myself with a knight in shining armor. I have my father to thank for that. There'd be no acting in a certain demeanor or even at the very least catering to my husband's expectations. I never knew marriage was about unity until I met Vassili and we became a team. Working at Billingsley Legal helps with that as well.

***

Later on, Danny and I are stuffed. The recipe to the lasagna she made is in my leather purse as she walks me past a marble fountain to her front door.

"I really am considering the housewarming in Italy," Danushka says. "We have yet to meet each other's husbands, and vacation makes for a good double date, right?"

I nod my head in agreement. There were too many times in the past that either Vassili was out of town, promoting an upcoming match, or her husband was away on business. "We can always set aside everything for some 'us' time, and Italy sounds just like the place to do it."

Vassili

Las Vegas, One Month Later…

I've read my Bible this morning to Natasha, yet anxiety tears through my soul. The faint thump of music through the cement walls in the background signifies that the second match is now beginning. I finish my prayer, kiss the cross around my neck and stand up.

Fight, Vassili. Get in fight mode. God has blessed you…

I've told myself a thousand times now isn't the time to fixate on bullshit, but to focus on my capabilities. What I can control, but before I can mentally offer the same credo again, I ask, "No news on Danushka?"

"Not now, Vassili," Vadim grumbles. "You've prayed, let's warm up. Nestor."

"I'm hot as fuck," I tell him. I address my uncle, Malich, who's sitting on the bench, with Yuri and Nestor, the lockers are behind them.

My arms swoosh out as I complete rapid punching combinations. I'm burning up inside, and I'm consumed with what the fuck my sister has been up to. Why email me?

FEARLESS II
by *Amarie Avant*

"*Dyadya?*" I nudge my chin to my uncle. Nestor settles back down.

"Not yet." Malich says. My uncle isn't much for traveling, and I can't believe I'm ruining one of the select few times he attends my matches with talk of Danushka.

He gets up, walks over and places his hands on my shoulders. "You have a belt to get back, Vassili. The best thing Danushka has going for herself is getting into your head."

Vadim takes over with, "Do you want Karsoff there as well? Fucking with your mind?"

I stare at them both, they already know the answer is 'no.' My little half-sister hasn't reached out since dropping the bomb that she knew of Frank Gaspar's death. Although there isn't a stream of dead bodies everywhere I walk, her motivation has unleashed the beast in me. What is her reasoning?

"Nestor," I cock my head to him. He jumps up. Time to spar.

***

I keep my head down. All the light is on me and it's blinding. There's a camera crew in front of me, tracking backward, as I head to the cage. The music is funneled into my ears with the buds that I'm wearing. Though I can't see a foot before me, the muffled sound of screaming tells me that not a single seat in the place is empty.

Fearless II
by *Amarie Avant*

"Karo..." The crowd's chant pierces through the rap music I'm listening to.

I stop at the cutman, feeling like a caged tiger in my own skin as he applies Vaseline. Then I'm climbing up the stairs, and once into the octagon, I flip three times, and land on my side of the canvas. I miss being the favorite, the last man out, to assess my opponent as he stands here, stalking the cage. Now, here I am, the announcer is running stats for the German as he comes out.

It takes forever for the opening bells to ring, Karsoff steps forward to touch gloves, I gesture for him to get the fuck back to his side, so we can get started.

We crash into each other. Like those fucking punching boxer toys I wished for but never got in the past, we're tossing bricks for fists when my left zeros straight for his nose, sending him stumbling backward. I press forward, taking the left jab, right jab to my chin with a sneer on my face. That mudak gets confident until my right hook strikes, sliding across his jaw. The one hit shakes Karsoff to the core, I continue hitting him every step of the way to the ground.

"Put the pressure on 'em!" Nestor shouts from my corner.

This was too easy...

I grapple over him. Karsoff beings to turn over. Instead of protecting himself or fighting back, he grasps at the canvas as if he wants to get up and run.

With this position, I loop my leg around him, and press my bicep around his neck, choking him back to me, into a triangle choke hold.

Karsoff reaches a hand around, punching my ear. The pounding causes my ear to ring. I let up, stand, shake my head. He's left in a vulnerable position. As I reach down, Karsoff's leg swipes out. He issues a rapid succession of turtle kicks. I glare at this bitch, jumping to defend myself from his right foot.

I step back, my glare telling him to get up. I'm going to bring this cunt back down. So far, he's tried to run and did a shitty job defending himself when I stood up. A few 'boos' break through the chanting crowd. I gesture for him to get up, because tonight, I feel like entertaining.

Karsoff rises. He's back to his cocky self. This mudak was afraid of the takedown. Just as we go back to tossing punches the bell signals the end of the first round. I glare at my opponent one last time before moving toward my corner.

"You good?" Vadim asks.

"Good, Good."

"Your knee—"

"I'm fucking good, Vadim. Knee, body. All of that. Good." I snatch the water he hands over. "*Spasibo*," I grunt out my thanks in Russian, toss the water back, pour a bit on my face, and then crunch the paper cup and flick it over my shoulder.

FEARLESS II
by *Amarie Avant*

At the commentator table, two casters are chatting it up.

"The ferocity in which Karo came into the cage woke me up just now."

"Me too. Almost forgot there were a few matches prior to this, and we aren't even at the main event."

"He's looking better than he ever has in his entire career. And c'mon let's face it. We can count on two fingers the time Karo didn't rise to the occasion. He's one of the toughest dudes in the circuit."

"Karsoff looks more mature in the ring tonight as well, Johnny. After the first takedown, he came back smoothly. What he had going for him is matching Karo's pace, and not flying off the handle."

"Karsoff has made an excellent recovery, and he may be the current favorite, but I'm going against the grain. The moment Karsoff hit the canvass, he was a scared animal. If Karo can get another takedown, I predict vengeance will play out."

That's right, Johnny, I mumble to myself, I'm going to serve Karsoff the beatdown of his life.

The bell chimes. Time for round two. This time, when I take my opponent down, his ass won't be getting back up.

FEARLESS II
by *Amarie Avant*

Zariah

My heart lodges into my throat. Damn, I prayed that Karsoff would be a punk. Okay, maybe not "prayed in Jesus name" per se, but my fingers were crossed, and I wished with all my might. Vassili and Karsoff are going toe-to-toe, trading bomb for bomb like the first round was just a warmup. The announcers are shouting, and the people around me are screaming so loudly my eardrums rock.

Granted, I do my best to keep the confidence for Vassili's sake. There may never come a day when I watch a match without squirming in my seat. Scratch that, his fight with Juggernaut last year, was over so swiftly that I didn't even get the chance to become a 'nervous nelly.'

Natasha is sitting in my lap, or more like standing there, jumping all over my legs. In her shimmery purple dress, with a matching ribbon in her curly hair, she makes for the perfect cheerleader for her father as Vassili does a cartwheel kick that lands on Karsoff's ear. My husband is showing his ass now! All these signature moves that I eagerly learned put my mind in this invincible superhero mode. I snatch up some of our daughter's energy.

FEARLESS II
by *Amarie Avant*

"Kill 'em, Karo!" I scream so loudly that Natasha glances back at me, her pupils dragging up and down my frame. This child of mine glares at me like: *no she didn't!*

"Sorry, baby." I chuckle, rubbing her ears. Is this child mine? This girl with her dramatic sense of humor?

"Give 'er here," Yuri says, seated to my left. The instant I hand Natasha over to him, I'm out of my chair screaming and performing gymnastics moves. I can't do a third round—damn, I'm not doing much. But I can't stomach one.

"Kill, Kill!" The vocal cords in my throat strain. *Jesus, give my baby some David versus Goliath strength! A shot and drop 'em!*

There are seconds left. My eyes dart from the two of them, going brick for brick. Finally, a missile of a right-hand lands against Karsoff's nose and a mean uppercut drops him.

He bounces up.

"Stay down, motherfucker!" I growl.

From my peripheral Yuri glances at me much like he did when I went into labor in Kentucky. Vassili stands there as Karsoff seems to forget where they are. He just popped up like a jack-in-the-box. Now, his legs are buckling like a newborn calf. Karsoff stumbles into the cage, his fingers grip onto the wiring. Vassili slams a looping right hook into the side of Karsoff's head.

I swear, for a split second, the fighter recollected exactly where he was and what he was doing because his hands finally clenched into fists as he hit the canvass.

Vassili goes in for the kill. He slaughters Karsoff with follow-up strikes and lets his fists rain down on him. Luckily, his enemy turtles up, and the referee tosses himself into the mix.

Vassili backs up and allows Karsoff to be rescued. My husband pounds a fist against his chest. It's barbaric, and I love every moment of it.

After a long cheer, the referee stands next to Vassili as the fight stats are announced. While Karsoff is receiving a whiff of one of those nasty sensor things that wake him with a disgusted jolt, the referee grips Vassili's fist and holds it up.

My husband is declared the winner.

Then the commentator steps up, with microphone in hand. "This is two fights in a row now, you've come in and been very dominant. Karo, what's been the difference?"

My husband's muscular frame is drenched in sweat. "I'm just thankful to be here. God keeps my hands up. With faith, there's only one way I'm going."

"You made a fadeaway overhand that caught Karsoff's temple early on. Then you gave the fans more entertainment and Karsoff a chance to redeem himself. This is one of the most entertaining matches of the season…"

FEARLESS II
by *Amarie Avant*

***

"Aw, baby." My lips caress a kiss on Vassili's eyebrow which has seven stitches. He just returned to the hotel room with Yuri. I expected them to go out and celebrate. That was the plan if Natasha dozed off. The alternative is painting the town as a family.

I glance him over. He's wearing Nike flip-flops. I can't recall a day when his left big toe ever survived a fight. The damn thing is always broken. When I start to hug him, he grimaces.

"I'm sorry, baby," I cringe. And then I reprimand him with, "Why don't you ever say you're hurt?"

I shake my head at him. I realize Yuri is watching us with longing in his eyes, and I try to be less lovey dovey, but Vassili pulls me into a bear hug with gritted teeth.

"Just one rib."

"Boy, why don't you ever say anything? I don't have x-ray vision." I softly press against his chest. "And I hate when you hurt."

He caresses my cheek. "If my wife wants a hug, fuck it, that's what she gets."

"Humph! Broken ribs and all?"

"One rib, girl."

He lets me go and heads to the bedroom, where a Disney movie is playing loudly on the Pay Per View channel. Natasha loves to sing to the music.

"I'll be back after a quick shower."

FEARLESS II
by *Amarie Avant*

"Okay," I smile and then address Yuri. "I'm sure Natasha will fall asleep in the stroller soon. You guys can just go hit the club."

"You look beautiful, Zariah. *Nyet*, I'm not feeling the club scene. What were your plans?" He asks.

"We were going to head to the dolphin exhibit at The Mirage," I begin. Due to how forlorn he's looked this weekend, I add, "would you like to tag along?"

"Of course, more time with my Chak Chak."

"Chalk what?" My eyebrow crinkles.

"Chak Chak. Vassili calls her that sometimes. But *dah*, I'll definitely come. Malich doesn't gamble, it's no fun alone. There's nothing else for me to do," he pouts. "Taryn is sick so…"

"Taryn is sick?" I repeat, having spoken with her earlier yesterday. She was bragging about a date with a New York Banker. The guy had sent her a first-class ticket to come see him. Feeling sorry for the big guy, I wave a hand and keep the manipulation on rotation with, "Oh, yeah, she is cramping."

"She told me she had a stomach ache," Yuri's eyes shade in thought.

"Which is it, girl?" Vassili's tone is curved as if he's testing me.

Where the heck did he come from? I turn around. He is definitely in a defensive stance, with his shirt off, jagged muscles, a bandage around his hard abdomen, and a bath towel in his hand. "Cramping or a stomach ache?" His gaze narrows.

by *Amarie Avant*

"It's the same thing, Vassili," I cut my husband a look. Then offer Yuri a reassuring smile. Taryn is fucked up. "Um, I'm going to help the big bully shower. If you hear Natasha getting restless, check in."

With a small nod, Yuri settles down on the couch. He sits, wide legged and fingers steepled in thought.

Vassili stands at the door to the bedroom as I enter.

"Congratulations, Zariah, you could've saved his life," Vassili tells me.

"How?" I scoff.

"He wants to marry the bitch."

"Oh God, that's a bad idea." Shit, I have no poker face unless I'm in a courtroom. We move out of the way since the television is across from the bed where Natasha is laying like the princess that she is. There's a scattering of pillows on the floor around the bed, although, our daughter is a pro at the pull-up and can shimmy down a rope if necessary.

"Ya think? Fuck yeah, it's an awful idea. This is the first time Yuri has dated a female for longer than a few months. He cares about that bitch, and evidently, she doesn't share his feelings. You should've said something."

I head to the luxurious bathroom. "Yuri's your cousin, why me?"

"It's easier when it comes from a girl, shit, I don't know. I've never been fucking cheated on." Vassili closes the bathroom door behind him. Crap, I'm locked in with him. My husband never argues or debates with me. First of all, he says a man should not argue period. It's for women. Sexist much. Secondly, he's afraid of confrontation—or he was before he had a broken patella. I won all fights by default. Meaning he'd be quiet until he was calm enough to chat. After his patella broke he used that forearm conditioning thingamajig to get under my skin while I tried to carry on a debate with him.

Right now, I'm not in the mood to defend Taryn, argue or chat. Because battle wounds are sexy.

I try to conclude my opposing argument with another tender kiss on his lips. Then I murmur, "And you will never be cheated on because I love you with all of me. I think the consensus is that either one of us would murder the other due to infidelity so let's get out of their business."

His frown deepens. "So, my cousin loses out tens of thousands of dollars on a wedding ring for that bitch, fuck that! You go tell him that his bitch is a *bitch*."

My hand goes to my hip. "Vassili, if you don't stop calling my friend—"

He corners me against the counter, his hands slamming down on either side of the edge. "What are you going to do?"

My fingers brush ever so softly against the "K" in KILLER across his left pectoral. My voice is silky as sex. "Vassili, may I suck your cock?"

FEARLESS II
by *Amarie Avant*

"*Nyet! ... Da!*" He growls and then nudges his head to the floor. I sink to my knees. Vassili leans back against the counter. The sound of his belt unbuckling and his zipper moving titillating slow sends a rush of saliva into my mouth.

I gulp it down, imagining his seed. Vassili fists his cock, running his large hand over his extremely long, thick erection. Damn, but I want that cock all over me. In my mouth, between my breasts, pounding my pussy, and he might not even have to get me drunk enough for some anal action.

My fighter looks ruggedly sexy. His bruises enhance how strong he is. I'm imagining him slaughtering my pussy as hard as he slaughtered Karsoff. Kill the cat. He hits his cockhead playfully against my cheek. "You wanna suck daddy's cock?"

"I want to suck daddy's cock and I want daddy's cum in my mouth. All over me..." Shit, did I just say that? I'm hypnotized by the way his hand works his cock. Wish it were me.

My husband's eyes glint a gorgeous obsidian and his mouth pitches into a cocky grin. "Okay."

Vassili stops fisting his dick and I throw my lips onto it with eagerness. My mouth is warm and wet against his hot, slick, titanium rod. I toss it back down my throat and attempt to gulp the head of him with my tonsils.

I glance up at him.

"Fuck, keep your eyes on me, Zar." He commands. "You my good girl?"

I hum the perfect response against his crown.

"*Nyet,* Zariah, you're my bad bitch tonight."

My eyes stay trained on him as his cock pounds my brains with each swish of my neck.

"I can cum over your face?"

I nod.

He grips my ponytail and I choke his cock deep into my mouth.

"Fuck yourself, Zar. If you want me to nut all over you, fuck yourself."

My neck action keeps my head bobbing up and down. Like I'm going for an apple in a water filled barrel each time I meet my goal, the tip of his dick slamming my tonsils. I reach down over my skin-tight dress and grab my tit. My body is hot, my pussy is aching.

"Fuck that pussy, girl. I can't cum over you unless you cum all over your fingers."

"Mmmm." I moan. I'm in love with the taste of his dick. It takes me a while. From tweaking my nipples to roaming my hand along my abdomen.

Vassili reaches down, growls at the pain from his rib and helps me pull my tight dress up over my hips. I press my thong to my side, shove his cock back into my mouth and three of my fingers into my treasure. The release of feeling something inside of me has me momentarily satiated.

by Amarie Avant

"Suck harder, or I won't cum, Zar."

My tongue swirls around his head, and then to the back of my throat, he goes.

"You wet?"

I do my best to nod while sucking his cock like it's solid gold.

"Work that pussy."

My fingers move rapidly. Vassili's hand twines in my hair, pumping me up and down. My lips glide over his cock at a rapid pace. A flash of ecstasy masks my face when I start drenching down rain on my fingers. His seed sprints into my mouth. He pulls out. I'm masturbating the long orgasm out of me as his warm cum shoots across my lips. I lock my mouth open, to catch as much as I can, and continue screwing myself.

When it's all done, I rub my index finger along my chin, drag the rest of his cream to my lips and lick my mouth clean. Vassili is staring at me like he wants to screw me now. Again...

And then he holds out a hand, helping me up. I start to kiss him. He turns away.

"Okay..." My eyes water instantly.

"*Nyet, nyet.*" He kisses my mouth hard, then rough, then tender. He feasts on my lips and tongues me down. "I'm sorry, Zariah."

"What? Vassili, did the doctor give you any pain meds?" I place a hand on my hip. The momentary lurch of my heart has ended, now I'm concerned. He's usually knocked out after norcos. But what's up with his ever-changing attitude?

"I shouldn't have called you a bitch."

"We're married, Vassili. We were having raunchy porno fun." I scoff. He seems consumed by anger at himself. Disappointment? I grin. "If you call me that while we are arguing I'll chop your balls off." Really, I'll try.

"I won't call you it ever again."

Natasha starts crying. The credits for the Disney movie are running.

I sigh heavily. "Vassili…"

He steps inside of the elongated shower and turns it on. I know without a shadow of a doubt that this discussion is over, no matter how much I want to resolve things.

Vassili

"You're looking for me?" Her voice is unforgettable. It's filled with jealousy, envy, and strife. And fuck it, I prefer it over the sound of me calling my wife a bitch. *What the fuck was I thinking?*

Zariah had asked me to come all over her. That's something I've done to cunts, who've asked.

But my wife?

I shouldn't have wanted to fuck her ass! I shouldn't have called her a—

Yeah, that shit was running through my brain in rapid succession. On repeat, prior to me answering my phone.

I head into the upstairs office, although it's just Natasha and I. She's playing in her playpen for now. "Danushka, fuck yeah, I've been looking for you. Where are you at?"

"What's this? My big brother is requesting a sibling date?"

"Why did you email me?"

There's a momentary silence. "Just to determine your level of connections. In your assumptions, it was either Anatoly or Washington, right?"

The bitch is playing the power card. "What the fuck do you know about Washington?"

FEARLESS II
by *Amarie Avant*

"Lots. He is easier to persuade than you've been going about. But then again, Vassili, you never give a damn about making friends."

I listen for any signs of familiarity. Rushing water. People in the background? Drilling wells! Something! It's silent on her end.

"Vassili. Or Karo. Which do you prefer?"

"I'd prefer you forgot my name entirely." I settle down into my custom leather chair.

"Oh, no. You're father's beloved. Everyone loves you. You're a legacy. There's no forgetting about you."

"*Dah?* And there are few people in this world that I love. Like my wife and daughter. You're aware of them. And whatever is up your sleeve better have nothing to do with them." My Russian accent thickens with each word. "You got that, or I choke the life out of you with my fucking hands." I imagine her pulse slipping.

"You know what, Vassili? Only you could get away with murder. The choice words. Let another one of our brothers or sisters make pointed threats, I believe our dad would give the order. Bang. Bang."

Grunting, I toss back, "*Tvoy otets, a ne moy—* your father, not mine."

"Stop it with the reverse psychology already, Anatoly loves you in spite of…"

"Everything Little Danushka does for praise?" I smile. She may have won the match by tossing out her awareness of Maxwell Washington, but I win the war. Our father's love is all she's ever wanted.

"Correct, Vassili. None of my endeavors matter," her voice almost breaks.

"What do you want?" There isn't a sympathetic bone in me for this bitch. Her mother ratted mine out the last time my mother attempted to flee Russia, and more importantly, my father.

"Just to keep you on your toes, big brother. For now, that is." The call goes dead.

I'm left sitting with my hands tightly bound into fists. Danushka is a hard woman to catch up with. The real kicker is not knowing her game plan. What is her motivation...

Zariah

Having just returned to work after an extended weekend in Vegas, I don't have much on my plate. The case I'm currently handling deals with the Versa family will. Edgar Versa, the owner of a line of upscale home improvement businesses in Southern California died. And with death and rich offspring, thus began a lengthy argument. Sarah Versa is my client, and Edgar's granddaughter was the black sheep of the family. A party hardy, pill popping, alcohol guzzling, toss a grand each night for fun, type of girl. Until her parents cut her off. She sobered up to care for Edgar when he was dying of cancer, now her mother believes she tampered with said will.

Sarah does have much to gain. And with her parents sticking it to her, Billingsley Legal was all she could afford. But the real kicker is, nobody, but her appeared to give a damn about their great-grandfather until he gave up the ghost.

In order to gather evidence of his frame of mind while altering the will during the few months prior to his death, I'm reviewing information regarding the grandfather's last days with his doctors and nurses when Lanetta pops her head inside of the door.

FEARLESS II
by *Amarie Avant*

"Mrs. Resnov, we have a mother who just arrived with her children." She chews her gum impatiently. "She's saying if she goes away, she might not come back... She received your card from that nonprofit, *The People's Love*. Tyrese is trying to handle it but she's asking for you."

Oh, Tyrese is it? Over half a year has passed since I became her boss, and I'm referred to by my last name, but the newbie is Tyrese?

"Okay," my eyebrow furrows. It's a quarter past five and the front door should've already been locked. The top attorneys, myself, Connie and Samuel work on rotation in the evening and our secretaries assist with lock up. Clearly, Lanetta has her shoes geared toward the back exit. It's summer, the nights are long, but why work overtime?

While reviewing the last note from the man's doctor, I mumble, "Just leave the keys, I'll place the alarm on my way out."

"Alright, you may want Ty to stay," she advises as I glance up, "just to make sure nothing happens. Look at me like that if you want, but..." her voice trails off, she shakes her head in disgust. And over her shoulder, mentions, "I'm leaving the keys on my desk. I have to get to the childcare center in a few."

Um hmm, she has until 6:30 and lives a few blocks down the road

"Thanks," I call out while logging off my computer. Rising to my feet, I slide into my cardigan and exchange the house shoes that have kept me comfy all afternoon for my high heels.

A woman with a Hispanic accent continues to ask for me as I walk around the cubicles surrounding the middle of the office. A voice, that I assume belongs to Tyrese, offers to help her.

"No, no, I talk to Zariah, just Zariah, *por favor,*" she says. As I near the bend to the front door, there's stifled crying.

"I don't think that's a good idea, Mrs. Noriega. Please bring your children to my office, and I'd be glad to assist you."

"No," she replies.

My eyebrows crinkle. If the woman insists on receiving help from myself why would Tyrese attempt to intervene? The doorbells chime, and my first line of vision is Tyrese taking a deep breath while placing his hands into his suit pants. His back is to me. The mother and children are gone.

"Mr. Nicks, why wouldn't you escort Mrs. Noriega and her children to my office if she was so insistent? This was a prime opportunity to empathize and help."

He scoffs. I haven't seen the man's dimples since I chewed him up and spit him out. "Mrs. Resnov, it'd be better if she received assistance from—"

I place up a hand, my expression is enough to get him to shut up. I stalk out the door, into the evening summer heat. Headed to the bus stop is a woman, who cannot be more than five feet tall, with two children clinging to either side of her, crying into her chest. There's another young mother with stroller already standing next to the bus stop sign. By process of elimination, I determine the shorter of the two mothers is Mrs. Noriega. My pace falters a few empty parking lot rows away as the sun gleams down onto what I assume is a neck brace.

"Mrs. Noriega," I call out while hustling over to her.

She turns around, eyes swallowed up by shiners, and glossed with tears. The apparition I assumed was a neck brace is actually some sort of anchor, wired to her jaw. The look on her face pains me, and I can almost feel how badly it hurts to talk. Intuition warns that Tyrese's attempt to keep this case was due to whoever caused Felicidad so much pain. My mind instantly goes to my family. Vassili would snatch me out of the workplace and slap an apron on me for the rest of my employable life. He doesn't want me defending cases like this.

"I am Zariah Resnov, nice to meet you." I extend a hand.

"Felicidad Noriega," her thin lips move with restriction.

"And you are," I hold my hand out to the oldest, her son is about ten, his fingernails are dirty, and his clothing is soiled.

"Juan," he gives my hand a hearty shake.

FEARLESS II
by *Amarie Avant*

Felicidad's daughter has her face burrowed into her voluptuous hip. I place the girl to be around five at most.

"My sister is Rosemary, she doesn't speak."

"Are you guys hungry? I'm starving."

"No, no," Felicidad has difficulty shaking her head.

"Yes," Juan replies at the same time.

Rosemary peeks at me. They're all hungry.

"Well, Felicidad, Hot Chilly's across the way might be a great place for us all to talk."

"That's a great idea," Tyrese speaks from behind me. "The chilly cheeseburger has your name on it, Juan."

"Oh yeah!" The boy agrees enthusiastically.

I glance back at him as he catches up to us.

Felicidad bites her lip. "Uh... I don't know, it might be too expensive."

Tyrese is finally at my side, he places a friendly arm around my shoulder. His hand clasps around my elbow to hold me into position. "On me." As he holds out the opposite hand to gesture toward the pedestrian walk, he whispers into my ear. "You might think I'm a jackass but there's no way in hell I'm leaving you with them."

I grind my teeth and glower at him. "Remove your arm, Mr. Nicks."

"Her husband is one of the top dogs of the Loco Dios gang. Nothing you say or do will get rid of me.

Call that my good deed for today, if you'd prefer, but I won't budge on this."

Damn, I've heard of the gang before. In the late 90s, my father was leader of the gang unit. He was in charge of cleaning the streets, and he did. The Loco Dios were rid of each of their highest-ranking members. Nobody is still aware of how, but just like with many gangs, what goes down must come up. By the next year, there were family members from Mexico, more illegal residents, and younger members flooding into the spots where the top dogs were.

We walk across the street, and I'm hesitant for the first time. Each of my domestic violence cases in the past has given women a voice. Helping them seems like I'm paying penance for not serving my own father the bear down he deserves. But the Loco Dios Gang? What about Natasha? She's my priority now.

Rosemary peeks over at me from her mother's arm and my heart swells with a wish to keep her safe. I have to help.

While pressing the pedestrian button, I wonder if the Noriega's are here illegally due to Felicidad's scattered speech. Yet, Juan seems like he has a very strong head on his shoulders, he met my eyes and introduced himself in perfect English.

Well, at least we are in a predominantly black neighborhood. So, I can't see any cholos, Loco Dios or not, attempting to start anything.

FEARLESS II
by *Amarie Avant*

There's a strong oil frying scent coming from Hot Chilly's as we enter. The restaurant has a seating area with old dusty red vinyl booths. But with no servers to bus tables, we all glance up at the backlit menu on the wall to determine what to purchase.

Juan goes for the chilly cheese hamburger Tyrese recommended and it takes prompting for Felicidad to choose two street tacos for herself. I opt for a wedge salad while Tyrese subtly convinces Rosemary to try what he and Juan are going to eat in a kiddie combo version.

It's a quarter to seven when we return to the law firm. True to form, Tyrese has not made any moves to leave me to lock up. I settle Rosemary in the toy area, in my office, across from the table.

"Juan, I don't have too many toys for a boy your age—"

"Toys," he shrieks, not an ounce of testosterone in his tone, "I am too old for toys."

Felicidad glances back and forth from us, something I noticed that she does when not comprehending.

Rosemary is predominantly Spanish speaking like her mother, but with hand movements and other gestures, she'd caught on at the fast food joint. So, I try out my high school Spanish, asking, "Toys… uh… yo quiero—you want. Uh… ¿Quieres jugar con juguetes?" I finally allow each word to slowly slip out asking if she'd like to play with the toys.

Her mother offers the most humble, beautiful smile I've ever seen, as she appreciates my attempts.

Rosemary moves in trepidation. She unwinds her arm from around Felicidad's waist and then takes tiny steps to the toy chest before something of interest must catch her eyes because she zips the few yards and hunkers down to play.

"Juan, I have a Nintendo Switch somewhere around here," I begin, sitting down and opening my left file cabinet. "And a whole lot of new games for you— "

"But I know everything you want to ask," Juan assures. "I have to help my mother say what she needs to say."

His mother eyes him as if attempting to read his lips. She's aware he's talking about her.

"Buddy," Tyrese leans against my file cabinet along the back wall. "Some of the stuff we'd like to ask your mother might not be appropriate for your ears."

I almost smile at his response. What can I say? That was a perfect age-appropriate rebuttal.

"But I know everything. My father beats my mother as you can see," He states matter-of-factly. "I'm too old to allow him to hit my mother anymore."

Tyrese and I exchange glances. For a man I can't pinpoint in time, we have an entire silent film conversation in less than a second. The few interpreters on payroll unattached from the world of work when off the clock. No cell phones. No calls. No nothing. This is time sensitive. We need to be aware of what Mr. Noriega has done. It's imperative to her welfare, and maybe even her children as well.

"What happened?" I hesitantly ask.

"My father hit me, too." He rubs a hand underneath his left eye. Upon peering closely, there's a grayish half-moon that I previously assumed was due to lack of sleep. "My teacher harped about being a mandated reporter. She called CPS. They didn't come. My mom is afraid to go to the cops. Yes, she's illegal, Rosemary is too. But we cannot go to the cops because some of those cops are friends with my father."

"Are you illegal?" I inquire.

"Nah, my father snuck my mother over here a long time ago, they had me. Mom got caught working at a cleaner, she was sent back. But I think my dad is the reason those people—I don't know the names of them—come and get illegals."

In his haste to speak, I decipher that he means ICE or another immigration official came to get his mother at his father's request.

"Why would your father rat out your mother?" I inquire, hoping my friendly jargon keeps him speaking. Much of what Juan has divulged can be verified.

"He had just beat up my mom, I was five. He had another woman on the side. Mom tried to fight him, that was the first time and last time she did that." He huffs.

"So, you've stayed with your father while your mother lived in Mexico?"

"No, I stayed with my *abuelita*. My father's mother. Then my father went to see my mother. She got pregnant with Rosemary."

I want to ask a question but can't get a word in edgewise as Juan continues to tell the story of how his father snuck his mother back to California after promising life would be better, and *he* would be better.

"Where's your grandmother?"

"Dead."

Shit, I keep a straight face. "I'm sorry to hear that. Does your mother have any other family in the states?"

"No. Her family isn't in Mexico either, they're dead, too. Or maybe they don't want to see my mom because of my dad. Sometimes I wonder." He licks his lips. "I've never been to Mexico and I ain't trying to go either. Can you help my mom and sister stay? Can you keep them safe from my dad?"

His dark brown orbs plead with me to work wonders. Which is harder? Our current president doesn't give a shit about Mrs. Noriega or keeping her near her son. Her husband, clearly, doesn't give a shit about her in general. And he has an entire dang family to assist with apprehending his wife and punishing her as he sees fit.

FEARLESS II
by *Amarie Avant*

"We'll speak with an immigration attorney about your mother and sister."

"Thanks. That would be great," he says.

I text Vassili that I'll be home late tonight, and mumble to Tyrese, "Can you call the Four Seasons and see if there's a vacancy?"

His eyes sparkle with hope. Did this fool think that myself and him would be frequenting the establishment?

I redirect his ass with, "We might not be in Noriega's neck of the woods, but let's have his family stay somewhere he's even less likely to frequent." *With the other half... rich white folks.*

"But we have vouchers for the general area."

"Unless you're on your way out for the evening, I would be so grateful."

"*We* will lock up together," he mumbles under his breath, hopping off the file cabinets and exiting the room.

***

It's past nine when low and behold, I end up at The Four Seasons *with* Tyrese Nicks. Felicidad is wiping away tears as she takes in the double bed with clean sheets.

"Can you tell your mother that you all should head to the welfare office tomorrow?"

"She won't go," Juan replies, truly parentified—a term I learned in child development, which indicated that the youth held on a parental role. He makes a good attorney in her defense.

"Please and thank you." I smile.

He starts off in Spanish. She makes scissor movements with her hands, saying "No, mijo, no."

"I told ya." Juan huffs.

"You have the right to have food stamps, Juan. Your mother and sister are undocumented and therefore won't be calculated into the amount. But you have the right."

He continues to shake his head. "No. I don't care. We will go hungry."

Tyrese tries. "It's against the law for the eligibility technician to— "

"But these are my mother's words. She's paranoid. Thinks my dad knows everybody in Cali."

"Alright," I say, dishing out a few dollars. I don't keep change around. Tyrese pulls out a money clip and gives them three crisp twenties.

Dang, I can agree with her paranoia. The Loco Dios has gained notoriety in recent years. They're even more infamous than in the past because of the new ties they made while resurrecting themselves. They're a ruthless, rowdy bunch backed by cartel connections. I need some intel as to how deep Noriega is with this gang.

I know exactly the person to apprehend that information from... my father.

FEARLESS II
by Amarie Avant

Vassili's

My entire day went to shit. You'd think all the trouble Malich endured to get a message for Danushka might make the situation more settling. But the logic behind what my half-sister is gunning for, while in my court, is still over my head.

Natasha is asleep, and I'm seated on the chair in the master suite, watching a recap of the fight from Vegas. Though there were no title matches last night, each one is enough to keep my eyes focused on the pound for pound bricks being tossed from each competitor. Shit, my very own fight held enough damage to fill an entire fight card. Karsoff and I went for blows, but as suspected, I came out the victor. My hands are clenched into fists at my side. There was a moment in the second round in which my knee started to knot up on me. Karsoff didn't use that to his advantage, but then again, the fire in my eyes made it seem like a grenade could've been tossed at me, and I wouldn't have given a fuck. Wouldn't have felt a thing.

My cell phone vibrates on my left leg.

ZARIAH: I'll be home in 15. No thx for dinner.

Is she texting while driving? I call her instead of replying.

FEARLESS II
by *Amarie Avant*

My wife's voice is cheerful as she speaks, "Hey, baby—"

"Girl, are you driving and playing with your phone?"

"*Boy*, you love to check in on me every few minutes when I'm out late." Her voice is filled with laughter, then she switches up her tone to attempt to sound like me. "Vassili, you texted, 'girl what's keeping you,' I respond about a client. You offer to *have borscht on the table when I get home.* Vassili, you have better luck adding a line of sugar to your cock and having me lick it up for a late dinner. So yes, the last few messages I replied to, may have been while I was driving."

"Are you hungry?" I ask her, eyeing a roundhouse kick, on the screen, from the main event that sent the loser into a frozen state before he fell back.

She cackles. "I love you, Vassili. You keep me safe, I'd never go cold or hungry, so I think I'll keep you around. And no, I'm not hungry for the last time."

"Shit, salad is not a dinner."

"Humph, coming from the man who tortured me with raw juice and roughhoused me enough to be afraid of entering a Jamba Juice within a hundred-mile radius."

"That fucking stuff isn't healthy, smoothie my ass." I quip, hearing the sound of the garage in the background.

FEARLESS II
by *Amarie Avant*

"Whatever, Vassili," she says. The faint sound of music is cut off. "I swear, I may have enjoyed the green machine with Kale more than you know what."

"That so?" I chuckle, rise from my chair, go down the hall, and shuffle downstairs. "There's probably one bite of kale in the juice. That shit is full of lime sherbet."

"For taste," Zariah says, her voice echoing as she rounds the corner near the laundry room. "I had a long day at work, why are we arguing?" She asks into the receiver, twenty yards away, glancing me up and down like she's really ready to lick a line of sugar off my cock.

"Nyet, I'm not arguing with you, beautiful." I hang up the phone and get an eyeful of my wife. How does this happen? Every instant I lay eyes on her, she's more beautiful than before. My hands brush over her shoulders as I remove the floppy sweater thing she calls a cardigan, and let it fall to the floor. Yeah, that's what I think about those stupid little sweater thingies. They cover the roundness of her ass, the fatness of her hips and pussy. Sometimes she's holding the knitting over her chest and I'm not even a breast man, but I still want to snatch it off of her.

My mouth goes to her forehead, and I brush a soft kiss there. I needed her softness to settle the anxious rage within me. Her essence filters through my nostrils, and I bestow soft kisses to her neck, my nose nudging into her skin, getting an addictive whiff of

by *Amarie Avant*

her. I fall to my knees. My hands clasp her ass, and I prod my nose at the apex of her thighs, breathing in deeply. And she smells so sweet like...

"Brown sugar," I groan.

"What?" Zariah licks her lips, her chocolate gaze glancing down at me.

"You had this on during our first encounters. You were at Vadim's Gym, and then again when I came to see you at home."

"More like breaking and entering. Yes, Vassili. It's my favorite from Bath and Body Works."

"Shit, girl, then why haven't you worn this in a while?"

Zariah shrugs. "I usually wear perfume these days. Just being a little more sophisticated, I guess."

Instantly I'm standing, and I've swept her off her feet. My wife lets out a fearful yelp before laughing and kicking her legs. "Can I get a little pre-warning, Vassili, dang!"

"Okay, I'm going to feed you," I kiss her mouth, "then I'll eat you." My tongue weaves around hers in a breathtaking kiss. "Then you tell me what caused you to return home so late. Da?"

"*Nyet.*" Zariah sounds too cute telling me no in Russian. She presses a hand against my chest, though her face is beaming from ear to ear. "How about we skip part one. Oh, and part two is confidential as well, Vassili. Let's just finish the evening with you tasting these sweets."

FEARLESS II
by *Amarie Avant*

I carry her upstairs. "Confidential my ass," is all I say. There'll be no arguing about it. I'll compromise about her dinner since she says she's not hungry. But family law or not, I prefer my wife in the kitchen and pregnant. It's the safest place for her. So, I'll eat her tonight, and ask about the new case assignment come morning. If it was an emergency to her, then it's a concern to me.

***

Only one of her gorgeous brown eyes is visible. Zariah has masked much of her face with the pillow. Her tone is delectably sultry, and groggy, "Why aren't you working out?"

"I meet with Vadim at 11 am. You know the drill," I tell her.

"Humph, I'm referencing your work out before your quote-unquote workout?" She finally pushes the pillow away enough to give me that look of hers which tells me she's about to toss a bomb my way. "Vassili, I am aware of your entire day. You're in our home gym at 5 am. Then you cart Natasha around Venice Beach to eye some hot ass, and I do mean hot as in stinky, funky asses swallowing up thong-kini's, before going to the gym. What a convenient location for all you guys. And if another fighter is behind schedule, you become a big bully."

"Stinky thong-kini's you say?" I arch an eyebrow.

"Um hmm!"

by Amarie Avant

I lay back against the pillow and roar with laughter.

My wife straddles me and issues an assault of hooks and jabs against my ribs. "Oh, so you do check out scantily clad chicks? I hate you, Vassili."

"Fuck," I growl, my chuckles fading out enough to allow me to grab the bulldozers she has for fists. She isn't that strong, but my broken rib has a few more weeks to heal. "My rib, girl, my rib."

"I don't give a damn about your rib." She pouts. "You were supposed to deny looking at those hoes. Deny it vehemently!"

I reach up and kiss her poked out bottom lip. Then my tongue soars into her mouth, my hand claims the back of her neck and I send this kiss to soaring heights. Zariah's breasts rise and fall rapidly against her tight negligee as she catches her breath. My eyes connect with hers, and I decree, "There's only one woman for me. I put that on my life."

"Okay..." she pretends to cave, as I wrap my arms around her in a bear hug.

"And I resent your statement, beautiful. There's only one girl I know in the entire world, whose thong can be perfectly eaten by her ass." My hand slams down on Zariah's butt.

"Oh, so you're calling me a –"

"I'm calling you my little *kholodets*," I bounce my hands over her ass cheeks.

FEARLESS II
by Amarie Avant

"Wait a minute, boy did you just say Kholodets?" Her eyes peel in thought. "That revolting Russian meat jelly?"

"I love it. That was Natasha's favorite when she first got a few teeth."

The smack against my face sends me into another hard laugh and I lay back again. Zariah pretends to lean down and choke me out for a second. "Meat Jelly? Can't you think of anything sexier? I know my ass is fat, you can see these cakes from the front," she says, her legs squeezing around my waist. Zariah glances back at her fatty and then her ponytail whips over her shoulder as she looks down at me again.

I rest my hands behind my head and lift my hips. My cock pierces the inside of her thigh, a reminder that too much playing in the bedroom leads to other things. I love these happy moments of joking with my wife, but really, with her straddling me, those breasts of hers are about to spill out.

Her eyes darken with desire. Zariah rocks her hips, letting her pussy slither over my cock. There's only one problem with our current dynamic. I slept in boxers and basketball shorts. She has on panties. I don't like friction.

"Stop playing, girl. I want to fuck."

"Humph, you better be glad I let you have something good to eat last night." She dips her tongue out and licks her lips.

FEARLESS II
by *Amarie Avant*

"*Dah*, I ate this succulent pussy all night, eh? Now that sweet tasty cunt of yours can eat my cock, okay." I press my hips up again, searing the inside of her thigh with my stiff erection.

She reaches toward me, her hands go to the headboard, and her mouth goes to mine. Zariah licks my jaw as she works her lower body like a snake. My dick is swollen with hunger. I clasp her hair. "Take your panties off, girl."

"Mmmm, you want them off?" She leans back up, grips the sides of her thong and pulls upward. Those fat folds of her labia are on display now as the material puckers between her lips.

Shit, precum is seeping from my cockhead.

"Take them off," I grit out. My hands are still comfortably behind my head. The only warning that she is in potential danger of me slamming her down and fucking her silly is the hardness in my eyes.

She again works the thong with her thumbs hooked at the side. "I think I might cum like this, Vassili." Her voice is trembling with desire. Zariah continues to work the material against her pussy. "It's rubbing my clit so rough, so rough…"

I go for the takedown.

Zariah

Did I even get a chance to blink? Nope, not at all. The air felt cool against my skin, for it to be a warm summer morning, the air literally chilled against me as swiftly as Vassili had me on my back. He doesn't even snatch off my thong, nor does he take off his clothes. His boxers and basketball shorts are pulled just over his ass, as he slams inside of my pussy. His hand claims the headboard like mine had just done a second ago.

"Ooooh, shit," I scream, as his cock batters my insides, assaulting my g-spot. He reaches between our bodies, his thumb finding that tiny bulb of mine that always makes more of my cum rushing against his cock. He works my clit with his thumb while pumping in and out of me. My left leg goes over Vassili's hip, and he bangs my back.

Missionary never looked so good.

Our hearts drum to the same beat as his cock glides in and out of my wetness.

"Vassili," I ground down on his dick. "I'm gonna—"

"Fuck," he growls like the incredible hulk. "Shit, I'm coming, Zariahhhhh."

by *Amarie Avant*

My eyes close and my head kisses the pillow. The raw tension dwindles down and a euphoric calm claims my body as I welcome Vassili's steel body on top of mine. I can't breathe, but I'm content. I press my arms around him, holding him against me. Delighting in his heaviness, strength, and power. He starts to roll over.

"Not yet," I moan. "Stay."

"You can't breathe."

Damn, it's a feat to give him a 'give a fuck' look that he likes to dish out on occasion. "Don't need to," I finally murmur.

Everything about him is heavy. His paws feel heavy as he rubs my face and kisses my forehead tenderly. *"Ya nikogda ne otpushchu tebya*—I will never let you go," he murmurs in Russian. Wetness instantly burns my eyes. I love the instances when he declares these kinds of words. Vassili rarely says them, but when he does our eyes connect, and it's more powerful than wishing on a star as an innocent child.

My husband is confident. Let him tell it, and he's invincible. He's fearless. I'm becoming fearless and shedding all worry and doubt. And in this moment, we are so very connected with each other.

My alarm goes off.

"Aw, no," I pout. It's not that I don't really want to go to work. God has blessed me with a career I enjoy, so Billingsley Legal isn't 'work' for me. But I love these moments. These moments that are solely for us.

"Turn it off," Vassili says, getting off of me.

I reach over, grab my phone and turn off the reminder. His thick bicep engulfs my tiny waist—well, it was tinier when we met—and pulls me closer. "We can stay in bed today."

"What about Natasha?" I ask.

"We can stay in bed until she bullies us to get out."

"Oh, she's a bully now? Like someone I know."

"When hungry, dah. When her pull-up is too wet, hell yeah. She," he nods, "is a bully. So, call in, and we will stay in bed until we're both punked."

I nuzzle my head beneath his chin. Something deep within my being just loves being so close to this man. I can be literally standing on top of him, breathing his air, and never be close enough. He's my slice of perfection, flaws and all. *Thank you, Jesus, for my husband.*

While I'm thankful for my blessings, I'm totally aware of someone who needs God's love.

Mrs. Noriega and her children cling to my cognition. My eyes close and I breathe in the sweaty sex of us. Then, even though it hurts my heart, I rise into a seated position. "I have to go to work, Vassili."

"Why?" He barks.

My bottom lip drops, my eyes narrow. "You know what, Vassili, you're a fucking asshole."

"Choice words, girl," he growls, sitting up, too.

"Don't throw the finger, Vassili, you just dismissed the hell out of my career. Tell me that my job isn't as important as playing the Neanderthal for … a lot more money, while all your doing is ancient human grunting and tossing fists in the air."

He rubs the back of his neck. "Okay, Zar, maybe I am being a bit of an asshole, I was born this way. But sometimes you work from home. We're having the best fucking day, girl. Can't we just have this day?"

I glance into his dark gaze. It's genuine. Something tells me that in retrospect, somewhere down the road, I'm going to wish I had set aside everything... life, for more moments with my husband. We live in a busy world, and the guilt I have for staying with my father, at my mother's insistence during the last year of high school still pervades my mind at times. Top that with me wishing I had the guts to try and go upside my father's head, starting back when I was four—the first instance I saw him hit her. Intuition told me it wasn't right, even at such a tender age.

I'm saving Felicidad Noriega from Juan Noriega Senior. I am.

"I can't, baby." I offer a weak smile. "I have a meeting this morning, it's unprofessional to call off, okay?"

Should I hand the case over to Tyrese Nicks? It's true. He came through on my way home, calling during Vassili's many texts, about having an immigration attorney push around her schedule to be able to meet this morning. Nevertheless, even though Mr. Nicks is more than capable of handling the situation, Felicidad requested me. And dammit, I keep seeing my mother through her eyes.

"Okay." His broad shoulders rise and fall in a shrug. "Tell me about this new case while you get dressed, though."

For a moment, I'm silently weighing the pros and cons. Can I handle this case? Will fighting Juan Noriega place my life, my child's life, in danger? Receiving help from a Resnov would be more beneficial than speaking to my father. Hell, I'm not even entirely sure my dad is interested in being bothered with me. But, Vassili will not have it. The instant I mention Juan Noriega, I *will* lose more than this case. My husband will bully me into the stay at home career he's always desired for me. *Safety first...*

With a heavy heart, I do what a lawyer does best... I lie.

The case regarding Sarah Versa, who cleaned herself up from alcohol, when her grandfather, Edgar Versa, was stricken with cancer and became his caretaker, becomes this fresh, new assignment. "Felicidad use to be the black sheep of the family. Her mother and father spent so much money on rehabilitation centers in the past in order to help clean her up. Felicidad told me that she met Lindsay Lohan, and listed off celebrities who she partied with, rehab was like a slumber party for grownups."

"Oh, daddy's little rich girl?" he asks, as I head to the dresser to pull out clothes.

"Yeah. Her parents had finally removed her from their own will, which, in a sense is connected with the paternal grandfathers, who owns Versa Home Improvements, it's like Home Depot but with top of the line stuff."

"Dah, I know them. I thought about having you a home built, in Calabasas, but your mother chose this one. And there was no fucking way I'd have it completed by our first Christmas together."

I snatch out a pair of undergarments and glance back at my husband. He sure knows how to make a person feel guilty for lying to him. With a smile on my face, I subtly gulp down the lump of remorse in my throat and head for the walk-in closet. "Felicidad hardly got by the past few years, because she receives a small trust fund from her grandmother, who died years ago. She had a career of attending college, it was a requirement for her to live a meager life," I say, snatching out a pair of burgundy pants. "And I mean meager as in she owns a home in the hood, and spent the rest of it on alcohol."

"Resnov Water?" He says from the bed.

In my shame, it hurts to chuckle at his joke. "Boy, I don't know. But she told me she got so bad with her drinking habit that she also had to panhandle. So, when grandpa got sick, Felicidad set aside the bottle and moved into his house in The Hills." I wipe a stray tear from my face and take my time with choosing a pair of shoes. Meaning, I'm numb to the lies I've told, and stare at the sea of designer stilettos for a few minutes, taking deep breaths.

"The good life returns for Ms. Felicidad," he says as I enter the bedroom. "Until her grandpa died?"

"The good life?" My eyebrow arches. "Felicidad isn't… living the good life now."

"I bet she's not. You watch too many lifetime movies. I'm guessing her family doesn't believe she cleaned up to help grandpa, out of the goodness of her heart."

"That's right. They'd gotten him to reconstruct his will in the past when she was estranged from everyone. The man had her last on his will, underneath various charitable organizations. But a few days before he died, Edgar Versa reinstated the previous clause in his will regarding Felicidad. She gets more than her parents."

"You have to prove he wasn't coerced?"

"Yup."

"Sounds like a hard case," Vassili says, grabbing my pillow and placing it against him.

"Yeah, this sort of litigation can be difficult. But I know what you mean by *hard* case, Vassili. You like me to debrief you regarding my cases because you worry that any of them has the potential to put me in harm's way. And no, I went to school entirely too long to become a housewife."

He holds out his hands as a sign of peace, and my heart begins to cry. Vassili is playing 'nice' while mentally considering how 'difficult' the Versa family can be. Little does he know how bad I feel for manipulating him.

     ***

Tyrese's dimples are deep and enchanting as he peeks into my room. And then he steps inside, holding a Harry Potter book. My eyebrow rises. "Good morning. So it's not coffee but sorcery that gets your day started?"

"Actually, I asked Lanetta if she had a few books to spare on her way into work. She picked up a few Spanish to English illustrated kid book for Rosemary from the library down the block, and a stack of her son's very own Harry Potter collection."

I blink twice. Well, damn, I learned not to ask her to file anything for me before ten am. And I sure as heck get my own coffee on the way to work, so the hoops she's jumping over, darting around, and army crawling through for Tyrese amazes me. "Oh, okay. Thanks, you can drop them off." My gaze returns to my laptop screen.

"The meeting with Mrs. Lopez is in an hour."

I smile my acknowledgment.

"My car or yours, Zariah," his tone is crisp. "I'm not allowing you to handle this one solo."

FEARLESS II
by *Amarie Avant*

Well, in my surprise of how thoughtful Tyrese was being this morning regarding books for Mrs. Noriega's children, I hadn't yet brought to his attention my concerns about the case, and I would've readily agreed that handling it alone against the best interest of ...well, my livelihood as a lawyer, at the very least. Vassili would blow up if he even knew I consulted regarding Juan Noriega. But Tyrese beat me to the punch, inserting himself as co-attorney on this assignment.

With a smirk, I close the laptop and determine to finish the memo I was currently working on later. "How about you drive? I'm sure that makes men feel like they're in charge, right?"

He offers up the sexiest chuckle he can muster. Pitiful fucker, there are plenty of other pairs of panties that need help getting wet. Mine belong only to my husband. "Alright, Zariah, I'll drive, and we can readdress the misconception that you have of me."

Well, damn! He's taking the wheels this morning. "I don't think so." I grab my purse from the bottom file cabinet next to my desk and arise from my chair.

"I rubbed you the wrong way. You've always been easily set off."

"On the way to the immigration attorney, we need to keep our minds sharp." My gaze darkens, and he seems smugly satisfied that he's gotten a rouse out of me. "You don't know me, Mr. Nicks. It would behoove you to refrain from such talk about how I've 'always been' this or that. Consider what you see as the new normal."

"Okay, too soon. I get it." He steps aside, and waves a hand, allowing me to exit the room first.

***

Later on, Tyrese and I are speaking with Mrs. Lopez as her assistant takes photos of Felicidad Noriega. Though the immigration firm is tinier than our own, there's an interpreter that assisted myself and Tyrese with understanding the discussion between Mrs. Lopez and Felicidad. Mrs. Lopez speaks English but wanted to streamline the entire interview by adding the interpreter to facilitate the meeting so that she could continue to speak with Mrs. Lopez, who reiterated her son's previous statement. Her relationship with Mr. Noriega is quite the love story. Apparently, he *was* a good guy in the past. Offering the standard 'honeymoon' phase in your typical domestic violence scenario. But even better, because as a lucrative criminal, Juan Noriega gave her shiny diamond rings with said *shiners*.

However, now, Juan Senior's not only a member of Loco Dios but his reasoning for being in the gang was to help him in the drug trade. He isn't the frontrunner for the cartel that the gang assists in Southern California, but he was running a drug mule operation and has quiet the intelligence. Noriega and a few others from Mexico helped connect the Cartel with the Loco Dios gang when the gang was at its weakest. Their alliance has started an army.

We are fucked.

"I don't want to know where you're keeping Mrs. Noriega," Mrs. Lopez says, "but I pray to St. Michael for protection that it is somewhere her husband will never get to her."

"Should we send her out of state?" Tyrese asks.

I had thought the same thing while the two women chatted. "Witness protection would be nice."

"You can do that," he tells me.

Mrs. Lopez has all her attention on me. "Do you have a connection that will ensure the Noriega's family's safety in another state? I fear shipping her back to Mexico will only increase the chance of corruption. Because it's either we hide her from Loco Dios in Los Angeles or hid her from the Cartel back home? These are trying times, Mrs. Resnov."

Shit, we have better luck sending her to Russia than me asking my father. I know, I know, I said I'd speak to my dad about Noriega. But Felicidad just dropped a nuclear bomb on us regarding the depth of his involvement with both entities.

"I can try."

"Without jeopardizing Mrs. Noriega's safety? She believes some of the LAPD are connected to the Loco Dios gang. These days, I'm inclined to agree."

"I can inquire without telling of her identity," I huff.

FEARLESS II
by Amarie Avant

I step out of the room. Across the way, in another immigration attorney office, little Juan is reading the words to Rosemary. Due to my awareness of some of the keywords she's speaking in Spanish, I believe, he's being quite the good brother and allowing her to stumble through a sentence in Spanish before he reads it in English. I smile. The girl is smart to be able to read already.

I slip out my cell phone and call my father. "Hello, princess," he grits out.

"Hi, Dad. Do you have time for lunch today?"

"No, it's Berenice's birthday. What can I help you with?"

Oh, so he still doesn't have time for his one and only daughter? Leaning against the wall I spit venom for his venom, "You can help me by setting aside your bitch, I am your daughter. I don't care if this is the day that she dedicates herself to our Lord and Savior. I need an hour of your time."

He breaths into the phone. "Very uncouth you've become, my daughter. But like I said, it's Bernice's birthday. We're in Temecula. Take this into account, Zariah Washington, it is you who has pushed me away. And I would love to be there for you, but unfortunately, I cannot in person. Is there something you'd like help with over the phone?"

"No. When will you return?"

FEARLESS II
by *Amarie Avant*

"Two days. Where's Sammy? He's the one you run to these days when you need fatherly advice, right?"

I bite my lip. Samuel is at a conference in Washington. And I don't need him aware of the case I just picked up. He'd tell Vassili...

Vassili

Today, Nestor and I are working on my takedowns. He has me pinned against the cage and the ground. This is where some fighters fuck up and get the shit slammed out of them. That's the difference between them and me. As he isolates my abdomen, I'm calculating my exit strategy in a split second. My arms are pressed against my sides, so I use my left leg, jamming it up and through his legs. Mind you, this motherfucker is padded and protected. So, the hits I'm dishing, which would otherwise hurt extremely bad, are being warded off from the Ukrainian.

"C'mon, Karo, get the fuck up," Nestor taunts.

I keep going at my abdomen. I suck in a breath.

"I see your fucking opening, get your way out!" He says, not dumb enough to go in for a submission.

I wedge my left arm out and jab at him.

"What the fuck, you ain't killing 'em today, Karo," he grunts out.

"Dah?" I finally have my leg anchored around his. Even with his upper body padding, my positioning hocks his entire body around, and I press him into a leg slicer submission hold. "So, I ain't Karo today, eh? Just regular ol' motherfucking Vassili?"

Fearless II
by *Amarie Avant*

Nestor isn't talking anymore. His breaths are slamming through his teeth as he mentally tapers off the pain.

Vadim steps over shaking his head. "Did I tell the two of you to work on submissions? *Nyet!*"

"*Dah!*" I correct my coach while tightening my thighs, in the leg slicer position. "You want me to perfect myself when my opponent has the takedown."

Nestor grits his teeth.

"Tap the fuck out, brah!" I tell him.

His hand slaps down on the canvas.

"Vassili, come see me before you leave." Vadim cocks his head to his office. He doesn't offer a chance for me to respond because he's already heading to the dog-face looking motherfucker, Rhy. The two of us mix like oil and water. I think Nestor put him in rotation with Vadim after me in order to screw us both because either I'm late or Rhy's early, and my sparring mate loves to fuck with me.

As Rhy glares at me like we're two gangbangers on the opposite side of the street, Vadim gestures toward the conditioning ropes. I grin and nod. Those ropes that Zariah can hardly lift up is something that we usually do in our spare time before Vadim works with us. Apparently, Vadim is cutting into his time for not being prepared.

"You did this?" I ask Nestor as we both take our stand.

He shakes out his leg and offers a lazy smile. "Yup. Keep you on your toes, Vassili."

I chuckle, open the door to the cage, and saunter down the steps.

"What does Vadim want with me?" I glare at my cousin, who is shaking a few more Cheetos, from the chip bag onto the table top in front of Natasha's stroller.

"The fuck would I know, kazen?" He shrugs.

"You know." I glare him down hard. My cousin's gaze never wavers, but instinct warns that Yuri is more aware than he's letting on. "Okay, come," I tell him while getting behind Natasha's stroller to steer.

"Follow you to Vadim's office?" Yuri moves like an old ass man, as if he's unsure about what I asked.

"*Dah*, you make a lot of money off me. It's all fun, fighting. Now, join in on the other shit," I toss over my shoulder, moving along, aware that Vadim has intentions to give me grief. Natasha's mini Jordan goes flying. I continue to cart her along, she looks back at me in confusion. My little girl is fucking with me, too. She loves to keep me running after her shoes.

"Oh, this is fun to you?" I tell her, although Yuri catches up to get the flyaway tennis shoe. "Maybe you should wear the old lady walking shoes your mom likes."

Her face falls into a frown since she doesn't notice my cousin toss the damn shoe into the undercarriage of her stroller.

FEARLESS II
by *Amarie Avant*

We head into the elevator and up to the second floor to Vadim's office. The place I cornered Zariah during our first encounter. MMA memorabilia still clutter each wall. And even more statues, that reach almost as tall as my own height, are placed around, making it an effort to squeeze Natasha's stroller inside. Retired belts are even on the wall. I glance at a place where my belt will be in the future, once I'm ready to call it a day.

Yuri stuffs in his stomach and moves around me to another seat. I choose to stand.

My coach is seated in his chair, scrawny white legs crossed at the ankles and propped up on the edge of his table. "Oh great, Yuri, you and Natasha can get the truth out of 'em."

Yuri grunts. There's more of a flicker of something in his eyes. One that reads he was previously aware of what Vadim has cornered me for and didn't want to be a part of telling me so.

"How's your fucking knee, Vassili?" Vadim asks. "And look at cutie pie before you answer anything other than the truth."

My eyebrow cocks. I glance over at Natasha, who rarely has an attitude with me, but the foul with her Jordan must've dug under her skin. Her pretty brown eyes seem to narrow in understanding. *Don't lie to me,* my child is saying.

Fuck.

FEARLESS II
by *Amarie Avant*

I rub a hand over my face. "*Khorosho. Khorosho*—Good. Good... *Nyet.*" I take it back. Using my hand as a lever, I gesture and add, "Okay."

"Okay?" Vadim's wrinkly face is spread into a frown.

"Okay as in you'll fight Rhy in October or okay as in surgery should be in the cards, first?" Yuri inquires.

My head tilts as I toss a glare in his direction. Rhy? The dog-faced fucker whose body conditioning at this very second? "What do you mean, I'll fight Rhy? He's nobody. And fuck no, no surgery necessary here, *brat.*"

"Rhy's making a name for himself in this world," Vadim sits up. "He fought Laquerre."

"Fuck Laquerrre, Kong is my next sub!"

"Like I just said, Rhy fought Laquerre, don't be so fucking cocky, Vassili. Laquerre and Kong are almost where *you* once were. And by process of elimination, Rhy might just very well put his paws on your belt before you do." He takes a deep breath. "You are both on my team. I talked with him about it first. You're money, Vassili. Fighting you puts money into his pockets while he guns for the belt."

I slam a closed paw against my chest. "And what the fuck does it do for me? I don't give a damn how many cocks he's sucked in the cage! My target is Gotti." *And you were my coach before you were his, so fuck that cunt!* Okay, *dah*, it's a little too much like a

269

bitch for me to actually say that out loud. My coach and mentor continues to keep his cool. Due to my outburst, he's content with making me wait a few moments before responding.

"Gotti will be out before you know it, Vassili." Vadim clucks. "Speaking of sucking cocks to get by, Rhy doesn't have as many decisions as you think. He's got Subs and TKO's. And if you close your cunt long enough to think, you'd realize this sport is like a game of chess. Any sudden movement can take the queen. In your instance, you did it to yourself. Your knee screwed you. So, can you fight Rhy or should I hold your fucking hand, call your doctor, schedule an appointment regarding your motherfucking knee, and shit, I'll even pay for the Uber on surgery day."

"You done?" I gesture.

He grunts.

"Kazen, are you okay?" Yuri stands up. His concern for me makes me glare hard back at him. "Vassili, you are as much my *brat*—brother as Igor. Sometimes you say I make money off ya—"

I hold up a hand to cut off his need for an emotional moment. "I'm just fucking with you, Yuri."

"But are you good, as in you can fight Rhy? Or are you good, as in you're capable of fighting Kong in Australia in six weeks?"

I glare at him. "I'm good enough."

"Gotti isn't shit. He fought a nobody after grabbing your belt. His fans are gonna call foul soon if he keeps it in the clutch. But tell me, should we set everything aside right now and have you visit the doctors? That's not the manager in me talking but blood."

Zariah

Two weeks later…

August sweeps in, bringing with it drier heat and mounds of luggage as I help my mother settle her items in the bedroom she's claimed since we bought our home.

"It's my birthday weekend, baby girl," she tells me, pulling out dresses and skirts from her rollaway.

"Move over Tina Knowles, Zamora Haskins is in town!" I rub a hand over a sequence dress with the tags still on it.

"Patience is a virtue, my dear daughter. Thanks to your father, it only took me two and a half alimony checks to purchase that dress." She chuckles.

"Mama, where and the heck did you get this dress?"

"Just kidding, it was on the clearance rack. Saks Fifth Avenue. So yes, it was a scary price, but I clicked my heels together and scoured the store top to bottom for my birthday."

I smile. The chat Martin and I had with her seems to have penetrated because I took a deep breath and gave her the once over when picking her up from LAX. Martin and his wife are also more available than they were in the past. And we almost have her agreement to attend counseling. Almost.

We head down stairs and outside to the outdoor kitchen where Vassili is grilling salmon and asparagus.

"Let's go see Maxwell tonight," my mother is all smiles as she holds Natasha on her hip.

With my mind still on Mrs. Noriega and being half a month into a rather extensive immigration process, I am confused as to why she'd like to see my father. "Mom, what exactly are you asking me?"

"Not your daddy, girl, the singer Maxwell. I got us tickets."

"Mom, I have to work in the morning." In actuality, I finally secured a spot on my father Maxwell's busy schedule. The issue of Mr. Noriega still needs to be addressed.

"But you want me to be happy, don't you?"

I groan.

"Ascension will make me happy. Bad Habits, Stop the *doggone* World, This Woman's Work, hell, everything Maxwell will make me happy. And when you get home, Vassili will be willing and waiting for you to make him happy."

"*Dah*, Zamora, good looking out." Vassili grunts turning the asparagus on a Himalayan salt block.

"Yuck, mom." I shake my head. My mom and I will never have what Taryn and Mrs. Takahashi have. So, I excuse myself. "Um, let me go see if those potatoes are soft enough to mash."

"Girl, we're all well aware of Maxwell's magic." She fans the tickets in her hands.

***

Later in the evening, while Vassili is studying his MMA textbooks and my mother spoils Natasha rotten with baby massage oil she purchased for the trip, I head upstairs and slip out my phone to call my new partner in crime.

"I expected more checking in," Tyrese flirts. There's mariachi music in the background, and I close my eyes considering how much I owe this man.

We've decided to move Felicidad and her children to a home Samuel suggested. He believes the case belongs to Tyrese for now, and I have yet to have a real conversation with my father about Mr. Noriega, but the paranoia of some imaginary entity tracking our calls causes me to forgo saying San Francisco when asking, "Humph, I believe in you. Are you almost there?"

"About an hour away. Did you finally buy your mother something for her birthday?"

I pause for a moment. The two of us have worked in tandem for almost a month in order to help secure a safe place for the Noriega family. He had insisted on facilitating their move, U-Haul and all. Although, I agreed that it would keep my family safe—namely my daughter and my husband's frame of mind—it took serious convincing with Felicidad to allow Tyrese to make the move instead of myself. She still has a distrust of men, but seems to be warming up to him. When Tyrese took the reins on their move to San Francisco, my mentor mentioned that I needed to get ready for my mother's birthday. Good ol' Sammy even made impeccably good gift suggestions for my mother. I have yet to ask him why he's still so afraid to try her Georgia Peach—just kidding, that's some crap my mother would say.

"Yes, I bought her a gift," I answer Tyrese.

"What did you get?"

"Let's keep this strictly business, counsellor."

"C'mon, this drive was… almost double the time it should've been, traffic."

"Hmmm," I note that Tyrese isn't using time frames either. Damn, I must seek out my father soon, regardless of what's new on his plate. "Okay, I purchased the most expensive pair of ostrich cowboy boots I could find. Although, I'm not sure what possessed my mother to ask for them."

"You got the photo album as well, didn't you?" He seems to smile through the receiver.

I feel uncomfortable chuckling. "Yeah, the silver one, engraved and all. I highly suspect that Sammy knows my mother more than she knows herself."

"What's the deal with those two?"

"Good evening, Mr. Nicks." I hang up the phone. There will be no crossing the line because I understand there is such a thing as an emotional affair, and that is not allowed either.

FEARLESS II
by *Amarie Avant*

Dear Lord, keep Felicidad and her family safe during this rough time....

***

"Wait a minute, wait a doggone minute, mama." I glance my mother up and down as she saunters down the steps. I'm wearing a gold-toned, sequined body-skimming dress that loves each and every one of my curves, but my mother takes the cake! "Place your hands at your sides."

Her head is held high. The shimmery eyeshadow brings out the hazel flecks in her orbs, so I can't address her age in this regard. But, I'll be damned if my mother is stepping out of my house in a skirt shorter than mine.

"What, why?" She does a 360 spin, in distressed denim jeans, a silk camisole and the boots I bought for her birthday. Lord knows she looks fit for a country concert, heck maybe even to see that Trace Adkins instead of Maxwell.

"Place your hands at your sides, mama! When I attended Pressley Preparatory Academy as an overprivileged wayward teenager, we not only outdid each other in the latest couture fashion, but we modified our checkered uniform skirts. If the tips of your fingers don't exceed the hem of your skirt, it's out!"

"Oh, hell, no," she chuckles. "You have that shape. Heck, if we want to be square, give me half your booty and I'll exchange my skirt for a pair of jeans."

I laugh, and it takes energy for me to force her arms down at her sides. We're almost in tears with chuckles as I get her to do what I told her to. True to form, her skirt is so short, it stops at her wrists.

"Mama! Go change, now," I halfheartedly gesture for her to head back upstairs.

It's a feat for Zamora to shake her head as she's in tears from laughter.

Vassili comes to the top of the landing. My mom shouts up at him. "Look, son, she's even more of a bully than cutie pie, or you."

"You both look very nice," Vassili tells her. It's hard as hell to get him to laugh, but that sinful gaze of his is twinkling with laughter. "If any man touches either one of you inappropriately let me know, I'll have it handled."

"Nope, because I wanna be touched inappropriately," My mother giggles.

"Vassili, you've learned well not to respond to my mom. I'm sure she's snuck a box of wine into her bedroom. Goodnight, baby," I blow a kiss to him.

"Oh, you think that's enough?" Vassili's bulky frame moves down the left side of the staircase, like a lion on the prowl. His gaze locks me down like a shiny new toy. "Zamora, please turn your head."

FEARLESS II
by *Amarie Avant*

His joke brings much more needed laughter to my mother. She's such a beautiful woman when she's happy.

My husband clutches me around the waist, his hand grabs for my ass, squeezing all the thickness.

"Will you be up when I return?" I cock a brow and lick my lips.

"If I'm not, kick me."

Vassili is reluctant to let my hand go. I reach to my tippy toes, even in six-inch heels, and taste his lips again. "I'll be thinking of you all night long," I whisper, my lips a fraction of a second away from his. He has an impending match with a fellow fighter at Vadim's Gym. He's being trained by Nestor, and the other guy has their coach, Vadim's attention. Needless, to say, I've juggled my 'secret' case and his dwindling time before we head to Australia. I need a resolution for Noriega first, or I may not be able to attend the fight.

On my heels, I go, turning around.

"Zar, call me when you're on your way home," he says.

"Okay, baby."

"Alright you two," My mom huffs. "Don't make me miss the comfort of a man's arms. Besides, this will be the best night of both your lives. I'm the one who has to return to a vibra—"

"MAMA!" I shout.

FEARLESS II
by *Amarie Avant*

She stifles a giggle, and I swear I smell white zinfandel on her as we head out to the garage. Although I'm ecstatic about going to a Maxwell's concert, an unsettled feeling coils around and makes itself at home in my abdomen. I attempt to tell myself that growing up in the middle of the warzone, that was my parents' home, is what makes me so pessimistic. There's a saying that troubles don't last always.

Where I'm from, the opposite is true.

FEARLESS II
by Amarie Avant

Vassili

I'm in a dead sleep when my cell phone rings. I left the damn thing on because Zariah was supposed to call me when they headed home. It's a little after ten pm, it can't be them. The concert doesn't end for another hour at the very least. Placing the pillow over my head, I groan and try to reclaim the sleep I had going. Then my cell phone goes off for a second time.

"Fuck, I am going to murder whoever this is," I grumble to myself. Blind to the night, I reach over and feel for my cell phone, snatch it up, and answer.

"Vassili, come over now!" It's Anna, Igor's wife. Her voice is heavy with anxiety. I can hear Malich shouting in the background.

Before my fucking brain can catch up, I'm out of the bed, tripping over the discarded high heels Zariah was unable to choose from for the concert. "What the fuck is going on, Anna?"

There's lots of sniffling and her voice breaks with each syllable, "They shot up the house."

Lightning streaks through my veins, and I stumble, losing my balance while shrugging into a pair of jeans. "What? Who the fuck shot up the house?"

FEARLESS II
by *Amarie Avant*

"Please come. Your uncle is talking to the cops. Oh shit, they're putting him in the back of the squad car. Vassili, we need you."

"Why are the cops taking Malich?" I shout. The phone goes dead. My uncle may have done bad things in his day, but he knows when to play by the rules. I dial Zariah. It rings and rings.

"Fuck," I hang up and dial her number again. What can I do with Natasha?

My baby starts crying the second I turn the light on to the nursery.

"I'm so fucking sorry, baby girl. Daddy's sorry," I grumble while picking her up. She's in some cotton footie pajamas. With the hot summer nights, I forgo a jacket for her, and shuffle down the stairs with her in my arms. When I put her in the car, I tell myself to drive safely while Natasha silently sobs, a desperate, sleepy cry.

"Everything will be okay," I tell her.

***

Twenty minutes later, I see the blue and red lights before I even hit the corner where my uncle's mansion is. The police cruisers line the entire block. Shit, I wonder if it's half the damn police force here tonight.

Anna is in a robe, with big curlers in her hair, talking to a uniformed cop. With nowhere else to park, I stop in the middle of the street, get out. I make a mad dash to the backseat, and scoop Natasha up. She offers a desperate little whimper. Before I can apologize again, a Mexican cop is shouting at me.

"Sir, you cannot park there!" He yells from the sidewalk. "Sir, you cannot park there!"

"Give me a fucking ticket," I tell him.

Anna comes running down the slope of wet grass. She slides and almost falls. Natasha is glancing around; her caramel complexion is already red from all the crying she's done. But she seems to be deciphering whether to continue crying or not. She yawns into my arms.

"Igor is… Igor is…" I shift Natasha into my left arm as Anna clings to my right side. I'm holding her 110-pound frame in one arm and Natasha in the other when she tells me something that makes me wanna fucking hit the ground. Anna sobs, "My husband is dead, Vassili."

I'm too in shock to make a move. I glance at her in confusion, but the cop asks, "Sir, what is your relationship to Mrs. Resnov?"

Anna sobs louder which prompts Natasha to burst into another round of waterworks.

"She is my cousin's wife. Igor Resnov, is he…" My jaw clenches. Fuck, I cannot say it. My pupils expand as I notice a bloody mess on the welcome mat near the door. There's yellow tape, a dude in a suit and more uniform cops there. Some other guy, with a SID uniform on, is taking photos. This is fucking real. I've seen dead bodies, mangled, tortured, all fucked-over looking. My father would have his enemies lined up. But that was a different time. They weren't family. The drum of my heart in my ears causes much difficulty for me to hear. "Igor is he…"

"Yes, sir, pronounced dead on the scene."

"Where is Malich and Yuri?" I ask him, rubbing Anna's back, and holding Natasha to my neck. Fuck, my baby isn't to see shit like this. Never.

"A man of the similar age as Igor Resnov was also taken to the hospital."

My legs fail me. Anna crumples to the ground, I go with her, placing Natasha in my lap as we fall. Yuri is closer than blood to me.

"He should make it, sir." The Latino says more sympathetically. "Malich Resnov was just escorted downtown for questioning."

***

I'm at Cedar Sinai, Natasha has fallen asleep in Anna's arms. The poor woman seemed to hold my one-year-older like a teddy bear, and it brings them both comfort, as I pace around, waiting for word on Yuri. Igor and Anna's four children are seated in the same row, heads all leaning to the left. The youngest, Albina was a few months younger than Natasha when I brought Zariah to the house for the first time. Albina is now a toddler; her head is rested on the side of Natasha. It's three in the morning when Malich is released from the jailhouse.

FEARLESS II
by *Amarie Avant*

He's still in his pajamas with a camel coat. My uncle's skin is white as snow as he enters.

I go to him. "What the fuck happened?"

"Your father." My uncle's searing glower moves away from me for a moment. There's a war within him. He's angry at *my* motherfucking father! Malich continues in a serious tone, "Anatoly left us wide open for retaliation. This has something to do with the government official in Italy that Danushka took out for him, I know it. They came up, disrespectful motherfuckers, drove by, shot up the house. Igor went out first. Then Yuri. Before your cousin went down, Yuri confirmed they were Italian."

I step away from Malich as he sinks down into a chair. I head down the hall to call my father when I see Zariah and Ms. Haskins rush into the double doors. My wife's face is wet with tears.

"Baby, we've called jails, hospitals! Why aren't you answering your phone?" She's angry and shaking. "I was just told a Resnov was here, I thought it was you. Don't ever do that, baby. Don't ever leave me wondering."

Zariah rushes into my arms. She's hugging and hitting me. "I almost died," she says. And then Zariah sniffles, rubs away her own tears and looks at me. She realizes I haven't been hugging her back.

"My kazen is dead," I say the words for the first time tonight.

"Oh," she clings to me again. "Yu—"

"Igor. Igor… is dead. Yuri is here. He's in the OR."

"Oh my god," Her mother says.

"Natasha is asleep, with Anna." I nudge my head. Ms. Haskins starts off as I finally hold Zariah tightly. I can feel tears burning in my eyes. The last time I was torn to tears, Sasha died.

Zariah

I have no words to express holding my husband, the fighter, as he cries. I'm clinging to cold, chiseled stone and his tears are falling like rain, dampening my hair. And then his tears turn into a roar. His hot muscles are on fire with rage. "Vassili, baby, you have to calm down."

I hold onto him tighter. *Jesus, we need you now,* I'm silently praying. Vassili begins to push me away. With all the strength I have in me, I try to cling onto him, but can't grasp him hard enough. He starts outside into the darkness, and I kick off my high heels to hurry after him.

"Vassili, wait, wait please," I call out, almost slipping on the tile. I run across the mat and through the sliding glass doors.

The cement is warm beneath my feet. It's truly one of those heat drenching nights, but I feel cold and alone. "Vassili, wait, baby!"

He doesn't. He continues past the stretch of grass and fountains. And then stops at the beginning of the parking lot to pull out his phone. Vassili is calling someone, I can hear the faint sound of it connecting. My heart lurches in my throat with each ring. My eyes plead with his, but I swear that he sees straight through me as if I'm not even there anymore. My stomach turns over. This isn't right. This isn't right.

He says something in Russian. Since he is teaching our daughter, I decipher the words, and believe he just called his 'father.' That's not right, he's never called Anatoly 'father.'

I listen as he makes a threat, "The next time I see you, you're dead. If you allowed this shit to fucking happen," Vassili stops speaking. "I will make due all those times I threatened to murder you with my bare hands, piz'da. You will be dead." He clicks the off button and fists the iPhone in his hand, again.

A rush of blood crashes through me. Vassili was addressing Anatoly in a voicemail. Damn, I tell myself that Vassili is not like his father, not like anyone else in his family. Tears cloud my visions as he finally stands before me. Thank god, the night is warm, because now, I pull away from his touch. "You promised me, Vassili."

"What the fuck is wrong with you, Zariah? I need you!"

"You need me? Hello, we are a team, we need each other, Vassili. You just threatened your father's life! You can't do that." I want to hug him, but Vassili needs to understand a few things. I glare him in the eye. "You cannot threaten your father's life, Vassili! He isn't just any person. He might try to kill—"

"The fuck I can't," his harsh tone feels like a tornado against my skin. "If Anatoly had anything to do with what occurred tonight, then I will do what I said, Zar. I am a man of my word."

"A man of your word?" I wipe the tears away and step closer to him. My body wavers, as my gaze seeks his. The darkness of his gaze is tangible, and it sends fear shooting through my spirit. I need to correct this now. Vassili is better than stooping to his father's level. So, I make the discussion personal. "Vassili, you told me you didn't want shit to do with what your family does! Vassili Karo Resnov, you promised to me, in my childhood bedroom, the day we broke up that you'd never allow yourself to become like them."

"Dah! I promised." He points a stiff hand. "I won't. But I promise you, now, my beautiful wife, anybody touches my family gets what they deserve. Thus said, any other assurances I made will have to be forfeited, no matter what."

I rub the tears from my face.

Malich steps outside. "Vassili, you need to go home with your wife."

His voice is dead. Gone is the always smiling man who in his generous ways loves to cook for people. The man that will ask you what your favorite dish is, if he hasn't perfected it, by the time you see him, he is a master of it by the next time. That man has disappeared. In his stead, is a man who looks just like the documentaries about ... Anatoly Resnov. Someone so far gone, without a soul, that it scares me to look into his eyes. And what hurts the most? Vassili just agreed to become the same type of man. I clutch my chest. These two men are better than this.

"Go home you two," Malich dismisses us.

"*Nyet!*" Vassili responds. "I will help rectify this."

"You are a fighter, Vassili, not a murderer. I don't fucking want your help, I don't need it." Malich turns around and heads back into the hospital.

"Listen to him," I tell my husband. Although, for the first time, I believe that his uncle had tossed the words out at him. Malich wasn't his usual proud self about Vassili's fighting skills, no, that was a low blow.

***

My mother drives my car home, and I drive Vassili's Mercedes. Though I've been praying within my mind for the last half an hour, I navigate the streets in silence. Vassili is ramrod still. He hasn't spoken a single word to me since my mother and Natasha came outside. My heart is conflicted about him. He's seated less than a foot away and I feel him growing even further from my heart.

"I'm sure that Yuri will be okay," I try.

I only have the subtle rise of his broad chest to remind me that he has heard me, even if my words do not penetrate.

***

At home, my mother's eyes are filled with sorrow as she heads to the nursery with Natasha. I close the double doors to our master suite, and turn around. Vassili is seated on the edge of the bed, his head in his hands.

"I'm so sorry, baby," I say kneeling down before him. My head goes to his lap, and I cry into it, reminiscing on a time not so long ago, Vassili hated to see my tears, sad or happy. He'd kiss them away. Malich's family is his family. Not Anatoly. And my husband still isn't over the abandonment by his mother at the hands of his father. It's in my heart to get the truth through to his thick skull but Vassili doesn't listen. Somewhere within him, he has to know that Malich is grieving, too, and that he doesn't have to take actions into his own hands.

"Stop, crying, Zariah." Vassili's thick, Russian accent breaks through the silence. There's no heart in his voice, but he says the words, "I fucking hate it when you cry."

Up until tonight, we've yet to be in a situation where I saw tears in Vassili's eyes. Even when he mentions morsels of time with his mother in the past, he seemed angrier at her and her situation that sympathetic. His dark gaze is glossed.

"Get in bed," he nudges his head.

Damn, his apathetic tone, and the way his jaw is sculpted in a marble scowl, warns me that there's nothing left for us tonight.

FEARLESS II
by *Amarie Avant*

"Vassili—"

"Zariah, take your ass to bed!"

I sit back on my heels, before him. "Talk to me."

He sits there, muscles stacked on muscles, glaring down at me like I'm one of his broken ribs. "There's nothing for us to fucking talk about, girl. Everything I told you outside the hospital, I meant it. If you feel it needs to be reiterated, we can chat tomorrow."

My arms fold. Vassili has never had such a nonchalant demeanor. "We are a team," I tell him, reaching up. I try to place my waist between his legs, and kiss him. He pushes my hands down with such quick movements I hadn't even seen them coming. Though there's no pain in his touch. I've never felt so hurt in my life.

"Girl, we are a team when I say so. And right now, isn't the time. I've told you some shit because I wanted to have you." His calloused thumb clasps my chin, and his voice is sarcastic. "*Dah.* I made promises that I hoped to fucking God I would never have to break, like I won't join teams with my father. Shit, that one's probably the only one I knew would be true. But if Anatoly sanctioned what happened tonight, like I already told you," he says gripping my chin, "I am going to deal with it."

Danushka consumes my mind. She said Horace was sweet, kind. Everything she didn't expect in a man of her own nationality. 'Russian men are ruthless, they don't give a fuck about anything but themselves...'

she had told me one day, angry that Horace wasn't splitting his time from his many companies with his new wife.

Only with Horace, he had never been put in the situation to choose.

What's more important?

Your wife?

Or, in Vassili's case, revenge?

Just as I had told Danny too, I speak up, ready to fight for my marriage. "Baby, you can't. Vengeance is like a seed, it sets roots. Talk to me, Vassili! Please!"

He starts to push me away. I clasp my hands onto his belt, and hold on for dear life. Sex can't fix us, but dammit, right now, it's the only thing I have of him.

"I don't want to fucking hurt you!" He screams into my face. Seems like the death grip I have on his belt is all I have of *him.* Vassili could slap me across the room, push me down on my ass, but he doesn't. I quickly undo his belt buckle and pull out his cock.

He eyes me with a dead gaze as my mouth goes to his dick. I suck for all I'm worth, for all the love we have. My lips wrap around his cock, and I'm banging it to the back of my throat faster than someone can shout 'Mississippi!' Using sex to my advantage is a new thing for me, and I hope to God it isn't a new normal. It's dysfunctional and most certainly not how you save a marriage, but for right now, it's working. Vassili grips the back of my neck. He grunts his approval and forces my head up and down. My tonsils are bruised by the strength of his erection, and I suck vigorously.

Vassili massages the base of his cock, since there's no way I can suck his XL dick all the way down my throat. I'm already gagging as it is. He then pushes off the bed, and I'm back on my ass, onto the plush pile carpet, with him on top of me.

He starts to unbuckle his belt. I push up my skirt.

"Put that ass in my face," he growls.

I tug off my panties in a flash, reach up to kiss him, but Vassili twirls his index finger. I turn over to my hands and knees. He enters my pussy with such force that my back arches.

"Fuck," I grit through my teeth. My walls begin to drench down on his cock as he clasps the back of my neck. He works his thumb into my ass. It feels good, gets my pussy quivering for more, but I guess that's all the motherfucker will offer in the form of foreplay, tonight. And I know that once this false closeness we have ends, I won't be crying tears of ecstasy, I'll be crying for my husband to open up, and talk to me again.

Vassili

Zariah is gone when I wake up on Friday morning. The moment I awaken, my mind is on the little things, like telling her 'have a great day at work.' Stuff that places a smile on her face. This is part of my routine. I do shit like this because for Christ sake, I can't be a man like my father. And there should be no doubt in my wife's mind of my love for her... like there was last night. So, as part of the usual routine, the thought pops into my mind to call her for virtually no fucking reason other than to just say I love you, and yeah, have a great day at work.

But reality slams into my chest, and the shit hurts so fucking bad. My heart isn't up to the little things. I turn on the shower, allowing it to get hot enough to burn my skin, to remind me what ... feeling *feels* like.

I'm torn between being the man I promised her I wouldn't be and the man who was given the opportunity to become the one she loves. That might sound confusing. But without Malich and his family around during summers in my childhood, and when I was a teen, getting the hell away from Anatoly, I would do more than *beat* Zariah's pussy. And I would've never known what true love is, because I'd have guarded myself with more cunts than I can satisfy myself with.

After showering, I have a towel around myself while digging into my top drawer for my passport. I dress quickly, and work over the words in my mind about what to say to my wife.

In the kitchen, Zamora has Natasha in her highchair, with scrambled eggs before her. She eyes my Louis Vuitton canvas duffle, and tilts her head at me. "Oh, Vassili. I made you breakfast. It's staying warm in the conventional oven, but will you do me a favor before you leave?"

Shit, I was just about to ask if she'd watch Natasha today... until I return. "Yeah, sure. Thanks for breakfast," I reply while opening the stainless-steel oven. Inside is a plate with more scrambled eggs, *kielbasa* sausage and toast.

"Sliced fruit is in the fridge," she says, still glancing at my duffel bag. "Vassili, you are a praying man. I owe you lots for being a good husband, the recent events with Mat—"

"*Nyet*, you don't owe me anything." I cut in, although I know where this is headed.

"Alright, well, will you pray before you leave? Wherever it is you're going, just pray about it."

"*Dah.*" I eat.

***

Ten minutes later, I've kissed my daughter, and officially asked Zamora if she'd watch her today. Her eyes were expectant, so I told her I prayed already—even though we both can tell that the mumble I sent to heaven landed on deaf ears.

While pressing the garage opener, I dial Zariah's number. Mid second ring I'm sent to voicemail. I close my eyes wishing I hadn't used her body like I did last night. Shit, she just sent me to voicemail on purpose.

"Zariah," I begin, still working in my mind on what to say to this woman I love with all of me. "I won't be home tonight," I start with the truth, while backing out of the windy driveway. "Probably not tomorrow night or the next."

Realizing that I haven't told her much of anything I add where I'll be. And end the call.

*** *The Next Day* ***

At LAX, I took the first available flight to Moscow, through KLM Royal Dutch Airlines. There was an extended layover in Amsterdam. By the time I arrive in my homeland it's the next morning. Grigor and Semion are posted at the terminal entrance when I arrive. My cousin's dog-ass of a face is set in a deep brown, while Grigor is wearing another power suit, breakfast bag and a cup in hand.

"*Privet, brat*—hello, brother." Grigor holds out the items.

Fearless II
by *Amarie Avant*

"I didn't fucking send for you," I tell him, glancing over his attempt at a kind gesture. "Don't the two of you have a demanding job? I'm well aware that Anatoly requests alerts every time I enter the fucking country, but damn, you're the right hand, and you," I address Semion, "are the left? Equal operation."

The ugly fuck's eyelid twitches. He's not a fan of equality, since he actually has the harder assignment.

Grigor drinks the coffee and eats the breakfast pastry as he drives us to the compound my father owns, Rublyovka. The mega mansions are suitable for trillionaires and dirty ass government officials. The gates open, and armed guards on each side track us as we enter.

My half-brother slurps down the last bits of the drink, and squeezes next to the cluttering of supercars that are parked around a lengthy lap pool. Shit, this man has become a hoarder. It's like a car dealership out here for the ultra-exclusive.

There are five armed men, even uglier than Semion surrounding Anatoly as my father meanders down the front steps of his home. His suit isn't a blinding highlighter color, but black. The many accessories he has on are all black.

"I've been in mourning," he says, holding his arms out. "Come, come, give your father a hug."

"Nyet, I'd rather not." My tone is calm and I'm my usual standoffish self with him. "Are you mourning your nephew, Igor?"

Fearless II
by *Amarie Avant*

My right hook shoots out like a missile landing against his chin.

Anatoly's brain snaps in place in his body, his legs anchor down and he falls backward.

A bunch of hammers cock back and machine guns are pointed into my face. A hard slam from behind goes to my left temple. Before I crumple down to the ground next to my father, I realize that of all these mudaks, it had to be my cunt of a brother, Grigor, who knocked me out.

Zariah

How do I breathe without any air? It feels like quicksand is consuming me and the devil has ahold of my ankle, speeding up the process, as I awake on day two without my husband. I'm torn between praying for God to keep him safe or hardening my heart to the only man I've ever fallen madly in love with. I called and called him last night, each ring took the air right from my lungs.

This morning, I open the facial foundation that I only use to make my face look super flawless for professional photos or those special date nights, and now I'm using it to hide the puff under my eyes. I shower and slip into a summer dress, the bright yellow brings my façade back to life, and for Natasha's sake, I step into the nursery with a smile. She's in the changing station, my mother has another new item from Mrs. Takahashi laid beside her.

Our beautiful baby's brown eyes sparkle as she looks me over. "Daddy?"

I clutch my chest and can't straighten my face when my mom turns around from Natasha, scooping her up onto a welcoming hip.

"Oh, honey."

"I'm okay, Mom." My voice tremors.

"You should stay home from work today."

An imaginary knife tears across my chest. Vassili suggested that I stay home so many times. He doesn't seem to believe in us. That I'd like to be there to help him work things out. But I know somewhere deep down, he believes in us. My husband just never had a chance to learn how to grieve as a child. Heck, I had trying times to learn, yet nowhere near as trying as his.

"No, I can't stay home. I have to work."

Zamora offers a faint smile. "I'm going to compare you to your dad now."

I scoff. "Don't—"

"No, he has his qualities. Resilience is one of them. Yet, balance? Not so much. Work can help get certain things off your mind, but there comes a time when you still must address said things."

"Humph, save this conversation for Vassili." I place up a hand, begging her not to continue with my gaze. "I'm so sorry, Mom. We ruined your birthday week."

"Why? I don't know how you or Vassili masterminded any of the travesties that occurred two nights ago. And if you ask me to watch my grandbaby, I'll find a belt."

I sniffle at her joke, with no energy to offer a comeback.

***

FEARLESS II
by *Amarie Avant*

My eyes land on a side profile of the balcony of my old bedroom and tears flood down my cheeks. I can still see Vassili climbing the tree effortlessly almost ten years ago to sneak into my room as I showered. *Jesus, please, please, please, I silently beg. Let him be okay. You are part of my marriage, we can't do this without You. Don't let us ...*

A hard sniffle rattles through me, and I flap my hands near my eyes to cool down the achy, hot feel of my skin. I scoff at myself, I'm sitting in my car, across the way from my father's home. My home. And I'm crying. Why didn't I just force him to give me attention at the end of July? He blew me off after returning from Temecula with Berenice. The asshole was too busy to see his only daughter. Now, I look like shit.

I clutch my keys and get out of the car, and head up the steps to the glossy black door. My fingers are crossed that he is home, and then I let myself into the house.

"Dad," I call out. "Dad?"

If memory serves me correctly, twice a week he stays home, to prepare for a golf match. Regardless of how 'busy' he's been in the past and unable to include me in the schedule, I'm sure golf is of the utmost importance. "Dad?" I call out again, ears perked, heading to the kitchen.

"Zariah?" There's shuffling upstairs.

FEARLESS II
by *Amarie Avant*

I start up the staircase, and head to my parents'— well, my father's bedroom. The door is open, so I hesitantly step inside hoping he's decent.

He is.

My father is in checkered shorts and a polo. The fucker does have time for golf! But on the other hand, Berenice isn't decent. I see a flash of her milky white breast as she covers herself.

"I hope you're comfortable in my mom's bed. Dad, did you at least have the decency to change the mattress?"

"Good morning, Zariah." He grabs my arm, and pulls me from the room while his mistress'-turned-whatever the fuck she is, face pales in color.

"What prompted this impromptu visit? Igor Resnov, eh?" he asks, hustling down the stairs on my heels.

"No. Wait, what do you know?" Suspicion has me eyeing him with an imaginary fine-tooth comb for any signs that he's had his hands in this.

"For your sake, Zariah, I have not inserted myself in the mistakes you've so chosen to make! What's with—" his hard tone cuts. Dad glances me over. "You've been crying?"

"I'm here about," I gulp, "About Juan Noriega."

He chuckles. "Russian money not good enough for you? That wetback is even worse. I'm telling you, stick with the white boy, and not further slumming in the gutter. At least you'll secure the throne when

Anatoly dies. Hell, they have the president in their pocket. No need screwing a roach and breeding a bunch of those babies too."

My eyebrows rise. Racist? I never pegged my father for a racist. Sexist, yes. Socialist, you betcha. But as Chief of Police, he must have some morals, right? I place my hand on my hip and utter one single word, "Sullivan."

My father's eyebrow cocks, he moves toward the marble mantle and readjusts a crystal figurine, as if he isn't all that concerned. "Why are you bringing him up?"

"The cop turned serial killer. You and Sammy weren't really good friends after the entire LAPD didn't do their fucking job and built a case for him to try. He had to use his own resources for the trial!"

"Zariah, check your tone with me."

"I remember, you and Lieutenant Sullivan were just as friendly as you and Sammy in the past. Heck, he should be golfing with you right now. Why did Sammy work so hard to put him away?" I spit sarcastically. "There are a lot of questions swimming through my mind, father. I can wake up, start being a bitch, if you'd like. Or would you prefer I keep my eyes closed and just allow you to tell me about Igor?"

"Allow! Cute, I'm being blackmailed by my daughter." My father grabs a silver case of cigars, moves away from the fireplace and sits on an antique chair, with his leg crossed. "Jesus! What has that fucking Resnov done to you?"

"Talk or I start digging," I tell him, as he opens up the silver case and grabs out a Cuban. "Sammy got his brakes tampered with during the Sullivan trial. Don't worry, I'm intelligent enough to know it wasn't you. But my IQ also keys me into the fact that you either sanctioned the request or turned the other way. Probably had your face in Berenice's bosoms, instead of at home with your wife, who was a little leery about you then. And I don't mean due to the hits. You were jealous about mom's concern for Sammy..."

"Zariah." He points the cigar at me, voice contrite. "Shut your fucking mouth, before—"

"I wish you would hit me." I stand before him, as he sits there. My dad takes his first puff of the cigar. I glare down at him, arguing, "I swear, before I sic my husband on you, I'm going to jump on your back, and try to take you down myself. Now, back to Sullivan. It isn't necessary for me to know about that skeleton. And here's how you can keep me from pulling even more skeletons out of your closet. Two things. First of them, tell me about Noriega; and second, you'll tell me what the hell you know about Igor Resnov's death!"

Maxwell rubs his knuckles along his lips. "Look at me, child, I don't know anything about Igor's death. That is assigned to a lower detective, not the Chef of police."

"Oh, I'm positive you insured the assignment went to one of the less seasoned detective."

He puffs more smoke. "Or maybe a burnt-out detective that doesn't give a damn."

"Humph, yeah, that scenario works, too. But you know more than you're letting on, father. Talk."

"Talk? Alright, let me gossip with my daughter, eh? There's talk about the Bertolucci family having done something, but none of my guys give a damn. It'll be a cold case soon."

"Thank you for the name." I shuffle Bertolucci to the back of my mind, aware when my father is telling the truth. It's a shame, he is. Family? What is that, some sort of an Italian mafia? I huff. What's next, the black mafia? "Now, Noriega."

"He has a few friends on the force."

"You allow that?"

"Me? Nope, bad for business. We have a guy who sends them to Internal Affairs when necessary, you know how I feel about IA, so it wouldn't be kosher for me to—"

"Snitch? Ha! What happened to handling it in the department or is it just the people who look like Noriega that you toss over to Internal Affairs?"

"Princess, I don't condone drug dealing."

"You condone everything else." I shake my head, ready to change the subject again. "I'm having Noriega subpoenaed today."

by Amarie Avant

"Why? You had better luck being one of his famous baby mamas. He doesn't slap them all around."

"His wife, I'm her divorce attorney."

My dad takes a long drag of his Cuban and contemplates for a moment. "Zariah, you come in my house making inferences that I do not appreciate. In some regard, you've been spot on. We keep our own safe."

The glint in my eye tells me that sick fuck Lieutenant Sullivan would've received a slap on the wrists and been sent away with his pension had my father been Chief of Police at the time.

"However, I am rigid in my ways, unpersuaded by some fucking Russians or no good Mexicans," he spits the words, and I take a step back.

"Well, damn, dad, tell me what you really think. Some of your friends would be appalled by your tone. Even your Latino political figures."

"I know how to put on a mask, and I don't hate all Mexicans just illegals and drug dealers."

I roll my eyes, my father has friends on the force who dip into evidence, especially when it involves cocaine.

"Since you've wiped your hands of me, Zariah, and now have chosen to come around," he glances down at me, "I see the ring still on your finger. For now, I'll have a police detail on you by the time you make it to the freeway. Because I love you, but that's all the love I can give, *Princess*. At least, while you're married."

"I don't want it. And I have no intentions of divorcing anytime in this lifetime. So, keep your detail." I argue.

"You're gonna need it."

Vassili

Aside from the boulder that must've fallen on my head, I wake up on day three, away from my family, and on a bed of clouds.

The mattress I'm lying on is halfway to the ceiling, and that's speaking volumes. I'm on the third floor of my father's home, and the walls soar high.

I touch a hand to my skull. It's bandaged.

"Fuck," I grunt, swinging my legs over the side of the bed. They're dangling because of how far I am from the floor. The room around me is fit for a king. Real gold wallpaper, antique furniture. Silk slippers are on the ground. I shove my feet inside of them and head to the door.

Once open, I'm stopped by a guard, with the barrel of his gun to my face.

My lips are in a tight line as I warn, "Move. Before you regret it."

He lowers it somewhat. "I'm going to tell your father you're up. Okay?"

"He isn't the boss of me, neither are you."

The man starts to pull a walkie talkie. My hand slams against the barrel, angling it over my shoulder, and I jab straight for his nose. Too easy.

FEARLESS II
by *Amarie Avant*

"*'Tchyo zag a 'lima*—what the fuck!" He screams, gripping at a waterfall of blood coming from his nose.

I snatch the walkie talkie. "Anatoly, can you hear me?"

"My son, you're up. I'm in the mud room." His tone is friendly. Sometimes he gets like this when angry. Either the punch I tossed rewired his brain, or he's in a psychotic episode.

In fifteen minutes, I've made it to the basement. The room is cave-like, with dome shaped walls, and even more shimmering 24 karat gold on them. My gaze shades to the darkness of the area. At the far side of the room, past a steaming jacuzzi, is my father, with his usual horde of model-type cunts. This time, they're in a mud bath.

One kissing his face, the other massaging mud into his back, not sure what the third is doing, her bare ass is to my face and she's down low, probably sucking his cock.

The kissy face chick moves, and I can see that Anatoly's eye is sealed shut, like Zamora's was the day Yuri and I came by her place in Atlanta.

"I'd offer you some pussy but," he gestures to his face. "My son, I regret never having attended one of your matches. That hook of yours, boy, oh boy! Semion, take notes your ugly motherfucker."

My cousin eyes me.

309

FEARLESS II
by *Amarie Avant*

"Where the fuck is Grigor? I'm surprised he got to me before you."

Semion grunts. "He was closer. I would have tried to kill you..."

Anatoly cuts in, "and I would have had to put your ass down like a fatted cow, Semion."

"Damn, kazen, we should switch parents. You'd be in my spot. Then that ugly face of yours might not look like a dog's ass, since you wouldn't have had to spend your days being jealous."

He lunges for me. The men around him stop him.

I don't flinch.

"Let him go," I say, smiling at Semion.

"*Nyet.*" My father waves them away. "The two of you can play later. You all leave now. Vassili, step into my office."

He gestures toward the mud jacuzzi. The women wave me over.

"I'll pass."

When everyone leaves, aside from his whores, Anatoly says, "You've gotta stop exciting your cousin. If he hurts you, I'll kill him, Vassili. And Semion is otherwise indispensable."

Semion hurt me? I grunt. "So, you're being a father today? How will you handle Grigor? He hit me."

Anatoly shrugs. "Grigor is my favorite. He gets as many passes as you do for being firstborn."

"Them make him your successor."

FEARLESS II
by *Amarie Avant*

"Nyet. Grigor is pale. Skinny. Looks like that Twilight vampire fuck."

I glare at him sideways. "Who?"

Anatoly groans. "Bitches, the most beautiful ones wrap you around their pinkie. One I use to have, she loved the Twilight Saga, I'm just saying… whatever, right? You aren't here for movie trivia. Maybe I'll never die? It costs me a mil a day to look so good. It's this drink I have. The maker says it's almost like the stream of eternity. You know I've been sick?"

"So, you say. But I'm not here to feed you borscht and nurse you back to health, either."

"That's what these women are for, my son." He kisses one. "But truly, I was dying until I drank from the stream of water."

He is delusional. I take on a wide-legged stance and ask, "Did you allow some Italians to shoot up your brother's home?"

He laughs, the girls do, too. "I'm appalled that you think so little of me."

"Did you?" My shout is amplified by the structure of the cave, the women jump.

"No." Anatoly offers a smug frown.

"Then how?"

"Must have something to do with that public official, Albert Bertolucci. He died a few weeks ago."

"What was he up to?"

"The guy was gunning for sanctions. Bertolucci wanted to increase the requirements for international claims at the ports in the area. One of the seats of the seven owns a steel company in Italy."

I rub the old scar along my jaw. The Seven Chairs or whatever the fuck he's referring to has been mentioned before. Malich always said that Anatoly wanted him to have a seat. Even with all power, it was best to have Resnovs take every seat. Semion's mother has a seat. The rest of my father's siblings do. There are about three seats that aren't claimed by Resnov's. But each seat is claimed by billionaires.

"Then why didn't the guy handle it?"

"He's a bitch, all paper no balls," my father huffs.

I shake my head. "And Bertolucci's family retaliated? You've had powerful men murdered around the nation. Seems like this one—"

"His family thinks they're the mafia or something."

"Did you hear about this quest for retaliation! And why, why did they go after Malich's family, not yours?"

"What the fuck do you mean, yours? Vassili, you are *moy syn*—my son. *You are my family!*"

"Make me believe you."

"Does my word not mean—"

"*Shit.* Anatoly your word doesn't mean a motherfucking thing to me."

Anatoly stands up from the mud bath, and slaps a hand against his chest. "I had nothing to do with my nephew's death!"

I stare at him like I have the eyes of a new man. One who doesn't have a history with this psychotic bastard. One who never hated his mom for running away from a monster like him. Now, I'm second guessing my father's manipulative ways. Maybe Anatoly didn't remove his blessing from Malich's family. Those Italians have always feared us…

Zariah

After the chat with my father, I head toward Billingsley Legal. While driving, I call the hospital and am connected to Yuri's room. "Hey, Yuri, how are you? Are you hanging in there?"

"Feel like shit. There's a gaping hole in my calf. But there's no getting me down. Where's Taryn?"

I silently take a breath. "Oh my, I'm so sorry. Vassili took off. And I never called to tell her you were in the hospital—"

"It's okay, Zariah, it's okay." He cuts into my sorry attempt for an apology. Hell, the guilt of knowing Taryn is a hoe is eating me alive. "Zar, I know you have that knucklehead to deal with. Vassili came to see me on his way to the airport. I told the mudak to stay home. Malich sent for my brothers."

"Oh no," I sigh, heading onto the freeway. Malich has bred mostly sons, Mikhail is the oldest of the brothers. He and five other brothers, who've made homes throughout the states, come around during New Year's, which I've learned is bigger than Christmas for their family. Each brother has a mainstream job, and a good head on their shoulders due to Malich's wisdom. Mikhail followed in Malich's footsteps and became a doctor. Igor's death is setting everyone into action.

FEARLESS II
by Amarie Avant

Yuri continues with, "It's just that, I've been calling Taryn, not like I can do anything else, and she doesn't answer." He huffs. "I'm worried."

My heart clutches. Yuri is a big ass cuddle bear. He's lying in the hospital worried about Taryn not answering his calls. When I finish my attempt to encourage him, and we get off the phone, I dial my high school friend and she promptly answers.

"Hola, Zariah," she chuckles endeavoring to speak Spanish.

"Girl, where are you at?" My lips are set in a frown.

"Cabo San Lucas, heifa! It's my man's birthday, and we are celebrating."

I can hear someone in the background, he has a dreamy Spanish tone. Can't be the guy who sent her to New York. That one sounded stuffy. "Taryn, c'mon, girl. Yuri is in the hospital, he keeps calling you."

"I know."

"We will be thirty in two short years, Taryn, damn. Not twenty. If you give a damn about him, answer him, and see how he's doing."

She huffs. The music in the background becomes muffled. "When I return, I'll go check up on him. I know I gotta break up with him sometime, so I will."

"Are you about to cry?" My lips tense. "Seriously, I don't want to hear it. There's a man here in California who has gladly given you his heart. Heck, Yuri doesn't need tears, he needs loyalty. I'll see you when you return," I finish the call, and hang up.

Through the rearview window, I notice an unmarked cop car a few spots back. My father didn't heed my stubborn response. He's got a security detail on my six. I take comfort in the fact that he must have some sort of love for me

It's lunchtime and the drive-thru line at Hot Chilly's is chaotic. I squeeze through the opening, where the cars are illegally jamming the intersection and make it into the Billingsley Legal parking lot.

My cell phone rings as I'm getting out of the car. The automatic tone says, "Incoming call from Husband."

I dig through my purse, and apprehend my iPhone. Too fixated on answering it in the allotted time, that I didn't remember I could have just pressed the radio button.

"Hello," I speak into the receiver.

"Baby," Vassili begins. Oh, the cold shoulder has been replaced. Another Resnov man that has an anxious tone. "I'm sending you—"

I cut in, "Where are you?"

"Still in Moscow."

"Then save it."

"Zariah, I'm sending you a photo of my sister."

"Dan... dan us... Danushka?" Damn, of all the times, I say the woman's name right, when my friend has the same exact name as Vassili's sister.

"Yes."

"Why, I have that photo ingrained in my memory. Pasty skin. Mousey brown hair. And a nose too big for her skinny ass body. What do you want!"

He breaths into the phone. "I don't think my father allowed the Bertolucci's to go after the family. Danushka might have, and I want you to stay away from her, if she ever comes around."

"Oh, so now you want to share information. Save it. I won't speak to you until you're right here in my face, so I can smack the dog shit out of you if need be. If it makes you feel better, rest easy knowing that I'm an obedient little wife and haven't forgotten about what your sister looks like. If she pops out of the bushes, I'll call you. Not sure how that will help, since you left our home, and left me a voicemail with half a cryptic ass message." I pause. Damn, I'm acting like a brat, but there were better ways to handle Igor's death. Hell, I kept seeing images of him an Anatoly murdering each other. Fighting fire with fire as Vassili is hell bent on doing, is not the way to go. So, I soften my tone, "Hello, Vassili? Are you still there."

"I'd never abandon you, Zar."

"I love you, Vassili." I hang up. The moment he returns home, I'll talk to him. But he'll have to be willing to be a team, and then *we* can seek out the Bertolucci family.

***

Samuel is standing next to Tyrese's office when I start to head past, with a respectful head nod, but he cocks his head at me.

"You, step inside, too."

"Alright..." I follow him inside. Tyrese isn't wearing his signature suit today, but a short sleeve button up as he sits behind his desk. He doesn't even offer his signature dimple. Either this heatwave has him lethargic or we are in deep trouble.

"Not sure how we secured such a high-profile case, as this firm usually works with a lower socioeconomic. However, the company on payroll, which issue out subpoenas called me personally," Sammy says. "Zariah, I know you've helped Tyrese become acclimated with the office, but no more assisting him with Mrs. Noriega's case—"

"Assisting me?" Tyrese's eyebrow piques.

"I won't." I glare at Mr. Nick's daring him to speak up. I'm still not ready for Samuel to know that Nicks and I are co-counsellors on the case. "What's going on?"

Samuel huffs. "Well, I had it in my mind to commend you, Nicks, on Mrs. Felicidad obtaining her green card in such a swift manner, it takes some serious connections, and balls. But now you're suing a US Citizen for half of everything that he owns, and that man so happens to be a known member of the Loco Dios. The company refuses to submit the subpoena. Zariah, I don't want you in this mess. Tyrese, it's not too late to back out."

"But Felicidad was," I stop myself, and resort to a more formal response, "Mrs. Noriega was abused by her husband. She has rights."

"You'll stay out of this, Zariah. I'm bringing this to your attention just to keep you aware, if Tyrese chooses to continue to represent Mrs. Noriega there might be consequences. He's new, so this is a warning to him, too. You..." he glances at me with all sincerity. "Your mother would kill me."

"Well, Mr. Nicks?" I cock a brow.

"I'll pay a bum off the street to serve him, if necessary." Tyrese asks.

"That might be necessary," Samuel stands up. "Zariah can no longer assist you. Any questions or consultation required, see me."

My mentor stalks out of the room.

"So," Tyrese speaks up. "I'm to assume Billingsley must've been so emotionally invested in keeping you away from this case, that he didn't look at the paperwork before telling you to stay away. Zariah, your name is all over the summons."

"Yes, good call on getting a transient to have him sign the papers. Will you go vet one, or should I?" I arise.

"Not so fast, Zariah."

Lips set into a line, I sink back down, arms folded. "This is my case, Nicks."

FEARLESS II
by *Amarie Avant*

"I'll see to it that the summons is delivered by this afternoon. But let me make something clear, Samuel has had conferences to attend, prior to attending court, he'll know. That is if the Noriega chooses not to retaliate once he gets the subpoena."

I scoff. "Look, we agreed to have your name on the subpoena. Lanetta made that mistake, when I requested her to write one up. She uses a generic form."

"We don't have time for mistakes, Zariah. For your safety. And I have talked with Lanetta about it," his tone is hard as if he reprimanded my assistant to the fullest extent, "because after you made the request, with Lanetta, I also told her to ensure that I'm on the line, not you. Shit, I could fire her ass myself."

"Thank you, Tyrese." I nod in agreement.

"I can't bring up your husband, right?" he shakes his head with a laugh. "I guess, I'll just be grateful he can keep you safe."

Our eyes connect. I'm too angry to read Mr. Nicks the wrong way. "Yes, he can. And I have the genetic makeup of a man who gets paid hand over fist to rub people the wrong way, too. I can handle myself. But we do not have time for mistakes."

"I'll revamp the subpoena with my information and it will be given to Noriega this afternoon, Zariah. I understand that you're going to continue assisting with this case for whatever reason, but I don't want you in court during litigation."

"Alright," I nod. "I'll write reports, but I'm going to continue to stay in communication with Felicidad and her children."

He bites his lip. And holds out a hand across the table. I reach over and shake it. "Zariah," he says, not letting me go. "I really like you, and despite the craziness of this case, I'm enjoying getting to know you."

"Okay," I narrow my eyes somewhat, as a sign for him to remove his hand.

"I'd prefer you had nothing else to do with the Noriega's, but you made a promise to Felicidad, so therein lies my agreement with you still having a hand in the case."

"I have no say," I tell him. "Just a cheerleader for Felicidad. Okay?"

"Shit, this is the moment where I offer a wisecrack, like I prefer it if you were my cheerleader."

I offer the usual sardonic look he always receives whenever he flirts, but there's genuine concern in his gaze. It's my cue to head out the door now.

***

Mom advised against working until I drop. This is a morsel of wisdom that I chose not to take today. My eyes burn from staring at the computer screen, and from staying wide open so as not to cry about Vassili. Like my mother warned, I've submerged myself in work so long, I'm unaware until Tyrese taps on the door.

Fearless II
by Amarie Avant

"It's almost eight, can I go home yet?"

With my mind on sleep and as I skim through the neurologist's statement about Edgar Versa, I mumble, "Go."

"You know exactly what I mean." He takes on a wide-legged stance.

"You chose to stay, Mr. Nicks. I've locked up shop more times than I can count. Besides, we shook hands, you have the Noriega case. I've been consigned to 'social worker' status whenever Felicidad needs." I have it in my mind to argue with him but end up yawning. He's right, it's time to head home. "Let me finish my sentence, okay?"

"Thank you."

Ten minutes later, I exit my office. Tyrese is in the hallway, leaning against the door. He glances me up and down. The dimples in his cheek deepen. "God, you are beautiful."

"Don't piss me off, Nicks."

"Look, I woke you up." When I give him a confused glare, he elaborates, "I watched you for a while, before I knocked. You were sitting in front of piles of documents, dosing. Your head kept ..." he starts to chuckle, as he gestures that my head continued to dip. "Since you aren't your usual sharp, sophisticated self, I snuck in the truth. Shoot me. It's cute, you know."

"Be respectful." I tell him, stalking to the alarm, and quickly punching in the code. Tyrese unlocks the front door, holds it open and we step outside. The air is hot, and the sky is a pretty light purple, with fragments of orange where the sun just dipped over the horizon, it's going to be a long summer night.

I've taken one step out of the door when I notice three Escalades are surrounding my car. There are enough Mexican gangsters to start their own sports team, leaning against the sides of each SUV.

"Zari…" Tyrese's tone dies as a man comes from the side of the wall. He was hidden by the door. He's holding a sawed-off shotgun to Tyrese's head.

"Ay dios, mis amigos, look at the two of you," Juan Noriega says. Has to be him. I can spot him on a Where's Waldo billboard in Vegas. I googled him. He has so many tattoos on his neck and chest, if I squint my eyes, it looks like he's wearing a turtleneck. And the motherfucker is all but five feet tall. "You scared, puta?"

Tyrese is pulling close to me. His tone is rather confident under the circumstances, "You all need to disburse at once!"

I glance down at Noriega and ask, "Do you own these SUVs? I've got an inventory of all your assets. Since Felicidad is taking half, how about I just take these two, you can keep the other one?"

Fuck! And I promised not to attend a court hearing! I am truly my father's child.

His laughs, all his teeth are capped in gold. "You're a hot little piece of ass, aren't you? Isn't she Chico?"

A brick house of a man, who I must assume is Chico steps forward. Now him, I'm afraid of. One of his arms is bigger than the combination of my thighs! His dark gaze shoots up and down my frame.

"Alright, guys, you need to get in your cars and leave," 'Tyrese tells them. "Noriega, I'm sure you have a slimy ass attorney just waiting to handle this case."

"Oh, no," Noriega shakes his head. "I like her. Tyrese Nick's, your name is all over the paperwork, but this bitch knows my bitch by first name. What's your name, sweetheart?"

Chico's gaze lands on mine, and then his pupils dilate. He mirrors the fear I'm internalizing. "I know this girl. Juan, we gotta go."

He nudges his chin. "Que chucha tienes?"

My eyebrows knead. I'm not certain what Noriega asked, but I assume, despite my verbal outburst, he isn't aware of my hand in assisting his wife.

Chico says, "She's that fighter's wife—"

Police sirens ring.

***

An hour has passed. The sky is dark and with the bad neighborhood I work in, there isn't much light. The red and blue lights on top of the masses of police cruisers bounces a glare off the window of each of the other cars. I can't see Noriega's face as he is seated in the back of the car furthest from me. But I swear, he's making connections as I give my statement to Officer Greene.

"How long are you going to hold them?" I ask.

Greene rubs his goatee, and then he looks into my eyes. "How long do you need us to? The guy with the sawed-off shotgun, is going away for a while. But there can be drugs beneath the dash, or anywhere else you'd like them to be found in those SUV's, Mrs. Washington." He makes sure to look me dead in the eye while giving my maiden name.

Lips pursed, I shake my head.

"You have time to consider it."

I bite my lip.

"Your call," he shrugs. And then walks away.

Tyrese comes to stand next to me. "Your husband should've texted or called you at least twenty times by now, Zariah. He had reached out to you at least five times by the time I ate my chilly burger on our first night working this case."

I rub a hand over my face, glad that my eyes aren't burning with the need to cry. Fatigue weighs down on me, and my mind is too muddled to lie. "He's got a fight coming up."

"Can I drive you home, please?"

"No."

Fearless II
by *Amarie Avant*

He rubs a strand of hair from my face before I can protest. "Follow you?"

"You're gonna do it anyway. You did it the night we got the case."

"So it's 'we' now."

"We did get guns put to our heads together." I smile to keep from crying. I just wanna go home and hold Natasha as Vassili spoons me.

His dimples deepen. "So are we friends now?"

"We're colleagues, Mr. Nicks." I shrug, my usual blasé self.

Tyrese backs up toward his Jaguar as I head to my car. And then Tyrese Nicks follows me home... So much for getting married, and believing my husband would always and forever be my savior—Okay, dammit, he isn't even aware of this. And won't be until the final remarks of the pending case, but Vassili just took off, without so much as a word, so I am being petty.

by Amarie Avant

Vassili

TWO NIGHTS LATER

Just as I was flagged for returning to my homeland, a police cruiser lines up behind my Mercedes, and BLURPS the lights at me. And I thought Mr. Washington had backed the fuck off? I pull over, grab my license and insurance and zip down my windows.

"Hands on the steering wheel," a masculine voice blares through the speakers. "Both windows down."

Doing as told, I shake my head.

The beloved boys in blue step out of their cruiser and come to both sides of my car, flashing the light in.

"What did I do, this evening, officer?" I start to grab my license and insurance from my lap.

"Hands on the steering wheel," he says again, flashing the light in my face.

The illumination burns my retinas. My hands clench the wheel. He pulls out his phone, and starts to make a call.

"Keep your head forward, too," the cop on the passenger side commands.

I lift my middle finger from the steering wheel as response. A few moments later, the cop on my side holds out his phone.

Keeping my head forward, hands glued down, I argue, "What the fuck? Is it for me? Are you going to hold it to my ear?"

"Take the damn phone, Resnov."

I snatch it from his hand. "Hello," I growl into the receiver.

"Are you keeping my daughter and grandchild safe? And why the fuck are you going on vacations to Russia for *five days*, without them? Got another family that I should be aware of?"

Damn, did Zariah go to her father about Igor's death? No, my wife wouldn't tell him our problems. "What do you want, Mr. Washington."

"You to choke on rat poison, but I'm a softy. My pretty princess loves you. When she takes her love away, Resnov," he chortles, "that's the end of you, buddy. She's a cop kid, should've married ... a cop. Should've become DA."

"This is fucking perfect, Maxwell," I laugh with him. "Your mentality is just like my father. Get the entire family into the business. Zariah can prosecute the cases that you deem necessary, and she wouldn't harp if you sent over investigation files with nothing on them. No reason to try the mudaks who are on your team, right?"

"I keep saying you were smart. Remember the first time we chatted? I came to that conclusion. You're a fighter, a strategist. Now, take your ass home. You've been gone for almost a week. Keep your family safe."

CLICK.

My chest is tight with anger. This motherfucker tells me to keep my family safe? I can handle my own! The cop reaches inside and grabs the phone. I have it in my mind to call Mr. Washington back, but I head home instead.

***

In the nursery, Natasha's back slowly rises and falls as she sleeps. I place my hand on her, she's warm and soft. It takes all my strength not to pick her up, and hold her to my chest. But my baby is a true fighter and a restless sleeper. She will riot if I wake her.

I feel someone watching and turn around, Zariah is standing at the door, in a nightgown. I head toward her, she pivots on her heels, and starts to our bedroom. Inside the room, she stalks past me and closes the double door. This is a signal that her mother stays. I expected loud cussing, and anger. She leans against the closed door for a moment.

I take her arm, she slaps me away.

"Zariah, I'm fucking sorry, baby," I try.

"No, I don't need your apologies, Vassili, I need you to understand something." She moves from my grasp, and goes to the dresser.

"Three months ago, we were in opposition of each other. Then we head to Brazil, and you had your comeback fight. We made promises…"

I'm a dick. I look like a piece of crap as I begin to grovel, "Zar—"

"No, let me finish," she has something fisted in her hands. "I stopped taking birth control, so Natasha could have a little sister or a little brother." She flings something at me. It bounces off my arm. "I'm pregnant, Vassili! And FYI that's from last night, this morning, I went to see the Obstetrician. Two months, Vassili. I have the photo. Would you like to see that, too?"

"*Dah*," I nod my head slowly. Can't show I'm fucking elated, I'm still in the dog house.

"Okay, but only if you promise to step up to the plate. What do I have to do, get you to pinkie swear, sign a fucking contract! What's gonna get you to put our children first, Vassili! Huh? We have a life here, you tell me you went home. Fuck you and your damn home, Vassili, this needs to be home."

"It is home, Zariah!"

Her look shuts me the fuck up from another attempt at an apology.

"Vassili, you go away to fight in Australia in three weeks, I swear, if you runoff before then, I will find you, and drag your ass home. Now, do you want to see the ultrasound? That's your gesture to me that you plan to *take care of home*."

FEARLESS II
by *Amarie Avant*

"I'm sorry," I step closer to her. She slaps my face, again, and again. I take every hit she offers. From my back pocket, I pull out a long jewelry box. "See, beautiful, I have something just for you, baby. I'm sorry."

Zariah gingerly takes the box, opens it up. It's a platinum tennis bracelet with seven-carat diamonds, I always get her seven carats. The damn thing cost 30k, but she's worth more. The box snaps shut.

"A tennis bracelet. Wow, I'm a fucking little girl now?" She tosses the thing over my shoulder. "I'm actually so very sorry about what happened to your cousin, Vassili. Yesterday evening, I met with Mikhail, and all the older brothers to help with funeral proceedings. Malich is mute, he isn't saying shit to anybody right now." She rubs tears from her face. "They're your family, damn it, and you know it! You should've been there."

I try to hug her again, but she slaps me. "I dreamed of Anatoly murdering you, Vassili," she screeches. "I dreamt that you'd try to retaliate, and your father killed you!"

I'm stunned, stock still, standing before her. Last week, she had tears falling down her face and I was too angry to give a fuck. Tonight, my heart feels like it's shredding in my chest, from the shit she just said. She worried about my dying?

I glance down at her, Zariah just stands there, hugging her hands around her chest. She's got my seed

Fearless II
by *Amarie Avant*

in her belly, and I'm being a dick! My hand goes to the back of her neck, and my lips go to hers.

Zariah turns her head. "Not right now, Vassili."

My teeth grit, I can't take her tears anymore. "You want me to sign a fucking contract or something? I'll do anything for you to forgive me, Zariah." I reach for my hair, my fucking mohawk is gone. There's nothing to tug. I rub a hand over my buzz cut, and then punch myself in the chest.

Zariah finally reaches out a hand to me. "I was just talking, but baby, I'm scared. If you ever leave…"

"Leave?" I bark. I plant kisses on her lips, more and more, tasting the soft sweetness of her mouth. "*Ya nikogda ne otpushchu tebya*—I will never let you go," I tell her. "No matter how much I might act a fool. I will never let you go."

"Yeah, well you can tell me more about your mother, Vassili." Her sweet voice makes my cock go flaccid. I just wanted to fuck her happy.

"Vassili, tell me why sometimes you can halfway screw me out in public, and then during other instances, your crazy ass plays the gentleman."

"Okay, I'll tell you." I nod, with a frown. My hands grope at her breast, and my tongue twines in her ear. My dick begins to stretch and harden again.

"Tell me," she folds her arms.

I press her hands back down at her sides, and kiss her again. "In a minute…"

"Now," she murmurs, eyes glittering with tears.

FEARLESS II
by *Amarie Avant*

Fuck now, I press my mouth over hers again. This time I bite her bottom lip until she opens up for me. My cock is straining against my jeans now, ready to leap out and fuck her. It's been five days, and I need pussy.

My wife pushes at my chest with all her might. I take a few steps back.

"Sex doesn't fix, everything, Vassili."

"I know," I shrug, but in my mind, I'm thinking yes it does. Sex will wipe away those tears and place a smile on that beautiful chocolate brown face of hers.

Zariah reaches up, places her hands on my jaw. "Baby, I'm not fucking you tonight. Sex isn't a means to an end, no matter how many times I've caved in the past, you're not getting any."

Fuck, she's right about sex. I close my eyes, breathe in the sugary goodness of her, and nod my head. I have to talk to her about my past, give her a little something.

Zariah

Vassili holds me tightly in his arms. I've showered for the second time tonight, this time with him, and without tears in my eyes. He was a gentleman and didn't try to screw me. Lord knows, I kept my gaze on his and not on all the ripped muscles of his body.

Now, we're lying in bed. He has this obsession with cocoa butter and my tummy. Although it's flat-ish, I told him during my pregnancy with Natasha that I didn't want stretch marks. Well, I had a few of those prior to, and he's kissed every one of them. But he got into the habit of massaging my belly.

Seems like the perfect slice of déjà vu as Vassili's big strong hands rub along my stomach. It's nothing short of therapeutic for him, because we have deeper conversations like this.

My husband is fearless and invincible. And I'm half the team. Now, I need to connect with him on a deeper level. I need to know more about his actions at the bar, more about his mother. "Tell me you trouble, my love," I sigh, sinking my head against his chest.

Vassili caresses my hair, kisses my forehead. But he doesn't utter a word.

FEARLESS II
by *Amarie Avant*

"You promised. I'll pay in ass in the near future, not tonight though." Damn, my joke was his level of crude, and still, my husband is quiet.

"You overheard my conversation with Malich about how my father tied my mother up to a street post?"

"Yes, baby. Tell me more."

"I'll tell you," he asserts himself. "Before she got up there, she was dragged to Anatoly's compound. I hadn't seen her in months... Had to be months. I always tried to forget about her. It was safe that way, and then Anatoly would go look for her. Bring her ass back. Shit seemed like years, since I was just a kid."

"Hmmm," my finger twirls a figure eight across his chest.

"One of his goons spotted her somewhere... I didn't know. He tossed her out of the trunk of his car, she was in the middle of the courtyard. The sound of her screams I can still fucking hear it now. Hear her begging for them to stop, to let her go."

My skin begins to burn as an image comes to fruition in my mind.

"The bitch, Anatoly had running the house told me not to go down. I said something to Sasha, scared the shit outta her. Made her stay with that cunt. Then I went outside. My father was ..." he pauses, his chiseled chest puffing with air before exhaling. "He raped her in front of them all. Sometimes I can't get

335

that shit from my head, and I don't want to disrespect you."

"Like when we were screwing in Vegas, and having fun, and you called me a bitch."

"*Dah*"

I lay on my side, and place my hands on his beautiful, stone carved face. Vassili seems so emotionless, but I swear it's eating him inside. "I'm going to ask you a question, Vassili."

"Girl, just ask———"

"What was in your heart?"

He blinks. This is a doggone trick question to him.

"Malicious intent? Were you angry when calling me a bitch?"

"*Nyet*. Fuck no!"

"Your father raped your mother. You saw it." I repeat to him the truth. His eyebrows knead as if the thought never occurred to him. "Rape is a means to gather power. To strip a person down in order to make the assailant *feel*.... good? I don't know. I'm just aware that it's all in the striping down, gaining control, showing of power, and causing humiliation. Have you ever kissed me crazy at the bar to shame me?"

He shakes his head.

"We have fun, we role play. Trust and believe, if we were just dating, I wouldn't have allowed very much of the stuff we do to happen. Yes, I can be sadidty when I want. And as your wife, I am bound to make all your sexual fantasies a reality. If I don't like something, I'm highly aware of how to say no."

I hold my husband tight. Yeah, he has a few visible scars that increase his sexiness, and on occasion, broken ... bones. My heart cries for those scars I never knew about. It's gonna take time for Vassili to fully open up to me. He just gave me one isolated incident of his childhood.

There's more.

I'll have to beg, plead, and sometimes even force him to share more with me in the future. And it'll break my heart to break his over again while he's divulging the past, but it's part of getting to know my husband.

Vassili

I'm dressed in all black. An expensive ass Westmancott suit, like the rest of my Russian family. Igor's funeral was held today and Malich still hasn't uttered a single word. Yuri walked around with a cane in his hand and a bone to pick with anybody who crosses his path. Mikhail handled everything.

I stand in the living room of my uncle's home, tossing Resnov Water back. The burn slams down my throat. I'm ready to hit the road. I need to fuck my wife, if she's willing, that is. It's been a week since I returned from Russia, and she's keeping those thick thighs locked. Don't get me wrong, my beautiful wife is still her nurturing self, but my leaving scared her, and the threats I made about murdering my father only heightened her fear.

Yuri pats my back. "Everything has been handled." We're an in a circle, the six of us, and I feel like one of the brothers.

"You tell dad?" Mikhail asks.

"*Dah*, he's in his room."

The oldest rubs a hand at the back of his neck. "Did he say anything?"

When Yuri shakes his head, a heaviness continues to weigh further on our shoulders.

FEARLESS II
by *Amarie Avant*

"All the Bertolucci's are dead, right down to the fucking kids," Yuri sneers. "A friend of ours owed dad a favor. I didn't think he'd do the kids," he mumbles.

I glance around for Zariah. She's seated with Albina and Natasha, and has done everything to keep the toddler from crying for her father. Anna's been popping pills like candy. With Malich's medical connections, she was a zombie at the funeral.

"We're family, we are fucking Resnovs," I tell them, in the words of my grandfather Anatoly Senior. "'Touch what's mine, and the funeral home becomes rich.'"

Yuri nods. Suddenly he isn't so sad about the Bertolucci kids that died. We all take a drink.

***

"Something bad happened yesterday?" Zariah asks, as she helps me take off my suit jacket. She'd already stripped down to just her panties and bra, and in my anger about putting my cousin in the ground earlier, I think I've been standing at the door to the bedroom for a while now.

I don't have it in me to lie. "What do you know, Zariah?"

"More than I need to." Her eyes warm with sadness. "Anna was bragging and crying about it before she took more meds." She wants to say more. Earlier, Zariah had mentioned learning how to cope. Well, apparently Anna's big ass mouth told her exactly how we Resnovs deal.

FEARLESS II
by Amarie Avant

"Are you mad?" I ask.

"No, baby. You didn't do anything."

I scoop her up, her hips go around my waist, and I place her on the bed. My wife is the most beautiful sight I've ever laid eyes on. Creamy, dark brown skin. Her hair waves over her shoulder, and caresses against her hard nipple. I push her tresses back over, pull out her breast and begin to suck.

"No more sad shit, Zariah," I say, tongue twining around the hard bulb of her breast. "Can I fuck you now, or am I still in trouble?"

She moans. See, and she said sex couldn't mend broken hearts.

"Soon as I taste you, baby," I reply. Unbuckling my pants and shoving them down. I work my way down to the sweetest scent I've ever breathed in. I push up her silky gown, so eager to get a whiff, I place my nose against her lace thong and growl.

"Vassili, fuck me, daddy," she groans.

My cock thumps against my thigh, begging like a panting dog for action. I tear the thong from her, and dig right in. My face is so far into her pussy, nose nudging against her clit, chin riding along her asshole, as my tongue digs deep into her candy core. My wife gets to cussing, and her leg starts to jerk.

I get to my knees, grab her ass, pick her up, and slam straight into that soaking wet pussy. All that moaning turns into sweet groaning. My tongue then presses into her mouth.

by *Amarie Avant*

With us in a seated position, Zariah works her hips, and grinds down on my cock. Damn, her pussy is just as wet as her mouth usually is.

"Yes! Yesssss!" Her long fingernails slash at my biceps. And I grip her ass as she works her hips.

"Damn, girl, you're having my baby."

She bites her lip, the perfect little fuck face of hers has me saying it again. "Girl, you're having my fucking baby."

"Shit, yeah, I'm gonna have your baby," she growls.

I flip her onto her back, grip the headpost, and pound into her pussy. "I fucking love you. I knew this pussy was wetter than usual, you got that pregnant pussy."

"Shit," she screams, her titties are bouncing. "Vassili, I'm coming."

"That's right cum all over daddy's dick." I'm beating her pussy like a speed bag. Zariah's hips angle upward and she grabs hold of my ass, taking every punch to her cunt. The slickness of her walls, has me clenching my toes, and I time my release just right.

Zariah

Three Weeks Later…

Chico was right about something. I'm not to be fucked with. Drugs were pinned on Noriega and his gangster friends, thanks to Officer Greene. However, the kilos of cocaine weren't "found" until their Escalades were processed—meaning, the morning I found out I was pregnant, three weeks ago, I called Greene and he was happy to oblige. It's karma for his ass, and guess what I'm actually guilty about?

My Fatburger with Rally's French Fries.

Natasha and I are holed up in the game room. She's at her toddler table chewing on a Baby fat with cheese. Needing elbow room while I eat, I chose to sit on the plush carpet and lean against the wall. And she has some nerve, eyeing my Rally's French Fries. Really? She didn't like them the first time, and, I suspected, gave them the stink eye due to the difference in color to her usual French fries. So, needless to say, I didn't purchase her any fries at all.

"Mommy, fry, fry?" she begs.

"Girl," I chuckle, my tone is as testy as Vassili's usually is when he calls me that himself. "You can't eat it all," I pluck a few of my fries and hand them over.

Damn, I close my eyes and moan at the taste of my own. When who do I hear? Yuri's loud mouth. He's gotten comfortable with his cane. The other night, we went out, he was the oddball, and women flocked around as he gave boisterous stories about the shot he received during deployment with the army.

"Natasha, shhhhh," I tell her.

"Zariah?" Vassili shouts up the stairs.

Please don't come up... please don't come up... This is déjà vu, but instead of me being almost ready to pop, I'm only three months pregnant now. He's right at the proper weight, and if you let him tell it, he prefers *kholodets*, that nasty ass meat jelly stuff over a good burger and fries. So, I'm not in the mood for his ass. Gulping down a lump of food, I shout a reply, "Be down in a sec."

He's hustling upstairs now, so I slide my food over. "Natasha," I start to get up, but that will defeat the entire purpose of hiding my stash on the opposite side of me.

"You are in so much trouble," Vassili stands there, arms folded.

"Why do you move so quickly?" I grumble with a smile.

He comes in, scoops Natasha into his arms and gives her crazy kisses on her neck. "So, you're the accomplice? Did she force you to eat this shit, or did you do it willingly?" He asks her as she giggles.

FEARLESS II
by Amarie Avant

"Language," Yuri says, walking into the room with a gait. "Hello, Zariah, cutie pie, don't allow that, he'll tickle you until you can't breathe."

Vassili swings Natasha high, and catches her a foot before she can hit the ground. I clutch a hand to my chest, right at my heart. "Yuri, get him before you two are sporting matching war wounds."

Yuri chuckles. "Hey, this right here has the pussy flying," he says, knocking his cane to his calf—which I suspect is more healed than he lets on.

"Now, you're cussing," I tell him.

"Aw, that's not a bad word, it's a... beautiful thing."

"Keep having this conversation with my wife, and find yourself waking up in that exact spot in a few hours," Vassili threatens. He pulls out a chair, and sits.

"French fry?" Natasha holds the fry so tightly the center mushes in her hand.

"No, sweetheart. I'll take some tea; can you make daddy some tea?" He asks her.

"Yay!" She hurries to get up. Falls, and then heads to the Mickey Mouse play kitchen she has.

"Zariah," Vassili says my name, rubbing the back of his neck. "I'm gonna change the flight itinerary."

"*Nyet, brat*—no, brother," Yuri huffs. "Mikhail is moving in the house; he and the rest of my brothers will stick around town until Danushka comes out from hiding."

FEARLESS II
by *Amarie Avant*

Vassili doesn't seem convinced. They set aside businesses and their lives after Igor—the baby, second only to Yuri, died.

While Mikhail is tasked with keeping his father from grieving it was Yuri who set in sequence the death of the Bertolucci family. I suspect that Vassili doesn't believe the other brothers were callus enough to handle it. And right now, he wants to keep me and Natasha safe.

"What if Danushka comes around?" Vassili spits the words at his cousins, eyeing myself and Natasha with a world of concern.

"You think I'd let that cunt hurt Cutie Pie?" Yuri clutches at his cane and comes over. "Zariah, you're my sister now."

My husband isn't moved by his cousin's sincerity. "We will all arrive the morning of the match. Together."

"No, baby, we'll not," I shake my head, climbing to my knees, I crawl over, and plant myself before him. We're eye to eye, with him in the tiny chair. "You have to be well rested. I'll be in Australia, before you even know it."

I'm comfortable. Noriega is rotting in jail, for at least 16 months on drug possession—pathetic, I know. He should be in jail for the abuse of his wife, but Felicidad is still afraid of him. His attorney is so busy fighting me over his assets. This fool is so flashy that his cars are worth more than his one home, but

Felicidad is stepping into her blessings. An involuntary termination of his parental rights is in the works as well. That should be slapped in his face tomorrow during, hopefully, the last of the contested court hearings for the Versa family will. My client's parents want the continued litigation hearings to dissuade my client.

So, the very next morning, if all things go to plan, I'll be on the plane with Natasha. Maybe I'll even sneak some Benadryl into her apple juice sippy cup so we can both get a few winks before the fight.

Zariah

The day death knocked at my door began like any other. Well, a little differently. Mikhail had followed me around everywhere since Vassili and Yuri had left. This morning, we both agreed that Natasha and I can make it to the airport ourselves.

So, I wake up with a pep in my step. The Hollywood attorney I fought with over the sizeable Versa family will had given in just yesterday afternoon.

While dressing Natasha, I facetime my mother on my iPad, and set it against her teddy bear.

"Aw, honey, I wish I was traveling with you today."

"Mom you have your very first appointment with Dr. Jester." I hold my tongue about my wishes to be there with her during her therapy session about her past issues of domestic violence abuse, but she must build rapport with Dr. Jester, and Martin tells me that I enable our mother.

"I can't believe I'm missing Australia! The men out there are made of solid gold," she joshes.

"Humph," I begin, slipping baby oil on Natasha's feet. I grab her calf as she flips over to get away, and pull her back down. "Actually, you're staying home sounds like even more of a good idea, with the way you continue to go on about it. Gushing over men."

"Tsk, just because your man is made of—"

"TMI, mama, I have no desire be made aware of your thoughts of my husband."

"Vassili is still a boy, and he's my son, so don't worry about this Georgia Peach! I need me a silver fox, honey. Now, let me see Cutie Pie."

"Just a sec." I'm like a NASCAR pit stop, in my endeavors to get Natasha's shoes on before she hightails it. When I sit her up on the changing table my heart melts. My little caramel drop is wearing a dress with green and pink hibiscus flowers on it. Her long curly eyelashes further make me fall in love with her. She's my everything.

"Honey, all those outfits. Seriously, you should've just put her in a pair of pajamas to go to the airport. Those folks run the air condition like they want you to get sick."

"I got you covered mom." I place Natasha on my hip, move to her vast closet and pull out an 18-month sized trench coat.

"Come closer..." My mom says, squinting.

When I turn around, I laugh and say, "Yikes!" at the sight of just Zamora's eyes glancing through the screen.

This prompts Natasha to giggle.

"Oh, I like, I like. Is this one of Taryn and her whore of a mother's purchases?"

Fearless II
by *Amarie Avant*

"Mama!"

"Now, Answer me, child."

"Yes."

"You know she propositioned your father. And her husband put the moves on me."

"There's a baby in the room." I warn.

"Natasha doesn't understand. Any who, Taryn is a miniature hoe, too. But you two have always been very good friends."

"We are. Nevertheless, we're getting older, and at different stages of our lives."

"Like Ronisha?"

"Aw, I miss Ro." I head to the diaper bag, and riffle through it to determine if all the necessities are packed. "Okay, Mom, I'm headed to the airport, you have an appointment to catch."

"Time for a quick prayer?"

I pick up the iPad, toggle to the main screen, and my eyes widen at the time. "Sorry, Mom. I'll call you once I start driving. We can pray then."

When we hang up, I carry Natasha and her diaper bag downstairs. Vassili packed my car two nights ago, prior to his departure. Although, Mikhail offered to do it. But this morning when I woke up, I took at least five trips to the garage to check everything, and now I have yet another duffle bag that I jog upstairs to get.

It feels like my head is screwed on backward when Natasha and I are finally buckled in.

FEARLESS II
by Amarie Avant

"Daddy, daddy," she says, as I glance back at her in the rearview while opening the garage.

"We're on our way to see Daddy, baby." I press the car in reverse, and then sigh. The thought pops into my head to open the diaper wipe container. Vassili has a habit of using them all, but not refilling the darn thing. Pressing the shift into park, I reach behind me, and grab the diaper bag. The container is in a side compartment, I pull it out and open it.

Damn you, Vassili, what the hell am I supposed to do with two measly diaper wipes? I get out of the car, unlatch Natasha from her car seat, and say, "Let's put the sippy cup down," as I give her the look that says, this is the reason we need an arsenal of baby wipes. Her chubby fists, hold on tight. I pluck her to my chest, press the garage button, and run down the hall.

I don't hear the garage door closing. I grumble. So much for extra precautions. Juice spills on me as I take the stairs two at a time. We're back downstairs in seconds. My cell phone buzzes in my pocket.

"Natasha, you wanna walk?" I huff, breathing heavy. She clings to my hip, as I reach around to grab the iPhone.

Vassili.

"Hey, baby," I huff, heading toward the hallway.

"Zariah, beautiful, you on your way?"

"I'm trying. Your child refuses to walk," I again try to remove the chubby baby at my side. "I opened

350

the garage. Forgot something. Now I'm headed back to the garage with Natasha on one hip, her favorite juice spilling on me."

"That's Natasha, mayhem with apple juice."

I chuckle. "Whatever, Vassili. I don't have time to be abused by your mini me."

My pupils expand as I glance toward the garage exit. The sun is beaming down on Juan Noriega Senior. The way our home is built, with the windy driveway, the tropical flowers are his background. He's wearing a jumpsuit from Twin Towers Correctional Facility. There's a Glock in his hand.

"I'm all sticky, and we have less than an hour to…" My thought drops, but I keep trying, "We ---we have…." I continue but my train of thought has smashed to smithereens.

Vassili is in my ear, saying, "Zariah, girl. What's wrong—"

"Mrs. Resnov," Noriega scratches his skull with the nozzle of his gun as he steps closer to us, "you've taken everything from me."

My baby is in my arm, a fist full of my hair in her hand, pulling. Not a worry in the world. "Mr. Noriega… wh-what are you doing at my house? How do you know where I live?"

"My attorney, he gets paid well."

"Zariah!" Vassili shouts into the phone. "Who is that?"

"Oh, is your husband on the phone?"

FEARLESS II
by Amarie Avant

It's on the tip of my tongue to beg and plead with Noriega, but Vassili's voice is lower. "ZARIAH, WHO IS—"

Noriega's lips bunch into a frown. "Tell him."

"It's Juan Noriega. I'm representing his wife in their divorce," I murmur into the phone, then I talk to my enemy. "Let's talk, Mr. Noriega, you and me. Let me put my child in the house so we can talk."

There's silence from the gang member as my husband asks, "Does he have a gun?"

"Yes…" I manage to say before Vassili orders me to give Noriega my phone.

"Okay," I reply to my husband. When I hand it over, Noriega's cold tone churns. "The infamous Vassili Resnov."

He proceeds to tell Vassil that he's already dead. My body wavers in disgust as he mentions his parental rights were terminated.

"Mommy? Mommy…" Natasha has stopped whacking me with her sippy cup and pulling my hair. Her sticky hand caresses my cheek. Oh, God, I have to keep her safe. And our baby. We aren't even aware of our baby's sex. The tiny embryo in my belly has yet to mold…

"Noriega, talk to me," I speak up. My husband is adding fuel to the fire, and the man before me is shooting bullets with his gaze as he speaks into the phone. "Talk to me." I start to set Natasha down, but he cocks the hammer back.

FEARLESS II
by *Amarie Avant*

Into the phone Noriega says, "You're capable of that, Mr. Resnov. The only problem is, I no longer have a heart. Adios, mi amigo."

He clicks the off button and drops my phone to the ground. "You're a bad bitch, aren't you," Noriega steps closer to me. This motherfucker is perfectly eye level with my forehead. He presses the gun against my forehead and breaths in my breasts.

"How did you get out?"

"Technicality, while you've been riding my cock, my attorney—" Noriega pauses, now pushing the barrel of his gun to my mouth. "You have been riding my dick, right?"

I keep my chin up, there's no denying him.

"Yeah, my attorney looked into Nicks. He's new. And my bitch is so afraid of men these days, I knew it was you. So, while I sat in fucking jail, my attorney made it a priority to see just what Zariah Resnov has been up to. Then he got around to looking into my case. All the little technicalities." He shrugs. "I should let you have that baby, raise the little fucker as my own. Screw you a few times before you die," He says, his mucous tongue twirling across the tops of my tits. "Shit, maybe drink that milk of yours, eh? Should I, Zariah, take you to Mexico, keep you locked up till that little baby is born."

His gun goes to Natasha's head.

"But this little puta right here, she can go." When the barrel of his gun goes to my daughter's mouth I

353

start to say the Lord's Prayer. There's no arguing or talking with Noriega, telling him how I feel will make it worse.

Then I hear footsteps.

"Zariah, yoo-hoo, Zariah, are you there?" A familiar feminine voice calls.

Noriega trains his gun to my belly as Danushka Molotov walks up to my garage like it's her personal runway, with an outfit that looks like it's meant for Paris. She's wearing a fur vest, blouse and skinny jeans, and her face is as oblivious as ever. "I was in the neighborhood," she holds up a flowery canvas material dessert case, with both hands.

"Bitch, who are you?" Noriega glances over his shoulder.

"I'm Danny," she offers Noriega her stuck up frown, and dismisses him as if he's one of the staff members at her home.

"Danny, just…" I swear, she is super blond today, because she doesn't see the horror in my eyes as she heads up to us.

"Horace has been super busy. I made tiramisu, you know, one of my new recipes, and I honestly thought you were gone. I was going to drop it off on the steps out front then I heard talking—"

"Are you stupid or something?" Noriega begins to turn around.

A shot rings out.

Blood splashes onto my face and in Natasha's hair as Noriega crumples to the ground.

Danushka drops the dessert case. "Actually, it came out dry, so I packed this instead," she holds up her own gun.

"You're Danushka Resnov?"

"I am."

"But you can't be. You don't look anything like her." I say, rooted to the same spot. She steps over Noriega, bypasses me and a shocked Natasha for the garage button.

"I'm filthy rich, Zariah. Let's go in the house to talk."

I walk into my home behind her, with my baby's face hidden in my neck. Natasha seems to be in tune with my worry still.

"But your name, Danushka," I say it right once again.

"Oh, you figured out how to say it," Danny offers a smile over her shoulder. She heads into the kitchen. "My logic was, why make up some name like Daria, and I don't look like a Viktoria. That would've made you even more suspicious."

"Are you going to kill me?" I ask, eyeing her gun.

"Oh this? *Nyet*." She gestures toward the gun and places it on the counter. "We're friends, Zariah. You are smart and rational. I took a chance by coming to you with my real name. Besides, when you searched me, an associate of mine had already altered my maiden name from Resnov to Petru. There is a Danushka Petru. Actually, there was."

"You killed her?"

"*Dah.* Horace thought it was a good idea." She opens the refrigerator and shuffles around while adding, "Speaking of my husband, he isn't away on business today. He's manning the jet himself. It should be fueled."

"Then what do you want from me?"

Danushka starts to open a string cheese. "Cutie Pie?"

"No," I shake my head.

"Alright, Zariah, my main goal is for us to continue to be friends." Danushka continues to hold out the string cheese. Natasha doesn't make a move to take it. With a frown on her face, she bites half of it. "I was a big girl, all muscle, but a big girl. I still love cheese."

"What do you want, Danushka?"

"For us to be friends. I feel like it'll be necessary to reiterate as much over again. Hopefully not during the entire flight to Australia. I also need you to tell Mikhail to play nice when he arrives in a few moments. That cousin of mine is such an educated man. Dr. Resnov. I smile every time I say it." She grins. "We have many doctors and high officials in our family, but Mikhail listened to his father, he works for the benefit of people in general."

"What else?" I lick my lips. Danushka is on a bigger mission, I can smell it.

"Also, you will not have any side conversations with Mikhail during our lengthy travel. Neither of you are to tell Vassili that I'm here yet. I prefer to make an entrance. Oh, and one last thing, Zariah, I'd like you to help me make friends with my *brat*."

It takes a while for me to process the many orders she just gave. This entire hour has been a hard pill to swallow, and now, Danushka is making orders. Vassili was vehement during the many times he told me to stay away from her.

The Danushka he 'stuffed down my throat' metaphorically speaking looked nothing like this. I have an entire rundown on 'this' Danushka's background, and due to her name being as common as Mary, Brittany, or Ashley, in their culture, I wrote it off as my Danny being different from the bitch of a sister of his.

How could I be so stupid?

And how the hell do I get away from this psycho? I realize, for my daughter's sake, that I won't. We will go to Vassili, but there'll be a Christian revival in hell before he agrees to make friends with his half-sister.

Vassili

"Mikhail is at the house, Vassil. Zariah is fine, Natasha is fine." Yuri attempts to catch my eye as he tugs on my arm. We're walking through the lobby of the hotel. He's stumbling with his cane. There are streams of water, designed throughout the area. I have to give it to my cousin, for keeping up.

My passport and wallet are in my back pocket. The rest of the shit is nonconsequential. I'm on my way to the airport. I don't give a fuck if the next flight to Los Angeles is filled and I have to hand over my entire wallet to someone for their seat, or if there are layovers in every country on the way.

I'm going home.

Past regrets flood through my mind as I sidestep tourist. *"I won't be home tonight... Probably not tomorrow night or the next."*

I was a dick when telling Zariah that very statement after Igor's death.

Then Zariah is in my ear, exclaiming, *"Okay, but only if you promise to step up to the plate. What do I have to do, get you to pinkie swear, sign a fucking contract! What's gonna get you to put our children first, Vassili! Huh? We have a life here, you tell me you went home. Fuck you and your damn home,*

FEARLESS II
by *Amarie Avant*

Vassili, this needs to be home. You go away to fight in Australia in three weeks, I swear if you runoff before then, I will find you, and drag your ass home. So do you want to see the ultrasound, that's your gesture to me that you plan to take care of home."

When the image of her crying for me fades, I'm out in front of the valet, preparing to ask one of these running fuckers to get me a taxi.

"Vassili, listen to me," Yuri grips at my collar.

My left hook snakes out, and I stop myself a fraction of a second before knocking my cousin into next week. I breath heavy. He grips the back of my neck.

"If you fucking leave, you stupid mudak, you will miss Natasha and Zariah. They are headed here in a few hours, do you understand?" His words are paced for my comprehension.

Did he already say this? Feels like he might have already mentioned something about them catching another flight.

"I don't want them riding alone."

"Mik-hail, my big motherfucking *brat* is with them, Va-ssil-iiiii!"

I rub the back of my neck in thought. "He's gonna—"

"Fly with them and come to the match tomorrow. They'll all be here by the time you wake up."

I start to tug at my mohawk, and recall that its gone. I rub a hand over my buzz cut, and nod. "Okay."

"Okay, okay? Kazen, are we good?" He gestures toward both of our eyes.

"Khorosho!" I shout.

He takes my hand, I snatch it away.

"Shit, I thought I'd have to guide you like my little god babies. I was gonna lead you back to your room, tuck you in like a little piz'da, the works, brat."

"How will they arrive by the time we wake up, Yuri?" I ask. "The flight they missed would've arrived at that time."

"Just shut the fuck up and thank God," he replies.

***

All night long, I toss and turn in the hotel bed. My dreams transform from nightmares to even worse night-terrors about my mom. About me.

Finally, I sit up in bed. It's early morning. "Fuck."

My mind is racing like a bitch. How will I fight tonight? I should give up. Won't be giving up, because I'll do something with my lounge. The Red Door has the perfect manager. I'll have the guy really show me the ropes this time, like Zariah suggested when I pulled Malich from my establishment. My wife and children are alive.

Time to be a family man....

I hear voices. What the hell is Yuri up to? In this large suite, his room is located on the opposite side of the living room. He's been hitting the porno hard since that bitch, Taryn, stopped coming around. Yet there's no moaning going on.

My eyes burn, and I stumble out of bed with a grunt. Mikhail? Is that him? My pace falters when I hear Zariah. They're here in record time, has to be under twelve hours.

"Let him sleep," I hear Yuri saying. "He has a fight later on."

"Okay, we will get another room for the night." This voice prickles goosebumps over my forearms. Danushka?

I finally make it around the bed, and open the door.

"Shit, I said 'let him sleep'," Yuri gripes.

Zariah is in my arms in seconds, hugging me tightly. I hold onto her, breathe her in, bestow a brutal kiss to her forehead while glancing down at my sleeping daughter, in her stroller. Then my gaze goes to Mikhail, a slimmer, ripped version of Yuri. The woman next to him is the only other person in the room. Her skin is the color of alabaster. Blonde hair almost as white. She cocks a smile at me.

"Moy mladshiy brat!"

Little brother? I don't have any older sisters. Who is this bitch?

She reaches up and pats my cheek like Danushka use to... Danushka... I glance into her eyes. They're pale blue. Her nose isn't so big.

"I'm the prettiest thing you've ever laid eyes on, eh?" She punches me in the arm, her tiny hand is like a brick. Still very powerful. "Cost me a 2.5 mil for all the upgrades."

Fucking bitch is just as dumb as her father—our father. She has gone under the knife.

"Alright, lets allow Vassili time to sleep." Yuri places his hand on Danushka's shoulder, but she doesn't budge.

"Hug me, Vassili, I saved your wife and daughter. I deserve some respect, seeing that you hit the ground running a few days before I came into this world."

It is her! Danushka was like a broken record, all the times she mentioned how she should've been Anatoly's first born. I beat her to the punch by a few days.

Not feeling any emotion, whatsoever, I give her a hug.

She grins. "Thanks, *brat*. Zariah is still mad at me for my deception, although she's great at being cordial. And I think if you give someone a ride on your private jet, it sort of tips the scales," she says, winking at my wife. "You really saved my marriage, Zar. Although, you did a background check and everything, I'll admit that I can be rather deceptive at times. But nothing I said was a lie. Horace is the reason I'm so pretty. I'd like for us to continue our friendship."

"You had Igor murdered." Zariah says.

Mikhail frowns harder.

"Oh, really?" Danushka scoffs. "Zariah, I said I'd play nice, and I'll continue to say so, but don't bring up bullshit."

"What?" Yuri has changed his demeanor from being a manager to a distraught brother. He growls at my half-sister. "How?"

"I didn't, I didn't." Danushka holds up a hand. She settles down into her chair, and doesn't sit with a wide-legged stance. Fuck, she's no longer the boy with a cunt between her legs. "My husband, Horace, owns Molotov Steel, an international manufacturing company. That little shit, Bertolucci, wanted to impose sanctions, even greater sanctions on Horace. He had to be put down. It was inevitable."

My eyes narrow in thought. Horace Molotov is one of the richest men in the world. He holds a seat at the seven chairs—or whatever the fuck they call it.

Danushka wriggles her eyebrows. "I may have done the job myself, you know, shopping in Milan gets boring sometimes." She offers her usual frown of disgust. "I left my Resnov card, like usual, because hey, one day, Anatoly has to notice me, right?"

I shake my head.

"The official's family thinks they're hot shit out there. Italian mobsters, my ass. Doesn't matter now, right? Yuri, your friends showed those mudaks who's boss."

"How did they shoot up my father's house!" Mikhail snaps.

"People talk, you know." Danushka shrugs. "Malich left Anatoly. Makes people paranoid, you know. They think that Malich is going off on his own. Biding his time, taking the Resnov name."

"My father could give a fuck about the bratva!" Yuri roars.

More of a slow to burn, in anger, Mikhail bites his fist. "So, our brother died for nothing?"

Both men are torn, eyes glossed with tears. I squeeze my own eyes closed so as not to get angry enough to cry.

"I would've attended the funeral, paid my respects."

"Fuck your respect, Danny!" I shout.

"*Dah*? Fuck me? Well, let's get to the point then. I have a proposition for you, Vassili. Seeing as I saved your wife, and your children." She grunts. "Heck, side note, Grigor thought you were going to murder Anatoly when you went to Moscow last. He still feels bad for popping you in the back of the head, my little brother. Isn't he the sweetest?"

I shrug. Grigor is her full-blooded brother. They share the same cunt of a mother. "What do you mean, Grigor thought I'd kill our father?"

"He went to pick you up at the airport. That ugly cousin of ours, hops into the car before Grigor can leave. Semion is loyal to Anatoly. I'm Grigor's big sister, he's loyalty resides with me. We would've corrected the Bertolucci family, but Yuri's associates got to them first. That's a promise."

"Okay?" I cock a brow. This bitch continues to make intercession for her actions by mentioning how she just saved Zariah and Natasha. My face is blank as I mentally determine how crazy my sister is. "What the fuck do you want, Danushka?"

"She wants you to be the new king," Zariah murmurs. To a round of applause from my psychotic little half-sister. My beautiful wife's eyes are sunken in with lack of sleep. This has been a long night for everyone. The only person who is elated is Danushka.

"We are a name, big brother, we are the Resnovs." Danushka grins. "Horace is one of the biggest investors for the Table of Seven. My husband has connections. And like Zar just said, the world needs a king. Resnov is the perfect brand. I will of course, be the true leader. People see pussy and run screaming." She shrugs. "Men are afraid of women. We all know I'm more than competent."

"You want to take down your father, right?" Zariah's eyes latch onto mine. "He did things to your mother, very bad things to her, Vassili."

My knees give out. I sink down before the rest of me decides it has a fuck to give. My head is down, I knead the back of my neck.

"You can kill him, or I can, Vassili," Danushka offers. "Horace is a billionaire, but we can all be richer. You'll continue to fight. You attend a few meetings at the Table of Seven every once in a while. On most occasions, I'll appear in your stead."

Zariah goes to her knees before me, placing herself between my legs. She caresses my cheek, and kisses my mouth. Her lips taste good, her mouth is sweet. Fuck, I was so afraid yesterday. I don't even have a moment to realize that I now know what fear looks like—losing my wife and children—because I'm blown away by Danushka.

"You two are beautiful. But you don't even know how to fuck yet. There's no sex like sex when you're made of money," Danushka assures.

I stop listening to the madness. This bitch is out of her mind. Zariah's tongue flicks against mine. My dick is hardening by the second. I want them all out of here, so I can screw my wife.

This must be a fucking dream…

Zariah nibbles my jawline, and up to my ear. Her tongue twines around.

"Fuck, I'm getting hot," Danushka says.

My blood is boiling, but something tells me not to move away, not to shout, not to act in anger as usual. Let Zariah lead.

She sucks on my earlobe and whispers. "We'll figure something out…"

Zariah

A new king is upon us. Vassili will hit the cages in a few minutes. He will dominate his opponent and go in for the kill. And then he will work with Danushka to … kill their father.

My husband won't do it, though. He's more of a man than Danushka will ever understand, or as it is apparent, than she wishes to be. So, he won't murder his father, because true vengeance is with the Lord. Anatoly Resnov will get what he deserves in this world, and or in the next.

Perhaps both Anatoly and Danushka will, with a daughter who was once so consumed by wanting his love that she now has decided to do away with it entirely. And him.

But Vassili and I are a team. There's a sea of people surrounding me. Yuri has Natasha seated in his lap, at my side, since he's still favoring his one knee.

I shoot up to my feet in a champagne-toned designer dress that Danushka stated was fit for a queen. The silk is like warm honey to my skin as I scream at the top of my lungs. "Kill 'em, Karo!"

She's at my side. For all intents and purposes, we are good friends now. I gave her a few makeup tips while we were dressing, and I swear, Danny could drop the madness and hit the catwalk in Paris to model.

The commentator was speaking with anticipation a minute ago, begging for a 'ground and pound' from Vassili and the Australian, Kong.

The bell rings.

Vassili and Kong lunge from their corners. Fists go flying. They're both hungry for murder, and I cannot blink watching the match.

My teeth grit, fists down at my sides. I must look like an angry royal, ready for war myself, because I watch the match without the coiling of my abdomen. Fearlessness is soaring through my veins as Kong pens Vassili to the cage.

He catches my husband with a jab before Vassili grabs his shoulders and knees him.

Vassili's arms swing rapidly, and like they weigh a ton. He kissed me before entering the octagon, promised the fight wouldn't last a minute.

He tosses a left so hard that it powers from his toes all the way through his shoulder. Kong's nose is shattered. Blood pours from his face like a waterfall. He crumbles in a heap.

"IT'S OVER. WOW! That nose will never, ever be the same!"

As I shout at the top of my lungs for my husband's victory, I'm already at work. Internally, I'm determining who will help my team. Vassili and I.

Should I go to Samuel Billingsley? He's the proper choice, he's my mentor, and he has a great relationship with Vassili.

Or Malich? He hasn't been the same since Igor died. Yuri mentioned that when their mother died, years trickled by before he felt like surviving, thriving again.

We'll hold off for now with Malich. He is wise in his ways, but only when he's in the right frame of mind.

There's always my father... I can tie his hands behind his back with information about the serial killer, Lieutenant Sullivan.

Vassili climbs to the top of the cage, straddling it. His dark gaze searches through the crowd. In a sea of a million people, the love of my life finds me. He pumps his fists into the air.

I blow a kiss to him, eyes burning with happy tears.

"I fucking love you!" he mouths.

HAPPY EVER AFTER... FOR NOW

Alright, so I ended it, again, without resolving everything. Since you waited so long, I have an **awesome, new FREE novella** that I'd like to offer you. Fingers crossed that I'll have Fearless III in your hands by March... April at the latest.

Author's Note:

I hope you liked Zariah and Vassili's story. It took me six long months to… no, not write this book, I'd go crazy. It took me three weeks. But for six long months, I was unable to write. Mostly due to not being where I'd like as an author. I want more good reviews LOL. So if you loved this, please write a review on <u>Amazon</u> letting me know what you think. If you feel like it sucked, and you'd prefer to offer a lengthy critique instead of review, email me, I may or may not agree and ask if you'd like to beta reader ☺.

Alright, so my Facebook group tells me that I'm a tease. And here's the part where I mention that Danushka is the ultimate manipulator. Anatoly and Maxwell have nothing on her. I know, I know, Maxwell didn't play much part in this book. He will in Book 3 when Danushka plays her cards right… I guess I'll try to wrap up the Fearless storyline so y'all don't riot with more than the standard three books… sighs.

CPSIA information can be obtained
at www.ICGtesting.com
Printed in the USA
LVHW02s2342060318
568948LV00007B/352/P